MY
LIFE
AS
A
FAKE

ALSO BY PETER CAREY

PETER CAREY

MY
LIFE
AS
A
FAKE

Excerpts from *The Darkening Ecliptic* by Ern Malley reproduced by arrangement with the copyright owners of the James McAuley Estate, c/- Curtis Brown (Aust) Pty Ltd; the literary estate of Harold Stewart; and with permission of the Max Harris Estate from Ern Malley's *Collected Poems* (ETT Imprint, Sydney, 1993).

The writings of Max Harris have been reproduced with permission of the Max Harris Estate from Ern Malley's *Collected Poems* (ETT Imprint, Sydney, 1993).

Excerpts from Ezra Pound's 'Hugh Selwyn Mauberly' and 'Homage to Sextus Propertius' from *Collected Shorter Poems* reproduced with permission of Faber and Faber.

A Knopf book
Published by Random House Australia Pty Ltd
20 Alfred Street, Milsons Point, NSW 2061
http://www.randomhouse.com.au

Sydney   New York   Toronto
London   Auckland   Johannesburg

First published in 2003

National Library of Australia
  Cataloguing-in-Publication Entry

  Carey, Peter, 1943– .
  My life as a fake.

  ISBN 1 74051 246 4.

  I. Title.
A823.3

Text design by Jenny Grigg
Typeset in 11.5/15.5pt Baskerville Classico by Midland Typesetters, Maryborough, Victoria
Printed and bound by Griffin Press, Netley, South Australia

10 9 8 7 6 5 4 3 2 1

For our sons, Sam and Charley

I beheld the wretch – the miserable monster whom I had created. He held up the curtain of the bed; and his eyes, if eyes they may be called, were fixed on me.

Mary Shelley
Frankenstein; or, The Modern Prometheus, 1818

1

The Old Rectory, Thornton, Berkshire. August 1985

I have known John Slater all my life. Perhaps you remember the public brawl with Dylan Thomas, or even have a copy of his famous book of 'dirty' poems. If it's an American edition you'll discover, on the inside flap, a photograph of the handsome, fair-haired author in cricket whites. *Dewsong* was published in 1930. Slater was twenty at the time, very nearly a prodigy.

That same year I was born Sarah Elizabeth Jane to a beautiful, impatient Australian mother and a no less handsome but rather posh English father, Lord William Wode-Douglass, generally known as Boofy.

Slater's own class background was rather ambiguous, though my mother, a dreadful snob, had a tin ear, and I know she thought Slater very grand and therefore permitted him excesses she would not have tolerated from the Chester grammar school boy he really was.

It was Slater who carved my father's thirtieth birthday cake with his bare hands, who rode a horse into the kitchen, who brought Unity Mitford to dinner during the period she was stealing stationery from Buckingham Palace and carrying that nasty little ferret around in her handbag.

I cannot say that I understood his role in my parents' marriage, and only when my mother killed herself – in a spectacularly awful style – did I suspect anything was amiss.

In the last minutes of her life I saw John Slater put his arms around her and finally I understood, or thought I did.

From that moment I hated everything about him: his self-absorption, his intense angry good looks, but most of all those electric blue eyes which inhabited my imagination as the incarnation of deceit.

When my mother died, poor Boofy fell apart completely. He drank and wept and roared, and after falling down the stairs the second time he packed me off to St Mary's Wantage in Berkshire, which I did not like at all. I ran away, was returned in a post-office van, fought with the headmistress, and adopted the perverse strategy of writing with my left hand, thus making almost all my schoolwork illegible. I was so busy being a bad girl that no-one noticed that I also had a brain. But even while I was receiving D's in English I somehow managed to see that Slater's celebrated verses were nothing so much as bowers constructed by a male in order to procure sex. This was far from being my only insight and I was not reluctant to let the Great Man know exactly what I thought. Somewhere in his papers there may still be evidence of my close reading of 'Eastern Oriental', with its impertinent corrections, its queries about his heavily enjambed lines, all of which I archly hoped might be 'helpful to him'.

I was, in short, a precocious horror and you will not be at all astonished that John Slater and I did not become friends. But, London being London, I did keep on running into him over the years, and as he continued to write poetry and I had ended up as the editor of *The Modern Review*, we knew many of the same people and had reason to sit at the same table more than once.

Time did not make the association easier. Indeed, as I grew older his physical presence became more and more disturbing. I will not say that I was obsessed with him, but I could not be in the same room without looking at him continually; I was drawn to him and repulsed by him all at once. He was an appallingly unapologetic narcissist and so full of iconoclastic opinion and territorial enthusiasms that there was not a dinner party, be it ever so packed with the Great and the Good, where one could escape his increasingly bardic presence. Of course I could not look at him without thinking of my poor unhappy mother.

In spite of the fact that we were so very intimately connected, it took all of thirty years for us to speak with more than superficial politeness. He was then sixty-two and while perhaps better known for his novels – *The Amersham Satyricon* had been a huge bestseller – he was still generally referred to as 'the poet John Slater'. Which was exactly how he looked: rather wild and windburned, as if he'd recently returned from tramping over the moors or following Basho's path all the way to Ogaki.

Slater does seem to have worked very hard at the social side of literature, and there was scarcely a British poet or novelist whom he could not call his friend, or for whom he had not, at some time, done a favour. The Faber crowd he cultivated particularly and it was at a Faber dinner party, at the home of Charles Monteith, where we finally came to talk to each other. Our conversation aside, I don't recall a great deal about the evening except that Robert Lowell – the guest of honour – had inadvertently revealed that he didn't know who Slater was. This, one could hypothesise, is why Slater chose to turn and talk to me so urgently, calling me 'Micks', a name belonging to my family and all that lost time at Allenhurst at High Wycombe.

What he had to say was not in the least personal, but his use of the nickname had already touched me and his voice, perhaps as a result of the famous American's careless judgement of his life, took on a wistful, elegiac tone which I found unexpectedly moving. For the first time in years I looked at him closely: his face was puffy, its colour, uncharacteristically, a little grey. When he began to talk about revisiting

Malaysia, a country where so much of *Dewsong* and its successors had their roots, it was hard not to wonder if he might be tidying up his affairs.

Come with me, he said suddenly.

I laughed sharply. He grasped my hand and held me with those damned eyes and of course he was such a Famous Crumpeteer that I looked away, embarrassed.

We *should* go, he said. Don't you think?

It was impossible to guess what he meant by 'we' and 'should'.

We *must* talk, he insisted. It is very bad that we never have.

This sudden intimacy was as off-putting as it was wished for.

I have no money, I said.

I have tons of it.

He watched me closely as I poured more wine.

You've got a boyfriend, he suggested.

I have a very jealous cat.

I adore cats, he said. I will come and talk to her.

And suddenly his cab arrived and he had to go on to a very glamorous party where he was expecting to meet John Lennon and as he rose there was a general clamour of farewells and it was my understanding that our conversation had been of no great moment – merely a cover for his embarrassment at the hands of Robert Lowell.

But he telephoned me, at home in Old Church Street, at eight o'clock the next morning and it was very quickly clear that this journey was not at all impulsive. He had already arranged for the British Council to pay for one ticket, while two thousand words for *Nova* would fund another. He would be delighted to foot all of my expenses.

My father had died just the year before in circumstances that were not at all happy – a sulky sort of estrangement on my part – and it was not in the least dotty for me to think that John Slater was offering this trip as an opportunity for

4

us to talk, for me to understand my own unhappy family a little better. Of course he never said so, and even now, all these years later, I cannot be sure what his intention was at the beginning. Certainly it was not sex. Let me dispense with that immediately. It was well known that I had no interest in it.

John, I said, I am an awful tourist. I have no intention of slogging through the bloody jungle with binoculars. I am an editor. It's all I do. I read. I have no other life.

You love to eat, he said. I saw you polish off that curry.

Well, it was very good curry.

Then Kuala Lumpur will be paradise for you. Darling, I've known K.L. for almost as long as I've known you.

Of course he did not 'know' me at all.

What's the worst thing that can happen? I'll make a pass at you? Micks, for God's sake – it's a bloody week of your life. We'll all be mouldering in the ground soon enough. Do come.

That did it – the mouldering. After lunch I burgled our safe and took the last of the magazine's petty cash. In the King's Road I purchased forty-five pounds in traveller's cheques, a pair of sandals, and a summer frock. So prepared, I entered that maze from which, thirteen years later, I have yet to escape.

In those days it was a thirty-hour flight from London to Kuala Lumpur, but we suffered a long delay in Tehran due to fog in Dubai, and then an interminable wait in Singapore. You would think that forty-two hours would be a sufficient opportunity for the two of us to begin our conversation, but it seemed that Slater liked to sleep on aeroplanes and he was so drugged with Phenobarb and whisky when we landed in Singapore that the air hostesses thought he was dead.

He passed through Malaysian Immigration in a wheelchair and so my very first memory of Kuala Lumpur involves the difficulties of transporting a large and meaty man into a taxi and from there into the extraordinarily kitsch foyer of the Merlin Hotel, and there his fame preceded him, thank God.

Apart from the awful gold and tartan decor of the Merlin, my only impressions of this foreign capital were heat and smells, sewage, floral scents, rotting fruit, and a general mustiness which seeped into my skin and permeated my large plain room where someone had written 'Fuck Little Duck' in grey pencil beside the toilet bowl.

The next day Slater did not answer his telephone and I became concerned that he really might have died. Then, on the off-chance, I checked with the desk and discovered he and his luggage had departed the hotel. No message. Just gone.

I immediately felt like someone who has been passionately seduced, fucked, and abandoned. This is not a pleasant feeling at the best of times and all my old animus against Slater came surging back. I was far too angry to read and far too agitated to sleep, and this was how I came to be inspecting the Indian haberdashers on Batu Road. I like to buy fabrics, but nothing pleased me here. The batik was rather coarse and opportunistic, not nearly as refined as the Indonesian fabrics, and yet I purchased a piece, as tourists do. From Batu Road I continued window-shopping, not liking anything, until I found myself in a noisy street of Chinese shophouses with the unlikely name of Jalan Campbell. I did not like it very much either, although the buildings offered a continuous colonnade and I was grateful for the shade, if not the interruptions offered by the shopkeepers who brought their chairs and hammers and plastic buckets out into the public thoroughfare.

It was here, glancing rather peevishly into one little store, that I saw in the gloom – amidst a tangle of bicycles, next to a Chinese woman who was ladling bright red fish into plastic bags – a middle-aged white man in a dirty sarong. He had lopsided eyebrows and very close-cropped hair which made me think of both a prisoner and a monk. However, what struck me most particularly were the angry red sores on his sturdy legs. He was sitting in a broken plastic chair and gazing out into the street and did not, when I paused, show so much as the slightest flicker of what I can only call racial connection.

I briefly wondered how he had got to this place where his sores were not being treated, but really I was too hot and sweaty, too offended by those Asian fish-paste smells, and generally too bad tempered to wonder about anything for very long. I crossed the muddy Klang River and was soon back in the musty air-conditioned Merlin, again trying to deal with the work of adequately talented English poets. I was still at it at eight o'clock that evening when Slater finally rang.

Micks, he cried. Isn't it a wonderful city?

How could I tell him that I'd waited all day to see him? He made me feel pathetic, childish.

What have you done? Tell me everything.

I walked a little, I admitted.

Good, good, wonderful. Darling, he said, I was hoping we could have dinner on Tuesday, but I'm rather caught up here. Could you write me on your card for the Wednesday?

John, it's Monday.

Yes. You see, I'm in Kuala Kangsar. Really just arrived. Outstation, as they say.

Kuala what?

You knew I was going to Kuala Kangsar.

He had said nothing about any such place. I know it. It was the first time I ever heard the words pronounced, and I was sure then — and am positive now – that as usual he had followed some opportunity, and not one of the mind. Recklessness and hedonism had fuelled the engine of his early genius, but they had also, ultimately, betrayed his promise. If he had written more and whored and sucked up just a little less, perhaps Lowell would've known exactly who he was.

Well, he said, I'll definitely be back for Wednesday dinner. Enjoy K.L. I really envy you discovering it.

And that was it. No apologies. No concern for my well-being. As I hung up the phone I finally understood poor Lizzie Slater, the second wife, the one who ended up in St Bart's with alcoholic poisoning.

The thing is, poor ruined pretty Lizzie told me, the thing about dear old Johnno, dear, he always does exactly as he damn well likes.

I am not a good tourist, as I said, but that second night I was too angry to stay in my comical hotel. I forced myself to eat satay in a street market in what is called Kampong Baru, a Malay's five minute walk from the Merlin.

The next day, likewise, I grumpily stepped out to stare at the Batu Caves, the Moorish railway station, the stinking Chinese wet markets. The smells were the most challenging aspect of my tourism, not merely the wet markets, but also the alien mixture of smoke and spice and sewer and two-stroke exhausts and all the sweet mouldy aroma of those broad-leafed tropical grasses. I preferred walking the streets very early in the cool morning as the Sikh bank guards were eating sweet *barfi* and drinking their beloved cow's milk in the street. The rain trees were lovely, all of Jalan Treacher heavy with green leaves and yellow flowers. Only the sight of a boy cutting a banana tree with a machete reminded me that, not three years before, the gentle smiling inhabitants of Kampong Baru had been butchering their Chinese neighbours. Blood had run along those deep drains beside which I now walked.

I wandered largely without harassment. This was 1972 after all, and one would've had to travel to the east coast to find people easily exercised by the length of a dress or the bareness of one's shoulders. Moreover, the British colonial past was still almost the present and one could pop off Batu Road into the Coliseum and find, on every one of the white-clothed tables, a bottle of Worcestershire sauce. This was all interesting enough, but what I had told Slater was true:

I was an editor, and *The Modern Review* was my life. I actually preferred to sit inside my hotel room and read, not only the poetry submitted to the magazine, but also *Paradise Lost*, which always reminded me, Mr Leavis notwithstanding, of what my life was given to. In the afternoon I again paid service to the word by writing long letters to my three most important board members: Lord Antrim, Wystan Auden, and a wonderful Mrs McKay, the divorced wife of a Manchester industrialist whose generosity had saved the magazine more than once. In each letter I mentioned our outstanding printers' bill but did not really expect anything to come of it. They had risen to the occasion too many times before and were, I suspected, exhausted by a magazine which might never be what we had all hoped.

Slater showed up on Thursday, unexpectedly falling into step beside me as I walked across the bridge towards Jalan Campbell where I had been anticipating the company of sodden red-faced planters who I hoped would say appalling raj-like things.

He was wearing walking shorts and heavy boots, and was still so sunny and unrepentant that I began to wonder if he had forgotten our conversation at the Faber dinner party, if he imagined that I would actually enjoy exploring a steaming Asian city on my own.

Micks, he said, I have something to tell you.

Ah, I thought – and was disappointed when he launched not into an apology but a very detailed account of his hike through the jungle with an Anglophile Chinese poet. As I listened, I wondered why a man would wear shorts in the jungle where his unprotected skin would be so badly scratched. Was it simply to show his legs?

Did you see that, he asked suddenly. No? Well, it was *Die Sonette an Orpheus*, in the 1923 Insel-Verlag edition. Must be worth a hundred quid.

For sale?

Don't be ridiculous. No, in that horrid shop back there. Come. You must look.

I actually did not wish to be controlled by John Slater, but he had his great paw on my forearm and I had no choice but to stare into the same bicycle repair shop which had taken my attention on Monday. The same white man with ulcers on his legs was sitting on the broken plastic chair and indeed was reading, by the light of a naked bulb, *Sonnet to Orpheus*.

See, said Slater.

Hearing this, the white man lifted his mild eyes and, having considered Slater for a moment, slowly raised his arm in salute.

Christ, said Slater.

His hand still clamped around my arm, he propelled me forcibly back along the street.

Do you know him?

He looked at me with his big chin working as if he were chewing something unpleasant. Know him? he said indignantly. Of course not.

And that is really where the story begins, for it was clear to me that he was lying.

2

The editors of literary magazines, while conceiving of themselves as priests, actually travel like brush salesmen, always making sure they have a sample of their wares packed along with socks and underwear, and it was not at all eccentric of me to bring several issues of *The Modern Review* to Malaysia. One of these had a very fine translation of Stefan George which I expected a reader of Rilke would admire and so the following morning, at half past six, I wrapped it in some pretty paper and set off back to Jalan Campbell. I had no notion of how this half mile walk was going to change my life. If I had only stayed in bed, I would not be where I am today, struggling in a web of mystery that I doubt I ever shall untangle.

Yet once I had started there was nothing to save me from myself. Indeed, all the obsessive tendencies which have made me a good editor were now brought to bear on this abandoned white man. I would not be happy until I knew who he was, although my curiosity wasn't quite so dispassionate, for I already imagined him to be 'lost' and wished, for my own personal guilty reasons, to give him comfort.

I found the shophouse very easily and was well inside its rather oily smelling interior before I realised that my man was not in residence. In his place was the Chinese woman I had previously seen packing fish in plastic bags. Close-up, she revealed herself to be a fierce little thing with a flat round face marked by two long jagged scars.

I greeted her as my phrase book ordered: *Selamat pagi*, I said, but she was working to a different script.

Wha you want?

There was nothing to do but offer my precious quarterly.

Wha for this?

English poetry, I said, for the man. *Orang*. Does he read English?

Her lip curled, giving an impression of implacable hostility, towards poetry perhaps, or England, or sweating white women – who could tell?

Poetry?

Will you please give it to him?

Not here now, she said, and tucked my proffered gift away as if she might later use it to wipe her bottom.

Selamat tingal, I said, and left the shop feeling very foolish, striding along the street with my head down, wishing that I had minded my own bloody imperial business. Most of all I wished I had not wasted my magazine.

Were it not for the squeal of a buckled bicycle wheel I might not have spotted my Rilke reader. In all the confusion of cars and trucks and motorbikes, it took a moment to recognise who was pushing the injured bicycle along the road. In the gritty, humid air, the white man did not look particularly alien, simply another human figure pressing forward under the clammy weight of the sky. I was by now rather at the limits of my social confidence, and if he had not stopped, I doubt I would have had the courage to address him.

Was that John Slater, he asked.

The moment I heard that nasal, reedy voice I understood he was Australian.

Yesterday, he said. That *mat saleh* with the camera?

Yes, I said.

He raised his thin black eyebrows but offered nothing more.

Do you know him? I said.

As he considered this, I admired his face, the impressive eyebrows falling away at a severe angle, the possibility of a smile hiding in the shadowy corners of his rather wistful mouth. He was bone and muscle, self-effacing, a little melancholy.

Not really-*lah*.

Are you a poet?

He looked a little startled. I thought it was Slater, he said, then blinked. Isn't it extraordinary how some people remain recognisable? One kind-*lah*.

Shall I remember you to him?

Oh, he wouldn't know me, he said, and with no more than a nod of farewell, he set off, pushing the squeaking bicycle along the edge of a treacherous storm-water drain. Nothing in his manner invited me to follow and so I wandered back towards the hotel wondering what curious events had led a cultured Australian to a repair shop in a street called Jalan Campbell.

3

At Heathrow John Slater had promised me chili crab and banana-leaf curry, but he was clearly a man who made his promises easily. I had been left alone to find what delicacies I could and had already wandered out into the dusty streets of Kampong Baru where there was a market, not in the street exactly, but in a sort of car park under a pair of giant mango trees. When I returned there it was already dark. It was not raining but I imagined it was the season that my father, who had done his stint in India, called Mango Showers, and in the yellow nimbus of the carbide lamps above the stalls and trolleys of the vendors, you could see and smell the damp, as it mixed with the odours of sandalwood and satay and the inevitable undercurrent of sewage. In the distance there were a few sodium streetlamps and in the liquid dark beneath the mangoes one could see the glistening possum eyes of Malay men and boys, whose idea of my rather tall white body seemed to have been formed by brightly lit images of American giants with ripped dresses and open thighs.

Where you come from?

They were not threatening but they were persistent and, finally, a little creepy.

Where your husband?

I had set out feeling angry with Slater but when I noticed

him, seated alone at a table beneath the mangoes, I felt considerable relief.

Seeing me, he rose, two long arms held high into the night, as if he had been waiting to greet me all this time. I am not being modest when I say that I looked a fright: frumpy cotton frock, no hat, no make-up, my hair cut in a style one can achieve only with two mirrors and a pair of nail scissors, a look I had mastered years before at St Mary's Wantage.

Ah, the White Goddess!

What tosh! Yet when his hand enclosed my own, it was persuasive. I cannot explain it – partly the size, but also a dry sort of heat, like a river rock. I was ridiculously relieved to see him.

Then he was doing everything at once, seating me in the most gallant style, calling for more beer, delivering a proprietary discourse on the etiquette of eating from a banana leaf.

I must say I do envy you, Micks, discovering everything yourself for the first time. You should write it all down. You know Lafcadio Hearn? 'Do not fail to write down your first impressions as soon as possible.' A tiny fellow, Hearn, very strange-looking. 'They are evanescent, you know; they will never come to you again.'

It was not hard to believe that he'd learned those inconsequential lines just now, and only in order to charm me. He was capable of it, I'm sure. Yet when he crushed my hand I was completely persuaded of his sincerity, also that his abandonment of me had been an exquisitely designed gift which I had insufficient character to properly appreciate. Thus, so easily, was my anger dealt with, and soon I was happily recounting my little adventure with the old Australian.

He said he knew you.

What else?

That you wouldn't know him.

He looked back over his shoulder – marginal rude, I decided.

Am I boring you, John?

I remember him, he said – but his eyes had become dull, even churlish.

And?

He shrugged and lit a cigarette.

Oh for God's sake, John, please don't make me draw you out.

He raised an eyebrow. Be nice, Micks.

You be bloody nice, John, I've been waiting four bloody days.

It was Christopher Chubb.

You know that means nothing to me.

Slater deftly paddled his fingers in his rice and curry. Really? I was sure he must have fallen before your pencil.

I sipped my watery iced beer in silence.

Seriously, he said, I cannot believe he has never crossed your desk. Formally very rigorous, a great fellow for the villanelle and the double sestina. Now *that* is an extraordinarily rigid form.

Yes, John, I do know what a double sestina is.

He smiled. Then you will know that our scrofulous friend was exactly that sort of fellow. Australian . . . 'born / in a half savage country, out of date; / Bent resolutely on wringing lilies from the acorn'. A very serious provincial academic poet, committed to a life of envy and disappointment.

Then you do know him?

Instead of answering, he patted the back of my hand. Did you go to Bruno Hat's opening, Micks? No, you would have been too young. He was an artist. Milo wrote a huge piece about it, I remember.

This was in London?

Ssh. Listen. I actually saw the so-called paintings, he said, tapping the hot ash of his cigarette with a naked finger. Not really my taste, bits of cork and wool and shards, but half of Chelsea was there wolfing down the Cypriot sherry. Later, I remembered a fellow sitting in the corner in a wheelchair, face all wrapped up as if he was dying of toothache. He hardly invited conversation but afterwards it turned out that he *was* Bruno Hat and it would have been hopeless to talk to him, so I was told, because he was Polish and spoke no word of English. Just the same, an extraordinary amount was said *about* the art. Milo wasn't the only one, but just as the whole thing reached a great crescendo 'Bruno Hat' quietly revealed that he was actually Bryan Howard.

Who actually spoke English rather well.

Yes, it was a prank. Made a few faces red, but no-one died, and even Milo – who made the most hysterical claims – still went on to be Sir Milo Wilson and no-one would bother mentioning it today. Don't be so impatient, Micks. My point is that a prank's a prank and Bruno Hat wasn't going to pull the whole of English culture down around our ears. Whereas if you take a country like Australia, you see the whole thing is much more fragile, and this old codger with the evil-looking boils, Chubb, was the author of a similar sort of prank. Have you heard of the McCorkle Hoax? No? Well, our Christopher Chubb was the villain.

The hoaxer, you mean.

Of a horribly prim, self-righteous sort. This all takes place in 1946. Imagine – twenty-four years after 'The Waste Land'. You'd think the battles had been fought and the bodies buried, but that's the rather splendid thing about your mother's people.

My heart actually leapt at the mention of my mother. Slater saw this. At least, I believe he did.

His eyes brightened. He slowed his pace. Remember, this is the country of the duck-billed platypus. When you are cut off from the rest of the world, things are bound to develop in interesting ways.

I thought to myself, he will talk about my mother now. But I was wrong. This is why, Micks, you can still have this fierce and bloody battle going on in 1946, when your friend in the sarong was a handsome shy young fellow seducing girls with his jazz piano. He was actually a little more 'chubby' in those days, if you'll forgive the pun, and when he was not drinking he had a sweet and rather passive manner which hid the fact that he had this awful chip on his shoulder.

Like Mummy in a way.

Slater paused, looking as if he was about to deny knowing the person I'd referred to. Oh darling, he sighed at last, your mother was never chippy. She was so absolutely Upper North Shore. Poor old Chubb came from the dreary lower-middle-class suburbs. I would say he *loathed* where he came from.

Exactly, I said. Mummy could never abide Australians.

He looked at me very directly, long enough to make me feel uncomfortable.

I thought, You bastard, you killed her.

In any case, he said, and his tone was very cool, our Mr Chubb had what you could only call a phantom pregnancy. That is, he gave birth to a phantom poet, a certain 'Bob McCorkle' who of course never really existed but to whom our bitter little Australian gave a ragingly modern opus: life, death, a whole biography – including, believe it or not, a birth certificate. And then he delivered the lot – with the exception of the birth certificate, which came later – to a journal with the rather pretentious name of *Personae*. He did a persuasive job, actually. Made a complete ass of the editor and became a celebrity along the way. Did you give him a copy of *The Modern Review*?

Why would I do that?

You're an *editor*, Micks. Of course you did. Which issue was it?

The one with the George translation.

He'll hate it, he said gleefully. You'll have him spitting chips all the way to Ulu Klang.

I thought how wounded he would be if I told him that someone would hate his magazine, if he ever had one. What happened to the editor, I asked.

He killed himself I do believe.

John! That's horrible.

He sipped his beer and crunched the ice blocks between his teeth. It is rather a long story. I forget the particulars. Look, here comes the satay. Probably loaded with parasites, but awfully good. We should get some of those Indian thing-ohs . . . those . . . Damn, my memory's going. I forget what they're called.

The Indian thing-ohs were *murtaba*, and as Slater rushed away to order some I realised that all my sentimental feelings for the old 'lost' man had completely evaporated. Chubb had preyed on the best, most vulnerable quality an editor has to offer. I mean that hopeful, optimistic part which has you reading garbage for half your life just so you might find, one day before you die, a great and unknown talent.

Fuck him, I thought. I hope he hates the George translation. I hope it fries his tiny antipodean brain.

4

The following morning Slater telephoned, with such an uncharacteristic concern for my health that I immediately asked if he was unwell.

Actually, yes. He paused. How are you?

Not wonderful.

Another pause. Stomach?

I suppose it was the satay, I said.

No, it was the fucking ice, he said. I can't believe I let them put ice in my beer, probably washed the damn stuff in the gutter. So much for the sainted Bumis. They pay for good ice and then get it so dirty they have to wash it in the filthy drain. You don't have any Enterovioform do you?

I have two left.

Micks?

Yes.

This is very humiliating . . . I don't dare stray far from the lavatory.

I waited for him to ask me to personally deliver my Enterovioform. Very few people would have done this, and fewer still would I have obliged. Just the same, I immediately began to dress.

When the phone rang again I answered it very crossly.

John, I said, I am very happy to bring you my drugs, but you must remember that I happen to be rather out of sorts myself.

Yes, hello, said a strange, papery voice. The remainder was drowned by the metallic roar of small engines.

Who is this?

Chubb, he shouted. Chubb here. Is that Miss Wode-Douglass?

How on earth did you find me?

Name in your magazine, he said. I'll come and see you, can or cannot?

Later I discovered this 'can or cannot' was very proper Malaysian English, but on this first encounter, hearing it delivered in Chubb's Australian accent, I judged it not only illiterate but disturbingly false.

I'm actually rather ill, I said.

I have medicine.

Having no enthusiasm for any diagnosis he might make, I remained silent.

Sarah Wode-Douglass? *The Times* of London?

Not for many years.

Please see me, he said. I can come to your hotel.

This, of course, is exactly what I had wished when I carried my magazine to his shop, but that was before I knew his history.

A fright in my sarong, he said. I'll wear my suit. Please. You show face for just a short while.

Mr Chubb, is this about the George?

Who is that?

Stefan George, the poet.

Sorry . . .

I thought you might have an opinion of the translation.

Forgive me, Miss Wode-Douglass. No time yet.

At this point there was a great thundering on my door. I opened it and a white-faced Slater pushed past me. As the bathroom door closed I saw a small green lizard flee for the corner of the room, where it slowly turned from green to grey. It was impossible not to hear the sounds of Slater's distress.

Mr Chubb?

Yes.

I'm sorry, I can't meet with you.

Mem, I have something extraordinary to show you. Absolutely unique. One kind only-*lah*.

Some poetry, perhaps. By Christopher Chubb.

No, no, not by me.

By whom then?

Please, let me bring it to you. Can or cannot? You won't be sorry.

I was rather surprised to find myself agreeing to meet him downstairs at the Highland Stream, which ran its tasteless course from the back wall of The Pub, beneath a wooden bridge, to a drain beside the gift shop.

5

By a quarter to two the rain had became torrential and, given the unsettled state of my stomach, I was relieved. The Australian, I was certain, would not venture out in this downpour. Fifteen minutes later he proved me wrong, appearing before me as I sipped weak green tea.

The sarong was gone. In its place was a double-breasted tweed suit made not only for a different age and climate but also, it seemed, for a more substantial man. Inside the framework of padded shoulders and wide lapels my visitor seemed shrunken, like a walnut left to wither in its shell. One could look at him and confidently guess that he had arrived in Kuala Lumpur in the late forties and had then, when the close-cropped hair on his beautifully shaped head was still black, displayed an almost sweet wistfulness around the shadowy corners of his mouth. Today he wore a white shirt and broad tie of a vaguely military design. He had done his best, as he had promised, yet the loose fit of his frayed collar gave him the appearance of even greater poverty and disenfranchisement than at that shocking moment when I spied him in his store.

I should add that although he carried no umbrella, Christopher Chubb was somehow completely dry, as if he had been recently unfolded from a camphor chest.

I offered him tea which he rejected rather brusquely. I am not here to bot on you, he said.

I made room on my settee but he chose to sit opposite me. He immediately produced two envelopes which he laid on the coffee table, then a small metal case from which he took a pair of old-fashioned horn-rimmed spectacles. He appeared somewhat pompous. Without looking at me he carefully examined each of the envelopes and finally chose one to give me, his manner very monkish. It was unsettling to remember that these same hands had once given another editor the fraudulent poetry which had destroyed his life.

What is this? I asked, looking into those seemingly mild eyes and discovering a sunken, sly intelligence.

Something you need.

There was nothing in the envelope but two roughly moulded brown pills. If he'd said they were the work of dung beetles I would have found it credible.

Pour les maladies des tropiques, he said in an appalling accent. I am not here to poison you, Mem. Please, take it. It will help, I promise.

The pill seemed so alien, and he no less so. I doubt I would have taken it had not a particularly violent spasm arrived at just that moment.

Watching me swallow, he smiled. In my interests that they work.

I was startled that he should so plainly confess to 'interests'.

He cast down his eyes, which produced an odd effect suggesting not whimsy or modesty but a sudden, secret, arrogance. I don't want you dashing off, he said. I need to speak to you.

He set down the second envelope. It was larger than the first and its flap had been closed with coarse black tape, clearly from the bicycle shop, and this he now fussily rolled away. From the envelope he extracted a single sheet of paper wrapped in thin clear polythene.

God knows why, but I was suddenly certain that he wished to sell me an autograph, and I did feel a twinge of compassion for this literary exile waiting for the chance to sell his little treasures. In this, I imagined, he was not unlike the boys who loitered in front of the Merlin with their rolls of batik, waiting for the Americans to come outside.

Very delicately, he removed the plastic sheath, folding it so particularly that my eyes were held and I really paid no attention to the treasure it had protected, not until the owner brought it to my attention.

It was a poem, or a part of a poem, composed in those thick rhythmic down-strokes which would later become, if only briefly, so familiar.

May I pick it up?

The tropics are not kind to paper.

And indeed the page showed the signs of both mould and water damage, having become so very fragile that it seemed likely to break in half or even shatter. It looked to have been sliced from a bound journal.

Read, Mem, read.

I did so, and I doubt it needs saying that I read with a full consciousness of the old man's history. I approached these twenty lines with both suspicion and hostility, and for a moment I thought I had him. It was a sort of oriental Tristan Tzara, but that was too glib a response to something with very complicated internal rhymes and, unlike Tzara, nothing felt the slightest bit false or old-fashioned. It slashed and stabbed its way across the page, at once familiar and alien. I wondered if the patois – Malay, Urdu – was disguising something as common as cod Eliot. But that did not fit either, for you really cannot counterfeit a voice. All I knew now, in my moment of greatest confusion and suspicion, was that my heart was beating very fast indeed. Rereading the fragment, I felt that excitement in my blood which is the only thing an editor should ever trust.

Who wrote this, I asked. I must have looked frightfully stern but in fact I was all atwitter. Where is the rest of it?

He removed his spectacles, rubbed his eyes, and sighed.

Oh shit, I thought, of course! It's him. It must be him. You wrote this?

No, no, not me.

Is the author a secret?

You will not believe me.

I should like to know, I said.

It is a man named McCorkle.

I do have a temper. My family knows I have a temper. It is probably true that I will die in a room by myself because I have savaged someone who was trying to help me, and I have seen good cause to write those notes of apology one of which – my grovelling little letter to Cyril Connolly – is apparently amongst his papers in the British Museum. But in this case it should not seem peculiar that I was angry, having been titillated by the prospect of a find only to be told that its author was the man upon the stair.

I am afraid, I said, that Mr McCorkle's notoriety precedes him.

Yes, he said, you know who he is. His manner was not as one might expect it to be – was oddly insistent, in fact. Oh, you know him certainly.

But not exactly?

He did not answer but returned the fragment to the safety of its plastic sleeve.

I doubt it has much commercial value, I said.

You think I come to hawk to you, he said brusquely.

Of course that was precisely so, but I shook my head.

Then what *do* you think-*lah*? He looked up at me with eyes still watery but also belligerent.

Oh no, I said, you are the one who sought the meeting.

He blinked. Perhaps a cup of tea, he said, and I saw what a strange and fragile creature he was, powerless, pathetic, filled with pride and self-importance.

While I poured his tea he made himself very busy with his

electrical tape, which he stubbornly forced to serve another time.

You have been out to the Batu Caves, he asked. His treasure was sealed but as he lifted his tea-cup there was a slight tremble to his hand.

I am a very bad tourist.

Yes, he said, I never liked foreign places. Still, should see the *kavadi* bearers. People seem to like that, bamboos driven into the flesh. He paused, staring at me intently. Slater told you all about the McCorkle business?

Yes.

He told you that Weiss died?

The editor?

He nodded and sipped his tea. The hand was now shaking violently.

You must've felt terrible.

Worse than that, he said in that papery, nasal voice.

At first I had been struck by his beauty, but there was now something very off-putting about him – neediness where I had seen strength, unsteady liver-spotted hands, and the disconcerting sensuality of those tea-wet lips.

You'll listen if I tell you a story?

I looked over his shoulder to where Jalan Treacher had disappeared behind the knotted skeins of rain.

I suppose I haven't anything better to do, I said, but in truth I had no interest in his story at all. I wished to read that fragment again, as he well knew, and so I must endure his tale.

6

I loathe dishonesty, he began, his grey eyes glittering. You would know that if you were familiar with my verse-*lah*. Like a good table or a chair, nothing there that does not do a useful job. So you see how bad it is that what I am remembered for is a fake. Smoke and mirrors, a joke, that's all it was.

He paused, glaring almost accusingly. Have you been to Australia? he demanded suddenly. No, of course not-*lah*.

Actually, I said, my mother was Australian.

Yes, we have a terror of being out of date.

Mother did not like to talk about Australia. She had rather a set against it.

Yes, she is Australian. She is wondering, what are people saying in France or wearing in London? That is the issue for her, isn't it? He raised his reedy voice but seemed unaware of the attention he was drawing to himself. No, we cannot wait, he cried, slapping his knee. We cannot wait another day to know, and yet we must wait-*lah*. They call it the Tyranny of Distance now, so I am told.

In the nineteenth century, he continued, energetically adding sugar to his tea, the women of Sydney would go down to Circular Quay to see what the English ladies were wearing when they stepped ashore. *Wah*, look at that. Must have one now. Whatever they saw there would be copied in the week. It will still be the same, take my word. Must have whatever fashion comes down the gangway. Osbert Sitwell, Edith Sitwell, we will have poems just like theirs on the streets tomorrow. Now, he said, one of the fashion spotters on the dock was a young man named David Weiss.

The editor?

A very handsome Jew. Parents were in the *shmatte* business. A man of letters also, so he thought – boy of letters really, so young. The parents were cultured in the way these people often are. I never went into a Jewish house until I met him. Who could believe it? My home bare as a cupboard, no books, dried-out plates of leftovers in the fridge. Here, suddenly – bloody walls of books, Turkish rugs, modern paintings, de Chirico, Léger. So shocking to me-*lah*. Unfair that anyone should have such a start in life.

Weiss and I, he said, were students at Fort Street, school for clever boys. Who would guess it now that I have become a mongrel? Then I won the exhibition in Greek and the Special Prize for an essay on the influence of Hokusai on Renoir – all this from reproductions, you understand. But it was through David Weiss – three years younger, imagine – I learned of Rilke and Mallarmé. He lent me *The Little Review*. We were friends, members only, but he was always foreign to me. You know these people, no natural reticence or modesty. Always thrusting themselves forward, must have a different table than the one they are shown to by the waiter. Soup has to be made hotter when any of us would eat it as it came. You must not think me an anti-Semite. Perhaps I sound like one.

Indeed he did.

Well, I was jealous of Weiss, won't say I wasn't. We were all struggling poets, trying to find our voices, to be published in little magazines printed on brown wrapping paper. It was the war, the end of civilisation, who could know? I was twenty-four, a private in the army in New Guinea. Weiss had some cushy job in the Department of Defence. He sat on his bum in Melbourne.

I was shot by bloody Japs, carried on a litter for sixty miles, dropped and bloody well abandoned in an ambush. *Cheh*. No end to it. Delivered to hospital in Rabaul; transferred to Townsville, where I was given this poetry magazine called *Personae*. No brown paper here-*lah*. Top-hole only, the best stock, a cover painting in colour. Inside, all the very latest fashions in poetry and art. And who was its editor? David Weiss! My first feeling? Jealousy. Why not? He was three years younger. No war for him, and now so far ahead. But then I read what he had chosen, and what I felt was not jealousy but . . . how pathetic, Mem. It was so fake, so half-past-six. No head, no tail. I truly could not bear it – sick in my gut. I will tell you the feeling – exactly like listening to my mother in the Church of England in Haberfield. Always the smell of something false about her. Holy, holy, holy. Bellowing the responses more loudly than anyone else, making an exhibition of herself. *Samah-samah*, all the same – fake is fake no matter where you find it.

In Australia they think I am the great conservative. Listen, I had spent more time reading Eliot and Pound than Weiss ever did, and later I would prove this. Even great poets have tics. No problem to trick a lazy reader with the mannerisms. Weiss knew of writers I had never heard of, but there was something shallow in his character. Send him a poem with the line 'Look, my Anopheles' as if it were some classical allusion and he would never admit he did not know Anopheles. He might try to look it up, but if he couldn't find it – forget it. Fake it. Never mind.

Well, Mem, Anopheles is a mosquito, and when I saw his magazine I had it in mind to sting him where his skin was bare. I know I said I would not bot on you . . .

Please, I said, whatever you want.

He ordered a cucumber sandwich, the cheapest item on the menu.

But you invented a whole life for your poet, I said. Is it true that you even produced a birth certificate?

He stared at me. Slater told you, yes or not? What *lagi*? That's all he said.

Weiss was a pinko, he said angrily. I would have made McCorkle a coal miner except they'd have gone looking for his union card. I gave birth to a bicycle mechanic instead. But his poems would be learned, so many classical allusions – from a grease monkey. Explain that. It cannot be. What a notion, that the ignorant can make great art.

It sounds as if you were very convincing, I said.

It *reeked* of rat-*lah*.

His sandwich arrived and he paused to pick it up, turning it this way and that as if he hadn't seen one for many years.

Reeked, he said, but I knew young Weiss had lost his schnozzle. He would so *want* pearls in the shit of swine, so want the genius to be a mechanic that he would never stop to question the evidence. So I wrote this letter. Meant to come from McCorkle's sister.

He replaced the cucumber sandwich, and as he did so his entire face changed, the cheeks sinking and the shadowy mouth becoming as tight and small as a widow's purse. The transformation was disturbing and did not become less so when I realised that he was taking on the sister's character.

'Beatrice McCorkle,' he announced in a careful nasal accent which was marked in equal part by its lack of education and its great desire for propriety.

'Dear Sir, When I was going through my brother's things after his death, I found some poetry he had written.'

Watching Chubb, I was reminded of a completely unnerving séance I once attended in Pimlico where an old Welsh woman suddenly began talking like a posh young man. That had been a striking mutation, and this performance now taking place on the tartan banks of the Highland Stream was more than its equal. Christopher Chubb was still sitting there in his oversized clothes with his large spotted hands, but the voice was from quite another place and body. As would happen often in the future, all those disturbing Malaysian locutions were suddenly leached away. Witnessing the depth and detail of the character, I wondered if this was not the mother he seemed to loathe so much.

'I am no judge of poetry myself,' said the voice of Beatrice McCorkle, 'but a friend who I showed it to thinks it is very good and told me it should be published. On his advice I am sending you the poems for an opinion.

'It would be a kindness if you would let me know whether you think there is anything in them. I am not a literary person myself and I do not feel I understand what he wrote, but I feel that I ought to do something about them. My brother Bob kept himself very much to himself and lived on his own of late years and he never said anything about writing poetry. He was very ill in the months before his death last July and it may have affected his outlook.

'I enclose a 2½d stamp for reply, and oblige. Yours sincerely. Beatrice McCorkle.'

At that moment, devouring his sandwich, Chubb appeared monstrous – malicious, anti-Semitic, so grotesque and self-deceiving in his love of 'truth and beauty'. I felt the Wode-Douglass temper rising like steam behind my eyes and I do believe I would've said something very sharp indeed had I not been interrupted by the Sikh doorman who'd met us on the traumatic night of our arrival.

Your friend, he said. Mr Slater. He is very sick. You must go to him.

7

Slater was waiting at his door. His face was green. From the gloomy room behind him there came the unpleasant aroma of a poorly ventilated lavatory.

I'm so sorry, he said as he accepted my last Enterovioform. I am a selfish beast, I know it.

Still standing in the open doorway, he gulped down the pill without aid of water. I rather hope it's not amoebic dysentery, he said. I did have that once. Lost two stone in a week. You really should get to a doctor if you're able, although they'll charge a bloody fortune if you're English. The Chinese chaps are better.

He retreated into the room, which rather incredibly showed the remnants of two breakfasts. He followed my eyes.

Yes, yes, he said, as he threw a napkin over the tray. I know, I know.

You had a visitor, I asked incredulously.

I'm a wretch, dear girl, I know I am. I thought a little massage might make me better.

Breakfast with a masseur? I have a visitor myself, I said.

This perked him up a little – though in retying his dressing gown he revealed a great deal more of his legs than I wished to see. You devil, he said.

No. It is Christopher Chubb.

Chubb? No!

He is downstairs still.

Slater sat heavily on the bed. Now listen to me, little Micks, he said. You tell him to go.

I'll do no such thing.

This is not a nice man.

But rather interesting nonetheless.

Oh he'll be bloody interesting all right, he said, grunting with effort as he reached for the telephone. Call the bloody desk. They'll get that big Sikh fellow on the door to see him off.

I took the phone from him and returned it to its cradle. He's my guest, I said.

Your guest is barking bloody mad. What's he selling?

He isn't selling anything. When you called he was telling me about the McCorkle Hoax.

Jesus, Sarah, you're the editor of an internationally respected poetry journal. You don't even want to *touch* a thing like this. Did he show you poetry?

No.

Are you sure?

Of course I'm sure.

Well, you stay away from Chubb. I should never have drawn your attention to the leech. Has he asked for money?

Only a cucumber sandwich.

Leave it at that, then. He is not at all well balanced. Why do you think he's here? Why do you think an educated man is sitting in that ghastly shop with those pustules on his legs?

I think they're tropical ulcers.

He is there, Micks, because he went mad.

To hear Slater speak so loudly and negatively about another poet was, to say the least, unusual. Setting Dylan Thomas aside, he was normally exceptionally careful. I was not deaf to him now, but if I can trust anything it is my taste – or, to risk a vulgarity, my heart. One's pulse rate is a very reliable indicator of what one encounters.

For a madman, I said, he seems rather credible. Why didn't you tell me how well you knew him?

I don't know him! I spent an evening with him in Sydney at the end of the war and he tried it on with me.

You mean sexually?

Of course bloody not sexually. He is really a despicable person. He will drag you into his delusional world, have you believing the most preposterous things.

You make him sound even more interesting.

This is my responsibility, and I cannot permit you to speak with him again.

Though intent on saying much more he was taken, at this moment, by a powerful colonic spasm and bent over in agony. Still doubled up, he stumbled to the bathroom. While he went about his business, I propped the door open with the telephone book and opened the windows to the rain, which hadn't relented in the least. The carpet was soon rather wet, but the room itself a little refreshed.

Slater returned, threw himself heavily on his bed, and burrowed under the covers.

Just send him away, he said. Trust me, Sarah.

I could not have been given a clearer warning of the consequence, and I really did go back to the foyer with the intention of terminating our interview.

You were talking to Slater? Chubb asked as I returned to my settee.

Yes, I was.

He told you I was mad?

No, of course not, I said, observing that the wrapped page of poetry had been returned to the middle of the table.

Wah – he got a fright the night he met me.

And why was that, Mr Chubb?

He looked at me keenly – suspiciously even – as if calculating the odds of my having heard the story already. I plan to tell you why, he said at last, after I have told

35

you what happened to the Jew. But I see Slater has put you off me.

No, not at all. Of course not.

He looked at me with an animal wariness, but of course continued with the story he had come to tell, pausing only occasionally to nibble at a sandwich. Although here again I was reminded of the way a dog or cat will eat, always cautious, concerned that a delicacy might be the bait inside a trap.

8

Jealous or not, said Chubb, I did submit my work to *Personae*, and Weiss took six months to reject it. But now I sent him the first two fakes by 'Bob McCorkle', and seven days later there was the envelope in the Townsville P.O. mailbox I'd rented for just this purpose. And Weiss was as *boh-doh* as a crayfish, in a great rush to crawl inside. So excited he could not write straight. Very difficult to read his scrawl. 'My assessment is that this is work of the very greatest importance. I should be very glad if you would send me any more of his poetry that is extant.' Extant, God save me. To Beatrice he writes '*extant*'? So *aiksy*.

Well, you designed the trap just for him, I said. Surely you can't blame the poor man for falling into it.

Oh I blamed him-*lah*. I blamed him very much at the beginning.

But you set out to destroy him.

No, Chubb cried, with such passion that his voice cut across the lounge like a hawker's, and a wall-faced Chinese gentleman in a boxy suit stepped out from behind the reception desk and stood watching, hands folded in the region of his crotch.

No! His watery eyes had turned a cold and cloudy blue. Please, no.

Mr Chubb –

No, he interrupted, you are plain wrong. I meant him no harm at all. No danger.

He died, I said, more angrily than I intended.

He stared so, it almost frightened me – white fissures in the iris, like those in fast-set ice.

I liked Weiss, he began again. Meant nothing but good. He was only twenty-one and so desperate to be in fashion. But don't you see? The boy writes drivel, publishes drivel. Does this matter, Mem? Perhaps I valued truth above friendship.

He looked to me, as if expecting me to endorse this view. I held my tongue.

Think what you like, I set out to prove the truth. These people had become so hooked on the latest fashion. No substance. Action only. The truth was dead or rotting. There had been a complete decay of meaning and craftsmanship in poetry.

When you say 'these people', I said, do you mean Jews?

He balked, staring at me fixedly, and I could not tell if I had hit the mark or gone so wide that he was stunned by my assumption.

Have you read the McCorkle poems, he asked at last. No? He leaned forward and laid his surprisingly moist hand against my arm. I stayed very still until he removed it.

'Swamps,' he recited mockingly in that wispy nasal voice, 'marshes, borrow-pits and other / Areas of stagnant water serve / As breeding-grounds . . .' There, he said. The genius of young Bob McCorkle. What do you say to that?

Naturally enough I said nothing.

'Areas of stagnant water serve as breeding-grounds.' Do you know what that is from?

I shook my head.

An army manual of mosquito eradication, You see, it meant nothing-*lah*. There is another poem I sent him, 'Colloquy with John Keats'. It begins, 'I have been bitter with you, my brother'. It is stolen. Any educated person would know from where.

How I disliked this prim pedagogy. Pound, I said: 'I make a pact with you, Walt Whitman – I have detested you long enough'.

Yes, he said, then listen to Bob McCorkle's lines to Keats: 'I have been bitter with you, my brother, / Remembering that saying of Lenin when the shadow / Was already on his face: "The emotions are not skilled workers"'. Of course Lenin never said such a preposterous thing.

With his frayed, gaping collar and his raised, crooked eyebrows he did look barking mad. *Hold off*! *unhand me, grey-beard loon*! I disagree, I said. The Lenin line is more witty than preposterous. And the opening line is quite different from Pound's.

Of course I had praised him without meaning to, so easy was it to forget that Chubb was the real author here. When I made this slip he could not quite contain his pleasure and he suddenly reminded me of those cunning old tramps who used to turn up at the kitchen door in High Wycombe with some story of the *great tragedy that befell me, Miss.*

Yet I must not make myself appear too cynical, for this was exactly the story I wished to hear. This must also have occurred to Chubb, of course.

If I had shown the first McCorkle poems to you, he said, you would have smelled the rat, I know you would.

But, Mr Chubb, you cannot have the slightest idea of my judgement.

Aiyah – I saw your magazine.

But as you said, you have not had time to read it.

Again he balked and stared at me. Anyway, he said at last, Weiss wrote back to little Beatrice, who – he lapsed into that horrid accent – was 'only too pleased to give the biographical information you requested'. Better she never wrote back, but no choice now. Bob McCorkle must be born. 'I could not stop

Bob from leaving school at fourteen', Beatrice wrote, 'and after that he was set on going to work. I have always thought he was very foolish not to have got his Intermediate'.

See how she writes to him-*ah*. So polite. Very respectful. Carrying his big leg, is what we say here.

'I am so pleased you think the poems are good enough to publish. I never thought they would be of interest to people overseas.' The writing in the letter, Chubb said, is even better than the poems. You can smell the suburbs in it. Cats' piss in the privet hedge. Leaking gas. Reeking odours of the petite bourgeoisie.

Could Beatrice, I said, bear any resemblance to your mother?

In the hour or so we had been talking Chubb had taken nothing stronger than tea, but now he showed a drunk's quick trigger. Don't get clever-*lah*, he hissed.

This sudden rage reminded me of Slater's warnings. I therefore signed and collected my purse.

Releks, he said urgently. Please. I know I am behaving badly. I promise I will stop it now.

Thank you, Mr Chubb, it has been very interesting.

You are *the* Sarah Wode-Douglass? You covered the Christie Murders for *The Times*? That was you? What the chances you ever come *jalan-jalan* past my door? And with John Slater? Me with Rilke? This is one chance in one million – but believe me, Mem, I have been waiting for you for the last eleven years.

I found myself, not for the last time, transfixed by him. I stood, holding my handbag, very aware not only of his earnest eyes but also of the tantalising parcel on the periphery of my vision.

It is not only poetry I want to tell you about, he said. Something much worse-*lah*. Sit.

9

It was to me that he issued his command to sit but John Slater also obeyed, appearing from nowhere to plop himself down untidily beside me, stretching his long arm protectively behind my back, extending his great bare legs beneath the table from which Chubb's plastic-clad offerings had disappeared.

Those two vertical frown marks above Slater's nose were the acid which had always stopped his good looks from being too saccharine. They drew attention to his very clear and active eyes and somehow, in the tugged and twisted skin of his forehead, suggested a sort of moral outrage. He could certainly look extremely fierce, and I should imagine his sheer size made him frightening to Chubb, whom he had obviously come to drive away.

First, as ever, he needed food and drink.

To the waitress he said: *Satu lagi* beer, one more Tiger, and do you have any of those little dried fish things. *Ikan ketcheel.* I forget what they're called.

You want the fried fish, *Tuan?*

No, no, small fish. Snacks.

I scowled at him ferociously.

Christopher, can you tell the waitress what I mean?

Ikan bilis.

The girl did not seem to hear him. A moment later, however, she returned with a bowl of dried fish – small pungent creatures, each the size of a jasmine leaf. Chubb thanked her, and then I realised she was somehow avoiding him. This was the first hint I had of his strange local reputation.

Slater leaned forward to sample the fish, made a face, and pushed the bowl away. I don't wish to be at all unfriendly, he said to Chubb, but if it's dough you've come for, Christopher, you are definitely barking up the wrong tree.

I could never have imagined Slater talking like this to a British poet, but Chubb did not seem in the least disconcerted. He merely lowered his papery eyelids and smiled.

She – Slater frowned in my direction – is not really worth your trouble. She may talk posh but the family has been in hock for several centuries and what little dough remained was all spent on some very lovely parties many years ago. As for me, I am reduced to being poet in residence on the *QE2*.

This was a lie.

So when you have had the beer, he concluded, you have pretty much drunk the well dry.

Yes, said Chubb.

It was a curious directionless response, and it caused Slater, whose best work was sometimes distinguished by exactly this type of unsettling effect, to pause.

Yes, Chubb said, and there you prove Auden's case against you, isn't it?

The expression of Slater's handsome face was that of someone unexpectedly and brutally slapped. Don't be a shit, old chap, he said quietly.

But Chubb leaned in towards him and I marked the thin elastic spittle, like the linkage of a mussel to its shell, joining his upper to his bottom lip. Can't remember Auden's sentence, he said, help me-*lah*. 'The author's inability to conceive of altruism', isn't it?

There was a silence then during which I remember thinking it must've been a very long time since anyone spoke to John Slater like this. In Britain he had somehow made himself so 'well liked' that it was hard to find another poet, even one who privately thought his work mawkish or pornographic, who would say a word against him. Certain I was about to witness the most awful row, I watched John sweep his great mane of grey hair back off his high and handsome brow, but when he finally responded it was in a rather small voice.

I'm sorry, he said.

Chubb gave nothing back except a sudden blink.

Wystan is a remarkable man, continued Slater, but he is capable of the most awful cruelty and he does not always hold himself to the ethical standards he demands of others. But that is not exactly the point in this case, he said, sadly watching the waitress pour the beer. He took a handful of the *ikan bilis* and dropped them back into the bowl. I behaved like a cunt, he said. You hit me back. Fair enough.

Chubb shrugged. I'm the hoaxer. No-one gives me face.

Oh, please. Enough. Do you really think anyone remembers that McCorkle business anymore? It's forgotten. Micks here never heard of you. The editor of *The Modern Review* never heard of you, or of Bob McCorkle.

Thank you for lying.

You know it is not a lie.

So gracious of you. There was nothing Australian in how he bowed his head, no sign of that dry and deadly sarcasm. Such a famous poet, he said.

The compliment caused Slater to swell physically in a way that reminded me, exactly, of Harold Wilson. Now, now, don't flatter me, he said.

Did I say *good* poet?

Touché, said Slater.

This conflict was not exactly boring, I suppose, but I had no interest in him fighting with Chubb, which he would surely do, at the next beer or the one after that. For the moment, however, he seemed mostly driven by a desire to prove himself a more decent man than Auden had thought. When he began to offer Chubb money, I was depressed but not surprised.

It would have to be a loan, of course, he said, but I could give you fifty quid. I could do it now.

He produced a pile of crumpled Malaysian dollars.

I do believe Chubb considered the money, but then he retreated, shifted sideways along the settee, shaking his head.

I'm not saying you're here for bloody money. I am saying that I will lend you fifty quid. Give face, old chap. Don't insult me.

Like a duck talking to a chicken.

What?

I don't want your money-*lah*.

What do you want?

He hesitated. Perhaps this lady will write up my story.

Dear chap, that is like asking Fangio to park your mini-moke. Don't you know who she is? She's not some bloody hack. She is the editor of an important magazine. Besides, no-one is interested in your story anymore. 'Unaffected by "the march of events," he passed from men's memory in *l'an trentuniesme'*. Really, if you're hiding here, the war – as they say – is over. Come out. Surrender. Go home.

Don't *lebeh*, you, said Chubb patiently. This my home now.

It was *twenty-six* bloody years ago, Slater insisted. Everyone is dead. He paused. Oh shit, I'm sorry. Really!

Apa? asked Chubb mildly.

No, no, I'm *sincerely* sorry. About the poor young editor fellow, of course.

I often carry notebooks, which normally contain nothing more interesting than my debts and schemes by which they might be settled. But when I produced one now Christopher Chubb's eyes fixed on it as hungrily as I had wished.

Slater also noticed. Oh Jesus, Micks, he said, you are so bloody perverse.

But he had not read that mottled manuscript. He could not imagine a wonder he could never have made.

I don't know what happened to David Weiss, I said.

I told you. The poor bugger hanged himself.

He did not hang himself, said Chubb.

Don't play tricks on her, Chubb, really. You cannot play this particular prank more than once.

Chubb completely ignored him, turning all his attention onto me. Great good fortune, he said, that someone who can understand this story has finally come my way. He smiled. Good things will come of this. Important things.

He is flattering you, Slater cried.

I do not flatter, said Chubb. I do not lie. I am the only person who knows how this young man was killed. I can tell you that story, or not tell you. What for you not wish to know?

10

I have no particular prejudice against middle-aged men, indeed I seem to collect them. However, at moments like this they become so intolerably *messy*. Chubb and Slater were like two dogs in a fight – deaf as posts, blood in their eyes, beyond my control. A Swissair flight crew who had been seated nearby moved into the fake pub, where presumably they would not have to endure Slater's booming voice. As they passed us, a very pretty young air hostess raised an eyebrow as if to say, You idiot – get rid of them. It must have been comic to observe, I'm sure, a pair of codgers competing for the attention of a dowdy Englishwoman. Just the same, I had my notebook out. Although where this cheap spiral-bound article would lead us all, no-one could have foretold.

Slater did not seem to notice the departing lovelies. The very nicest thing we could say about this prank of yours, he said, is that it misfired.

He then stretched back, his hands behind his head, exposing the entire length of his rather well-preserved body as if he were beyond any possibility of attack. Chubb, by contrast, presumed nothing. He was like a foot soldier, a knife man. He leaned forward with his elbows resting on his shiny, worn-out knees.

He is right, he said quietly. The hoax misfired. I wished to make a point, but only to a few. Who cares about poetry? Fifty people in Australia? Ten with minds you might respect. Once Weiss had declared my fake was a work of genius, I wished those ten people to know. That was it, Mem. I never wanted the tabloids. Who would expect the Melbourne *Argus* would ever be interested in poetry. This was not their business, but what a caning-*lah*, what a public lashing poor old Weiss was given. I could never have foreseen that.

To be correct, old chap, Slater interrupted, you were responsible for him receiving, actually, two quite separate sets of canings.

Cheh, cried Chubb. I know, I know. But you must understand – none of this was planned, Mem.

You see, Mem, said Slater, mauling me ever so affectionately as he spoke, the poor bugger was prosecuted for publishing obscenities.

Christopher? I asked. Why was he prosecuted?

No, not him. David Weiss.

How could I know? Chubb demanded. So *boh-doh* stupid. It is impossible to conceive.

Well, old mate, you wrote the bloody poems.

Yes, and I made damn sure that they were foolish and pretentious, but they were not obscene. You know that, John. Tell her the truth. Listen, Mem, please, let me recite just a little to you. I promise you will suffer no embarrassment. And he did so, quickly, rather plainly, in an uninflected whisper.

Only a part of me shall triumph in this
(I am not Pericles)
Though I have your silken eyes to kiss
And maiden-knees
Part of me remains, wench, Boult-upright
The rest of me drops off into the night.

And that was all? I asked. Bolt upright?
B-o-u-l-t.

Chubb smiled. The bard's servant in *Pericles*. As a pun it makes sense, but not as a prosecution. Nothing is clear until you understand that obscenity was not the issue here.

Very well. What was?

He was prosecuted, Chubb said solemnly, for being a Jew.

Oh, listen to him, Micks. You make rather a big thing about that, old chap. Take the blame yourself.

Chubb blinked. Yes, listen. You cannot change the fact – Weiss was a Jew. If he had been ugly, it might not have mattered, but he was handsome, tall. High forehead. Thick wavy hair. A little conceited also. Am I allowed to say that? Let me tell you, he had cut a swathe through those clean-limbed girls at Melbourne University. Fresh off the beach at Portsea and Frankston. An Anglo-Saxon would have known to apologise for such extraordinary success. Not David. He was so *aiksy*, he would not bow and scrape and make himself a humble fellow.

Micks, Slater told me, just remember this is reported by his enemy.

No, no, Chubb said, I was not his enemy. Weiss's great enemy was himself. Also the Chief Magistrate of Victoria. He had not made this opponent in the ordinary way but by having this Magistrate's daughter fall in love with him – she was a fresher at the university – and then dumping her. *Wah* – so brutal. You never knew that, yes or not? There are many things you do not know, John Slater. How long in Melbourne? One week? How long in Sydney? One year? The Chief Magistrate was a member of the Melbourne Club. Do you know what that is? Three facts about that club-*lah*. First: stand in Little Collins Street and stare up at the high brick wall and see, on the other side, the top of a giant palm tree in the middle of a huge garden. Second: you will never be invited to stand on the other side of the wall. Third: you have a thousand times more chance than the wealthiest Jew in Toorak.

I don't know what Sir David Gibbons's feelings were

about the Jews or if he personally blamed Weiss for the death of Jesus Christ. His head-*lah*, I can't see in there. But the man was a member of the Melbourne Club. Also – he used all his power to destroy his daughter's former Jewish boyfriend.

Slater, affecting boredom, was waving to the waitresses. It was dark now and a percussive sound came from the disco behind the pub, like some creature thumping its great flat tail against the earth. Chubb did not seem to notice. He leaned forward, talking, and one could still see in him the earnest schoolboy from Haberfield who dreamed of a sophisticated city where poets would argue the merits of the Great and the Good.

How Weiss learned of his ludicrous ill fortune, he said to me, is very well known. May I tell you? Please?

I nodded.

Personae had a little office, he said, above a Russian restaurant in Acland Street. This office was a rendezvous – bohemians, theosophists, free-lovers, all dressed the part in corduroys. But when the cops arrived – no members present. Weiss was alone, wearing the Anglo-Saxon uniform, Fair Isle sweater, and big-bowled pipe. He could've worn the bloody crown of England and it would not have saved him from these gents. One of the policemen was in uniform. The real frightener was in plain clothes. I am Detective Vogelesang, et cetera, this is my colleague Sergeant Barker.

Wah! Like the poor beast in Kafka, Weiss had not the least idea of his crime. McCorkle's poems? Already paid for that offence. Every day he paid, repaid, public, private, without relent.

Are you the editor of a publication named *Personae*? Vogelesang asked. I saw him later, Chubb said. Big, powerful blond man. Pugnacious chin and weathered face like a very pissed-off soldier-settler. He wore a pork-pie hat like he was heading to change his fortune at the trots.

Weiss became the clever boy. Cassius Clay dancing

around his enemy. He said he was the editor. He said he was not. He said *Personae* had a publication committee which was government over the editor. He opened a copy to show Vogelesang the masthead. He succeeded in having this copy confiscated by nifty little Barker.

Well, are you and the committee responsible for these poems? said Vogelesang.

Barker leafed through the magazine, fresh from the printer, then licked the lead of his pencil and began to underline certain words.

I say, goes Weiss. You can't do that.

Barker could, no question.

In the case of this McCorkle chap, said Vogelesang, who made the decision to publish?

You want me to say I did?

I don't want you to say anything, sir.

Oh, it's me, said Weiss. What the hell.

You wrote an introduction to the work, did you not?

You bloody know I did.

Did you cause it to be published?

What is this about?

It is in reference to the magazine *Personae*.

What do you want to know?

Are we speaking to a person responsible for its publication and distribution?

Said Weiss, I don't know whether I ought to answer your questions.

Said Vogelesang, You can please yourself about that, *Tuan*. As for us, we have been instructed to make enquiries in connection with the provisions of the Police Act with respect to immoral or indecent publications.

There are two headlines that are burned into my brain, said Chubb. The first is WAR WITH GERMANY. The second, seven years later, is 'BOB MCCORKLE' TO BE PROSECUTED FOR OBSCENITY. I was still in military hospital in Townsville. A lieutenant in the next bed was reading the *Townsville Advocate*. Poetry on the front page! Imagine! The photograph I recognised as one I made myself, patched together from three different men. My creature. Over six feet tall. Fantastic head, huge powerful nose and cheekbones, great forehead like the bust of Shakespeare. I had put him together with the help of my friend Tess McMahon. Chopped him up and glued him. I forget where we got the head, but the chest belonged to the famous Aussie Rules footballer Keith Guinnane. What resurrectionists we were-*lah*. Tess laid a sixty-five-screen stipple over it all, and the papers had to rescreen it. After that, no scars visible.

It took a long time for me to get the *Advocate* from my mate and only then did I discover it was Weiss who was now to be punished for this so-called obscenity. At that point, Chubb whispered, my lovely joke was truly dead, like some pretty tree snake left smeared across the Ipoh Road.

I looked to Slater, but he was gone, standing back against the wall joking with the waitresses. The women were in their twenties, he was sixty-two. They did not seem to notice.

You must remember, said Chubb, how to call long distance just after the war. Trunk calls, that's what we said at home. *Adoi*! Painful, you know. Very expensive. Every three minutes the operator is going: Three minutes, are you extending? Every time another two pounds and two shillings. That was the cost of a three-minute call. Two pounds and two shillings, I spent it all. Some thanks I got.

You shit, Weiss said to me, you've got a nerve.

I told him sorry. I knew why he was angry.

I bet you do.

Was there something I could do-*lah*?

Go fuck yourself.

Would he like me as a witness?

For what?

I said I should be prosecuted. Put my head right on the chopping block for him.

Said he, You mean you want to share the glory.

Typical of him, Mem. That is his character. I laughed out loud.

He then told me that these poems are far beyond me. That was what he said. Incredible. He said I was incapable of writing what I wrote. What hubris-*lah*. Takes the breath away. I reminded him that I was the one who made Bob McCorkle, not just the words, but also cut up his head and legs and body. I physically pasted him together.

Doesn't matter, he said. I am his publisher.

Three minutes, are you extending?

The poems are bloody nonsense, David.

Oh, really, Chris? Is that so?

So sarcky but still I did not lose my temper. I told him he did not deserve this prosecution. This is a dreadful, dreadful country. It was, it is. They crush the butterfly upon the wheel. But did he care?

Yes, he says, I have published this 'dreadful country's' first great poet and you have proven yourself to be a jealous, reactionary little shit.

Three minutes, are you extending?

Little shit! I was two inches taller.

'Hurry up please it's time', Weiss said. Quoting Eliot, of course, but the operator cut us off.

All this was recorded in my notebook. Hotel Merlin, Kuala Lumpur, Saturday, August 10, 1972. Thirteen years later, the pages still smell of *ikan bilis*.

II

Chubb claimed that he did not travel to Melbourne with the intention of attending Weiss's trial. He said he'd been promised a job at J. Walter Thompson as a copywriter. However there are two thousand miles between Townsville and Melbourne, and by the time he completed the final leg – sitting on the freezing metal floor of an injured Hudson bomber – his friend the copy chief had punched his creative director in the nose and Chubb was left no better connected than any of the thousands of soldiers trying to get on their feet again in peacetime. He began the dispiriting business of finding work but, having no better qualification than a bachelor of arts and a piece of Japanese shrapnel resting against his spine, seems not to have been spectacularly successful. The advertising agencies all relished telling him, You will find no poetry here. He tried for book-reviewing from the papers but got no encouragement from anyone except the *Argus*, where his role in the McCorkle business was known. Their books editor offered him a freelance assignment covering Weiss's trial.

He was desperate for money but could not bring himself to feed on Weiss's humiliation. Finally, however, he joined that peculiar group which waited each morning for the doors of the Supreme Court of Victoria to open. It was a crowd not unlike the one you might find outside the Melbourne Library at a similar hour. That is, it had a fair representation of bookish individuals and the occasional mad mutterer who – had this been the library – could be expected to head straight for the reading room and go to sleep. Weiss's parents, grey-haired and elegantly dressed, were also present, though Chubb succeeded in avoiding them. There were also a number of neatly if not fashionably dressed men, members of Catholic Action, and some wide fellows whose distinctive misshapen overcoat pockets marked them as reporters from the tabloid press.

The month of May, as I have since discovered, is miserable in Melbourne. You get a very melancholy light as a result of all that cold water swelling up in Bass Strait, and even when there is warmth in the sunshine there is something in the light that chills the heart. Chubb leaned against the iron palisades, shivering inside his AIF greatcoat, smoking, waiting for the day to begin.

The interior of the courts is surprisingly warm in appearance, with a vast amount of cedar, some of it beautifully carved, and the twenty-foot ceilings are very handsome indeed. But there is never enough heating in Australia, particularly in government buildings, and this was doubtless the cause of the rather cruel atmosphere in court number four. Chubb found the cedar benches so deeply, unremittingly cold that they might as well have been forged from iron. This he could tolerate, but the smell of the place – stale bread, cheese, orange peel – provoked in him a deep unease. The Supreme Court of Victoria smelled like the shelter shed in a school playground and evoked a dark, merciless world where you were not wanted and never would belong.

Here was where the apparatus of the state would decide if the poetry he'd written as a joke would fail the test contrived by a Justice Cockburn in 1868 to determine 'whether the tendency of the matter charged as obscenity is to deprave and corrupt those whose minds are open to such immoral influences, and into whose hands a publication of this sort may fall'.

There was a church-like aspect to the court, and the order of procession reminded Chubb of the church in Haberfield, the scraping of shoes as the clergyman entered, the rising swell of the organ, the distinctive noise of Psalters being returned to their shelves.

Into this Christian machine David Weiss was brought each day to take his place, either standing in the dock or sitting beside his long-necked, bird-beaked solicitor. The first day was the most shocking, not simply because the defendant appeared so very beautiful and, in comparison to the huge judge and the plank-solid Vogelesang, slender, but because he had chosen – for what reason, who could know – to dress in a long flocked-velvet smoking jacket and a drooping black silk bow tie. Even a brief visit to Melbourne would tell you this was a mistaken strategy, but Weiss nonetheless stood before his accusers as an aesthete, an alien. As Chubb had said, he would not bow down.

When called to take the oath he declared he could not and there was some confusion about why this was, the court assuming it was because he was a Jew and Weiss finally making it clear that he did not believe in God at all. All this you can read in the transcript of the trial and I have used my own copy to jog my memory here and there.

The thing that struck the horrified Chubb was not how preposterous it was to convict someone for a culturally pre-tentious pun like 'Boult-upright' but how relentlessly the government brought down all its power on this young man.

The judge in fact was not Sir David Gibbons but Alfred Cousins, who turns out to have been the godfather of the girl Weiss had spurned. He displayed a very obvious physical power – a swimmer's shoulders, large hands, a wide but inexpressive mouth. Vogelesang, the chief witness, was also a sportsman and is nowadays more remembered as a cele-brated contestant in that wild, anarchic, rather Gaelic football they play down there. Even the prosecutor, who was red-faced and decidedly out of shape, had a crushed, pugnacious face from which he had managed to exclude any evidence of human sympathy.

The trial began with Vogelesang being called to the stand and recounting his meeting with Weiss at Acland Street.

This, of course, must have been a very dreary perform- ance, with the stolid detective reading from his notebook in an uninflected nasal drawl, but Chubb, sitting in the Merlin Hotel years later, played the parts of Weiss and Vogelesang to considerable comic effect. It was only later, when I read the transcript, that I appreciated the accuracy of his recollection, as if the grotesque inquisition had been burned into his living brain.

> DET. VOGELESANG: Are you acquainted with the poems of Bob McCorkle?
>
> WEISS: Yes.
>
> DET. VOGELESANG: There is a poem titled 'Boult to Marina'. What is your opinion of that poem?
>
> WEISS: I don't know what the author intended by that poem. You'd better ask him what he meant.
>
> DET. VOGELESANG: What do you think it means?
>
> WEISS: Ask the author. I am not going to express an opinion.
>
> DET. VOGELESANG: That means that you have an opinion but you are not prepared to express it.
>
> WEISS: I would have to give it two or three hours' con- sideration before I could determine what it means.
>
> DET. VOGELESANG: Do you think it is suggestive of indecency?
>
> WEISS: Do you know anything about the classical characters?
>
> DET. VOGELESANG: What I want to know is what it means.
>
> WEISS: Pericles and Boult are both classical characters.
>
> DET. VOGELESANG: Do you think the poem is suggestive of indecency?

WEISS: No more than Shakespeare or Chaucer.

DET. VOGELESANG: Ah, so you do admit that there is a suggestion of indecency about the poem.

WEISS: No, I don't.

DET. VOGELESANG: What does it mean when it says, 'Part of me remains, wench, Boult-upright'? Do you think some people could place an indecent interpretation on it?

WEISS: I'm very sure that some people could place an indecent interpretation on anything.

At this comment the public gallery burst into laughter and the judge made a stern speech about his courtroom not being a place of entertainment. Personally, Chubb needed no reminding. The machinery of justice intimidated him; and the more intimidated he felt, the greater his admiration became for Weiss, who refused to bend to its dull and bullying will.

It quickly became clear to Chubb that his victim was the only other person in court who understood how well made the hoax had been. The rest of the cast, he said, the defence included, could not have read a poem to save their lives. Allegedly esteemed psychologists from the Melbourne Tech were called to attest that these verses were high art. These opinions Chubb called worthless, but Weiss mostly explicated the issues very elegantly, laying out the cross-references to *Pericles* or *The Tempest*, the parodies of Eliot and Read, the manner in which the hoax itself was both subject and key to the mystery of the poems.

Yet while he was at times effective he suffered a single but considerable disadvantage: McCorkle's verse was almost impossible to explicate, with the result that Weiss sometimes seemed like a bright but lazy post-graduate hiding behind obfuscation.

The florid prosecutor then asked Weiss to take one of the stanzas of 'McCorkle's' 'Egyptian Register' and tell the court what it meant.

WEISS: The poem starts off with the man examining the body.

PROSECUTION: What man?

WEISS: The man in the poem.

PROSECUTION: Where does that come from – examining the body? I don't see that in the poem.

WEISS: Each thing he takes up suggests to him the inexplicability of human life . . .

PROSECUTION: Where does it say anything about the inexplicability of human life?

PROCEEDINGS INTERRUPTED

How were they interrupted? The transcript does not say, but Chubb remembered everything and thus this lunatic event may be roughly reconstructed.

Dunce, cried a rasping untutored voice.

Weiss flinched.

Silence! cried the judge.

Answer the question, demanded the prosecutor.

But Weiss was staring at the heckler, his complexion turning the colour of boiled tripe.

Mr Weiss, you may continue.

Haltingly, Weiss argued that the actual point of the poem was 'vagueness and inexplicability'. He was interrupted by a chair scraping violently in the front row. He tried to argue that the spine mentioned in the sixth line was actually 'a part of the brain' and that the poet had linked it with the 'harsh and enquiring element of the brain' which attempts to pierce 'the obscurity of life'.

PROSECUTION: Where is the harsh and inquiring element of a brain. Where do you get that from?

PROCEEDINGS INTERRUPTED

The transcript makes no mention of the heckler or his raw, uneducated voice. Ask the bloody author, he cried. Ask the author, you fucking philistine.

No mention of the bailiffs either. They rushed loudly in. A woman screamed and a chair crashed to the floor. From this scrum the bailiffs emerged, somehow joined to a massive man with wild dark eyes and black, shoulder-length hair.

Here's to culture, the wild man roared. *Sieg Heil.*

He turned to face the court, raising his arms not in the salute suggested by his cry but as if in benediction. Then, like a man shrugging off a coat that had suddenly become too hot, he dropped the bailiffs to the floor and walked – with remarkable grace, lightly on his toes, back and shoulders straight – out of the completely silent court.

What transpired next seemed even more shocking to Chubb: the prosecutor, apparently in complete denial of this interruption, simply resumed his questioning.

> PROSECUTION: You don't think that it would be possible for any fair-minded person to think that the author in using the word 'index' was referring to a penis in the state of erection?
>
> *PROCEEDINGS INTERRUPTED*

And here Weiss angrily jabbed a finger at where Chubb sat, huddled miserably in his cedar bench.

I will not continue, the defendant informed the court, while that man is sitting there.

And so, in a state of considerable embarrassment and confusion, Christopher Chubb stumbled out onto William Street. He never entered the court again.

12

During this story Slater had wandered off, and I was not at all pleased to see him returning with a brimming goblet of red wine in his hand.

Apart from complaining that the wine was off, a process which involved two waitresses and took an extraordinary length of time, he pretty much behaved himself. Only when I asked Chubb to explain why Weiss had acted as he had in court did Slater begin to roll his eyes and tap his head.

You want to hear? Chubb snapped. Yes? No? Which is it?

Slater was not in the least discomfited by having been caught out.

Of course, of course. Always very interested.

Chubb leaned forward, as if speaking directly to my notebook, which prop I seemed to be using more energetically than was my original intention. I went, he said firmly, back to Gordon Featherstone's place in Collins Street.

A very hospitable man, Gordon, said Slater.

You wish to hear why Weiss went so queer in court, but perhaps you know already?

I scowled at Slater but he would not shut up.

Gordon's place, he said, was in what was laughably called the Paris end of Collins Street. It's very posh these days, Micks, but after the war all sorts of reprobates were living there. And that gorgeous creature. He turned to Chubb. God, what was her name?

I don't know.

Oh yes you do.

That would be Noussette, I suppose.

Whatever did happen to Noussette? God, she was beautiful. I could have married her. *Chili-padi* type, no? Isn't that the expression? Hot like a chili. He kissed his fingers.

Cheh! You talk too much.

Wasn't Noussette a girlfriend of Weiss's before she was with Gordon?

You know nothing about her, mate.

Mate? Slater folded his arms and smiled delightedly. *Mem*! *Mate*!

Weiss climbed the fire escape, Chubb told me. Came in through Gordon's bedroom window. Drunk-*lah*. Had his wobbly boot on, as they say. There was a great ruckus. I slept right through. I woke up to find myself being shaken.

Weiss, Chubb told us, was very fastidious, known for his habit of changing his shirt twice a day and carrying a toothbrush in his pocket at all times. But there was no toothpaste on his breath as he shook the sleeping hoaxer, waking him to a noxious effluvium of garlic and red wine. Why are you trying to destroy me? he said, seizing Chubb by the shoulders and slamming him back down in the bed.

By now Chubb felt he deserved almost any punishment. He was completely responsible for Weiss's nightmare and so did nothing to protect himself. When Weiss clambered onto the bed and lay with his muddy boots upon his pillow, he did not protest. Indeed he took this opportunity, once again, to offer to accept whatever public blame he could for the so-called obscenity.

The trouble was, Weiss was an editor. He loved those poems. He would stake his life on them. On the one hand he would not concede that Chubb had written them, they were far too good; on the other he blamed him for publicly humiliating a friend. Weiss's voice rose higher in complaint. Why? He pushed his muddy boots against Chubb's head. Why did you do it, Christopher?

To prove a point, Chubb said.

It's sheer jealousy, Weiss said. I am more intelligent. I am better-looking. I am better known. I understand that you were jealous but why, when you finally had me in the bloody dock, would you keep twisting the knife? You are mentally unwell, Christopher. You are a sadist.

David, what on earth are you talking about?

I mean your bloody little theatre piece this afternoon. Did you pay that appalling actor? If so, you were robbed.

What actor?

What *actor*? The bloody giant! In the front row of the court. Author, author? I have already been humiliated like no-one has ever been humiliated, but that is not enough for you, is it? You must employ this creature to taunt me.

What creature?

Ask the bloody author, mate. There has never been a decent actor over five foot eleven and this one's a fucking ham. You found someone to look like McCorkle's photograph. It was very clever, but so malicious. It is the malice, Christopher, that sickens me. You came to my home. You had Seder at our table. You take my breath away.

Only now did Chubb understand that Weiss had seen the interjector in the court as his hired assassin, but in Melbourne you did not need to imagine conspiracies to explain this character. That part of the city was always filled with drunks – derelict, unstable people from the Salvation Army home on Victoria Street. You saw them in the reading rooms of the public library and Chubb, earlier in his history, supplied one of them with a daily buttered bun. So the big man with the long hair concerned him not at all. What was shocking, though, was that Weiss should imagine his own motives were malicious, ad hominem, which in turn meant he hadn't the foggiest notion why Chubb had perpetrated the hoax in the first place. This he could not bear. He rose from the bed and managed to get Weiss into the kitchen, where he unearthed a bottle of two-shilling red plonk from Jimmy Watson's. Once this had been decanted into two jam jars they sat on opposite sides of the table while Chubb attempted to explain his concerns about the decay of meaning. This was, as he would say in Kuala Lumpur, when his own language had become marinated with the homilies of Kampong Baru, like a chicken talking to a duck.

Weiss would not hear a word he said. The only positive thing that arose from their conversation was that Chubb finally managed to convince him that the madman was a madman and nothing more. He also congratulated his old friend, telling him that he'd been a lion before the court. He had shamed them all.

By way of thanks Weiss informed him that his poetry was second-rate. He said the only thing Chubb would ever be remembered for was the work of Bob McCorkle.

I thought him entitled to this, Chubb told me. He caned me with such obvious satisfaction that by the time he left Gordon's flat he was in a very fine mood, ready to go and fight his next round. We walked down the cluttered stairs together and I let him out into Collins Street as the first trams came around the corner past the Treasury building. See you in court – that is what Weiss said to me, Mem. Not the sort of comment made by a man who is going home to hang himself.

13

Well, said Slater, we *all* must go to bed now.

I looked at him with astonishment for he was suddenly a great storm of physical activity, miming bill-signing to the waitresses who were clustered by the suit of armour beside the moulded plastic fireplace.

John!

He leaned forward and took my hand. You will go to bed, he said, smiling while secretly hurting me. You are still a sick girl.

I tried to peel his big fingers back but he easily pulled me to my feet. Actually, John, I feel much better.

Doctor's orders, he said. His eyes cold.

I was furious, and if I contained myself it was only because I wished nothing to intensify Chubb's very obvious humiliation. I could easily have slapped John Slater's face. Instead I stretched and yawned. Perhaps we could hear more another time, I said.

Yes, said Chubb, though his eyes would not engage with mine, and he busied himself hiding his documents within his suit. I doubt Slater noticed, for he would have been alert to any sign of paper. He was impatient only to send the man away.

It was wonderful to meet you again, he said. And to remember dear old Gordon.

Chubb immediately turned towards the entrance. I cast Slater a hateful glance and caught up with my visitor, walking at his side with my own eyes cast down on the impossible tartan carpet. I had the most complicated thoughts about him, feelings which went beyond the covetous emotions stirred by that single page of manuscript. This old man had somehow touched me. Impulsively, I tucked my arm through his and did not release my hold until we were both together in the soupy night. Slater trailed behind; had he been an Intourist guide, he could not have attended us more closely.

Perhaps we can talk some more tomorrow, I said.

Chubb looked at me directly. Thank you, he said, then turned abruptly and limped along the narrow concrete path beside the taxis.

Returning to that vulgar foyer, I glimpsed Slater's following figure in the reflective golden columns and rushed towards the lift.

Sarah! He beat the door and got inside the car.

You shit, I said.

Sarah, listen to me.

No. You are an irredeemable shit.

When he pushed the button for my floor, I chose the one for his, but of course my floor was first and he got out with me.

I don't want to talk to you, John. Please do not come in.

He might easily have forced his way into the room, so I left the hulking key inside my purse and returned to the lifts. He then accompanied me back down to the foyer, where he had the nerve to take me by the hand again.

I could see the Sikh at the door watching us but did not care if I made an exhibition. Let me go, John, or I will make you very sorry.

He knew me of old, and obeyed. Sarah, he said, do you really believe this fellow?

I have no idea. You didn't let me find out.

He is totally bonkers. Can't you see it in his eyes? Look at his skin – it's all soapy, like a priest's.

So? You think he is sexless? Castrated? What on earth do you mean about his skin?

Micks, I know so much more about him than you do. Wouldn't you like to know why he's so dangerous?

No.

No?

No.

Please yourself, he said, and to my enormous relief he walked away. As the lift doors closed he was already heading out into Jalan Treacher, in the direction, as I found out much later, of the notorious Eastern Oriental Cabaret which had, long ago, lent its name to his enormously popular erotic poem.

14

That night I dreamed that I was dead. My body lay in a
potter's field in the Essex marshes and all the contents of my
Charlotte Street office were strewn about in the vile morass
of mud. There was a sexton who soon turned into a tinker
sorting through the remnants of my life. He snaffled the ugly
little Staffordshire figure my brother had given me, but all my
careful files he cast aside. Enraged that my estate was being
handled by someone so uneducated, I grappled fiercely with
him – but while scratching his face I saw it was Lord Antrim,
and I understood my dream and began to cry.

It was raining when I woke, so I called the desk to ask if
I might borrow an umbrella. They claimed to have none. I
ordered breakfast in my room where I would be safe from
Slater. The bowl of cornflakes arrived on a big trolley with
an orchid in a vase, and the waiter, perhaps driven by a
sense of humour I did not give him credit for, wheeled it
over by the window where the view was of a wall of water,
the smudgy outlines of trees on a steep jungle hillside, and
the drifting, ghostly fish which were the cars and trucks
below.

I called the desk again. They promised the rain would
shortly cease and I sat down to await this miracle. I picked up
my Milton but was far too agitated to concentrate. The rain
was often rather green, and sometimes a yellowish white. One

could occasionally make out more of the road below, or else nothing at all, but as I gazed out I thought I saw one of those huge black rubbish bags abandoned in the middle of the broken footpath. When I checked again it seemed to have shifted a little farther along the street.

Some time after nine o'clock, I looked up from my book and saw the bag move by itself. It did not travel far, perhaps a yard or so, and I was appalled to understand that a human being was living inside it, a kind of hermit crab. I waited for more movement. There was none. I had my shower, dressed, and went down to the Balmoral Gift Shop, where I bought a second-rate umbrella for twice what one would've paid at Asprey, but I had such a short time left in Kuala Lumpur and I was determined to reach that manuscript again.

The doorman of course wanted to put me into a taxi, and only then did I realise I could've had ten taxi rides for the price of the umbrella, but having no more money to waste I grimly set off into the monsoon. In less than a minute my feet were soaking wet, and then a passing truck drenched my skirt with water.

As I came splashing along the opposite footpath, careful not to slip on the big yellow flowers the storm was stripping from the trees, my useless little umbrella prevented me from seeing where I was going. Which is how I collided with the human rubbish bag. It had been almost comic from the imperial detachment of my room but was not in the least amusing on the street. I tried to step around the thing, but it would not let me. From deep in the folds of plastic, a pair of strangely determined eyes confronted me.

It said my name, or so I thought. The rain was loud and the storm water roaring along the deep drains and I had that feeling of alienation, of disconnectedness, one gets when talking in the middle of a set in Ronnie Scott's. But there was no mistaking the sodden tweed trousers protruding below the plastic.

Mr Chubb?

Miss Wode-Douglass.

In the shouted conversation that ensued, he made me understand that the Sikh had refused him entrance to the hotel.

You could have telephoned me.

I tried. You had instructed the operator not to disturb you.

Of course I made no such request. This could only have been Slater's doing, and for the first time I appreciated how unbearable a busybody he was.

I escorted my peculiar friend back across Jalan Treacher to the gleaming canopy of the hotel. Here, under the watchful eye of the turbaned doorman, I shook out my umbrella and waited while Christopher Chubb carefully removed the plastic bag and, much as he had with the manuscript's protective wrapper, fastidiously refolded it for later use. For all this great care, his ancient suit was sodden.

The doorman was waiting, ready for us. Memsahib, he said, I am so sorry, this man cannot come into the hotel.

He is my guest.

Yes, I am sorry. It is forbidden.

I was not ignorant of the role of Sikhs as warriors, but I am English and it is sometimes forgotten that we are fearsome warriors as well. Please get out of my way, I said.

If need be I would have struck his testicles with my umbrella and doubtless he saw my face, which has always, so my father said, betrayed my intentions as clearly as a traffic light.

It is forbidden, he said, but I was a hateful imperialist with an angry, goaty face. He stepped aside to let us in.

As Chubb and I crossed the foyer, both of us literally dripping wet, we had similar encounters with three other members of staff, each of whom retreated before my obvious resolve. So it was with no small sense of triumph that I brought my guest to the sixth floor and escorted him into my room.

I had barely closed the door behind us when the phone rang.

You are being very foolish, said John Slater.

I hung up but he called right back.

Don't you think you should listen to my story, Micks?

No.

Darling, you do expect me to pay for your room.

That really did anger me and I was quickly on the brink of that dizzy precipice from which I might launch into delicious actions I would later regret. However, I had learned a thing or two since I slapped my father's face in the Café Royal. John, I said, I will meet you in The Pub at five o'clock.

I then took the phone off the hook and double-locked and chained the door. With that achieved I could consider my wretched guest: a monk hunched inside his hairy suit.

I'm so pleased you could come, I said, but even while escorting him to the window, where two chairs faced each other across the breakfast trolley, I became aware of an odour. It was reminiscent of cabbage, cheese, apricot jam, and something unidentifiable but decidedly local. It was, not to be too polite about it, a repulsive smell, produced by adding water to a well-loved suit. A dab of Vicks at the nostrils might have masked it, but I had nothing mentholated, merely a slightly hysterical response to alien smells.

I'm so sorry about your suit, I said.

Been through worse, Mem.

Then I recalled the batik I'd bought on Batu Road. I had intended it as a gift for my friend Annabelle but now donated it to Christopher Chubb. Give me your suit, I said.

He backed away, holding out his palms as if to keep me away. No, no, so old already.

I suppose I wrinkled my nose. I do believe I may have opened the window. Whatever I did, it is hardly to my credit that he was made to understand.

Very, very sorry, he said.

I was mortified on his behalf but there was no choice but to fill out the dry-cleaning list.

It stinks, isn't it?

I'm sorry the batik isn't nicer, I said, signing my name to the chit.

My suit smells, he demanded. That's what you mean?

It's hardly your fault it got soaked, I said, but we need it picked up by ten o'clock if you are to have it back before you leave.

Nodding bitterly, he took the batik and the laundry bag into the bathroom.

15

He sat very stiffly at my breakfast trolley, silently displaying what I assumed to be the complete 'McCorkle' manuscript. It was wrapped like poor man's luggage, in two quite different plastic bags, one blue, the other white, then sealed with three broad bands of black electrical tape.

He blinked. Slater says I will hurt you?

No, I said.

I had intended to ask to read the poems, but when he moved his package skittishly to one side I changed my mind. I opened my notebook and asked after the facts of the handsome young editor's death.

Ask his friends, he said brusquely. They say Weiss hanged himself, no doubt about it. Ask the police, in which case he fell off a kitchen chair. He paused. You have your pen?

Only when my biro was uncapped did he begin to explain how, on a grim and rainy afternoon, he had attended Weiss's funeral. In this he felt he had no choice, for although he might expect rudeness or even injury, he would be put outside the pale forever if he stayed away.

It is hard to imagine why this would be worth his bother, for he was not, as I was later to discover in Australia, a popular figure to begin with. In the correspondence of the Contemporary Art Society, for instance, he is described more than once as a fascist. This should not be taken to accurately describe his political position – which was more libertarian than anything else – but does show him to be out of temper with the surrealists, imagists, anarchists, and communists in the funeral party.

In the Melbourne General Cemetery Weiss's parents accepted his condolences with dignity while other mourners were not reluctant to offer threats. The nicest of them cut him dead.

As the Weiss family was not religious, the burial took place within sight of the tomb of a billiard player named Lindsay Waltzer. In Melbourne a billiard player will always outrank a poet, so this is still the best way to ask directions to the grave. If one sights along the marble cue laid on Waltzer's final table, the eye is led directly to the black marble tombstone on which is inscribed:

Set this down too:
I have pursued rhyme, image, and metre,
Known all the clefts in which the foot may stick,
Stumbled often, stammered,
But in time the fading voice grows wise
And seizing the co-ordinates of all existence
Traces the inevitable graph

These were the lines – from Bob McCorkle's 'Petit Testament' – that Weiss's mother and father recited in their heart-rending accented voices. Did they mean to insist on the worth of the poetry or mark the tombstone with the instrument of their son's destruction? It was not clear.

To Chubb it seemed that these words he'd written in such savage jest had been chiselled into granite much as the crime of Kafka's warden in 'The Penal Colony' is tattooed into his living skin.

Once the plain pine coffin had been lowered into the ground, he knew, the crowd would drift back to the Café Latin to recite poetry and weep and finally become pugnacious on their dead friend's behalf. A part of him wished to go with them, to take his punishment and have it done with, but it would have taken a thicker skin than he possessed and so he withdrew deeper into the cemetery.

It had rained in the morning and the air smelled of mud and smoke from the cottages of Carlton, and he headed at a brisk pace towards the very northern end of the cemetery, near the so-called children's graveyard which dates from the influenza epidemic of 1921. Later, when he was a father, he could not have endured the place, but now he sought it out in order to find peace of mind.

He heard his pursuer before he saw him. He recognised the noise – shoes fitted with those parsimonious little metal plates, the hallmark of the petit bourgeois and therefore as vile to Chubb as they had been beloved by his mother. This sound came nearer and nearer and it soon became clear that he would not be able to escape his pursuer without running, and he had already suffered humiliation enough. After rounding a bend in the path he stopped and turned, ready to face whatever punishment awaited him.

When the figure appeared at the corner of a cypress hedge, Chubb saw the lunatic who had provided such embarrassment in court. Although not technically a giant, he was very close to seven feet in height. Chubb had noted his strong Australian accent and had formed an impression of someone working-class, not well educated. He was therefore surprised that the man was dressed expensively, in black. His long-flowing hair, being also dark, served to accentuate his pale skin and his striking features, all of them distinguished by their individual size: strong chin, large prowed nose, prominent cheekbones, high forehead from which the mane of hair was brushed straight back. It was a powerful face – masculine, intelligent, and rather angry.

When he reached out his hand Chubb thought he

intended to shake, but instead found his right hand swiftly seized and held. No matter how he struggled he could not disengage, so when the stranger started up the bitumen path his only recourse would have been to cry for help.

What do you want of me, he asked.

There is no other bugger I can tell apart from you, the stranger said, for there is no-one but you who is as bad as me.

Saying this, he wrenched Chubb roughly after him. As they stumbled together along the uneven path, his captor continued speaking.

I could not bear that fucking detective, he said. I loathed him. Vogelesang! What a bloody name for the enemy of poetry. It means 'birdsong', I hope you know that. If the bugger was a bird then he was a vulture, ripping the liver from a living man. I could not stand it.

I did not like it either, said Chubb.

His captor paused and blinked but was not diverted from his speech. After I was evicted from the so-called court, he said, I hung around in William Street to see where Mr Birdsing would go, for I wished him punished in the court of Art. He was not difficult to follow with his big square head and his duck-leg march. He headed down the hill to Swanston Street, past all the homo newsboys screaming, HERALD, HERALD, DIRTY POEMS, READ ALL ABOUT IT. If he'd had a car or a taxi I might not have tracked him half so bloody easy, but he was just a bloody copper, so he got the 15 tram and I had him from that moment on. Birdsing bought a ticket to Glen Iris and stood scratching his balls amongst all the men in the open centre bit of the tram. I also bought a ticket to Glen Iris and sat myself up in the glassed compartment with the women. The old biddies did not like me being in their little chook yard, but no matter how they swayed and muttered I would not give up my seat. I hated them, you know, their prim little mouths, their closed purses in their laps.

At this stage, I really had no plan except to prevent all

further insult to my publisher. I was determined it would not continue a second day.

Chubb asked him was he McCorkle and, in the answering gaze, was reminded not merely of an eagle's fierceness but also its dire unknowability.

I am he.

By now McCorkle had dragged him quite far north, and what had seemed safe refuge had become something altogether different. Not unnaturally, Chubb began to have concerns for his safety and these were not lessened by his captor's passionate address as they left the path and set off squelching rapidly across a sodden lawn.

Have you ever looked up 'publisher' in the Oxford dictionary? the giant demanded. It will surprise you if you ever do. 'One whose business is the issuing of books . . . one who undertakes the printing or production of copies of such works, and their distribution to the booksellers and other dealers, or to the public.' Who could write a bloody thing like that? he shouted, his voice echoing amongst the mausoleums. A cypress hedge blocked out the yellow sky.

It was, the madman continued, as if no-one at Oxford had ever met a bloody publisher. You know what a publisher is? I bloody hope so.

This, Chubb told me, was not a casual question. He feared he might be strangled if he answered wrongly. A friend, he suggested. A defender of the work?

Bloody right, a friend. A defender of the work. And here was this flat-footed policeman intent on jailing him. How could we let that be? How could any of us stand there and let that crime be done? Would the French do this? he demanded as he stamped across the undrained ground where the old graves were sunken and neglected and thistles choked the rusting fences. Would any civilised nation do such a thing? They have made me hate my country. I tried to speak up, but the fascists evicted me, so I hid in the tram, crouching amongst the boilers like an old goanna in the chookhouse. Vogelesang stayed in the middle, reading about himself in the *Herald* all the way to the terminus.

When he got off I followed. You would not know Vogelesang's reputation in St Kilda. The working girls all call him Basher, but I was not afraid and followed, not three yards behind, until he stopped at a garden gate. As he opened the latch he turned and looked me in the eye.

He thought he marked me, but he'd never tangled with a poet before. He could not guess what lay ahead.

I continued strolling until I found a café run by a little reffo fellow in a dirty singlet. I got him to make me a chicken-and-lettuce sandwich and a chocolate malted milk. At dusk I returned to Birdsing's residence. I pushed down the side, past the lemon tree. From the middle of his iris beds I could clearly see the accused through his window. He had a bottle of Victoria Bitter and a meat pie for his dinner. I also live alone and know what it is to spend these hours of solitude when I would rather have a wife and baby and the smell of stew bubbling in the pot. But what civilised person can sit down to a meal like this and not pick up a book to read? Detective Birdshit read nothing and the table he ate from was as bare and shiny as a bloody war memorial.

I was very soon bored by his miserable life so I gave a little wee tap on the window with a shilling and he came out fast enough. It was now too dark for him to see properly but he'd had sufficient chance when I passed him at the gate. He said he would give me a hiding if I did not get off his irises straight away. I said he could make me if he liked.

He rushed back into the house and came out with handcuffs which he was in an awful bloody hurry to apply. I forced him to trample up and down his flowers and made him lose his temper badly, the result being I had no great difficulty in throwing him down. Don't hurt the irises, he cried. I dragged him back into his pathetic little kitchen. Irises were all he could think about until I got him sitting on his chair and there I officially informed him that he had no right to hurt a publisher.

If he had agreed to leave Melbourne or simply take a holiday, then nothing bad would have happened. He was a little roughed up. Some mud on his face and dirt and bits of iris hanging off his daks. He should've known it could get worse but failed to understand the authority given me as a poet. He told me it did not matter what I did. I could not prevent David Weiss being found guilty.

Then I went too far. I wish I hadn't now, but you also went too far, Mr Chubb, so you must have some sympathy for me in this. I found an old yellow-handled carving knife in his drawer and then I chased him round the table until I got his block-head in a grip and I took a good piece of scalp and hair, no more than two inches square, certainly not enough to damage him, although there are a great many vessels in the scalp and so blood did stream down his face and into his eyes. I don't know if he could see enough to be frightened by his reflection in the dresser mirror.

Now at least I had his attention and he suddenly had no trouble swearing to desist from attacking my publisher in court. Then he also went too far, promising he could get the prosecutor's house burgled and his car set alight. I told him his life was at stake and if he thought to make any promises lightly then I would come back while he slept and break his neck. All this I did not just for the sake of David Weiss but of art itself, and for a country where we seldom understand that we must be prepared to fight for issues bigger than an umpire's decision at the Melbourne Cricket Ground. If what I did sounds cruel it will only be to people with no appreciation of art. I would take any amount of skin and hair for the cause of poetry.

Chubb asked him if he was referring to 'The Darkening Ecliptic'.

I mean all poetry, he said, even yours.

It was hard to know what the creature meant by this, for of course Chubb had written Bob McCorkle's 'The Darkening Ecliptic'.

I did not leave Vogelesang with his injury unattended, he continued. I swabbed him with mercurochrome and made a bandage from a pillowcase. As you would expect of a bully, Birdshit was very meek by now and went directly to his bed when I ordered him.

Now all this doctoring, said the creature as he led Chubb into a place where last summer's weeds had fallen in a matted brown tangle, had taken more time than anyone could imagine. The trams had stopped running, which means it was after midnight and I had been out at Glen Iris for five hours. I therefore was forced to take shanks's pony to the city but I am used to walking, which is why I have these metal caps on my toes and heels – they save a great deal of leather. I would cover as much as thirty miles in an average day.

Now I was off to see David Weiss, to give him the good news that the prosecution had been nobbled. I went to Mrs O'Brien's in Grattan Street and bought a bottle of sparkling burgundy at the back door. I was by then in a great excitement. You must understand that David Weiss was like a mother, for he had brought me into the world, had given me life, had stood by me no matter what my enemies had said. When they called me a fake, he never once doubted me.

Yet here is the strange thing – we had not met personally. All he had were letters from my so-called sister. I have no sister but these were written by *someone* who claimed that I was dead. Certain of the allegations were fair enough. I had been a bicycle mechanic and I still work for Mass Mutual, where I happen to be a very successful salesman. But I had not died and the person who wrote those letters was a liar many times over.

And here, said Chubb, he glared at me. *Choy*! God save me. What eyes he had.

In Kuala Lumpur, Christopher Chubb rose and, for perhaps the tenth time, retied that brown and yellow sarong. Of course, he said, I was that liar, but I couldn't be sure how much he knew. Was this anger all for me? Nothing was clear except that he was mad as a bloody hatter. I did not try to argue, I held my breath. *Sarung tebuan jangan dijolok, mati kena ketubung.* Do not stir up a hornets' nest, as we say, you'll only be stung to death.

Yet there was no escaping either the teller or the tale. He was held like a cow in a crush. My first disappointment, his captor continued relentlessly, was to discover Weiss was not in his bed, and it was only after hours of wandering from Café Latin to Molina's and back to Café Latin that I found him, saying goodnight to you at the top of Collins Street. It was by then almost five in the morning, but my bottle of wine was still ready in my coat pocket and there he was, my publisher. I could not have been more well disposed towards another soul on earth.

Of course I did not doubt that it would be a shock for him to meet me. Given that he thought me dead. Rather than frighten him in the street I decided to confront him in the safety of his own home. He lived in a flat in Flinders Lane, a very short walk from Collins Street.

You are doubtless more worldly than I am, the madman told Chubb as he brought him within sight of the children's graveyard, where, beyond the cemetery's perimeter, they could see the solitary Skipping Girl sign glowing in the dark-blue eastern sky. I have been called a genius by some, he said without irony, and perhaps that's why I have very little experience of this world. What I know and what I don't know are difficult to categorise for people like you – who understand so much about the world and so little about me.

He paused. Chubb felt a moment of crisis had come and he glanced around looking for something that might serve as a weapon.

His captor glowered at him. Is my story dull?

No, not at all. I was thinking that I wished I knew more about you.

Well, I will tell you this, he finally said. I have a very thorough knowledge of the internal-combustion engine but a simple term like 'silk stockings' can throw me into the greatest of confusion. Explain that to me if you can?

Not knowing the currents of that injured brain, Chubb was afraid to answer the riddle. He said he did not get it, not at all.

I am trying to tell you, the giant said simply, that I behaved unwisely by forcing Weiss's front door when he would not answer it.

You broke the door?

For a moment all that great weight of animus seemed to dissolve. His shoulders slumped and he released Chubb's wrist, raising his large hands to his cheeks.

Alas, he said, I frightened him. I did announce myself, of course. I am Bob McCorkle, I said. And it was not as if he had not seen my photograph. He'd published it himself. You must have seen it too.

Chubb thought, He knows I made that photograph. He is challenging me, but for what end?

I am Bob McCorkle, I told him, he said again. I am your author, Mr Weiss. But he shrieked at me to get out. Shrieked! At *me*! He was dressed only in shirt and underpants, but he was my publisher. I loved him. I took off my coat and held it out so he could cover himself but he struck it from my hand and cried, Monster!

I tried not to be upset by this. I had come through that door because all my best thoughts and wishes were centred on his person and all I wished to offer him was release from the suffering he had met on my behalf. I picked up my rejected coat and discovered the bottle I had brought to share with him had been shattered. The whole garment was soaked with wine, the pocket filled with broken glass. It was wrong of me to be offended. I am Bob McCorkle, I repeated. And to prove it I began to recite my poems.

And there and then, in Melbourne General Cemetery at six o'clock on a winter evening, he set his great heavy legs astride and, having once more taken Chubb's wrist, commenced a strange and passionate recitation.

'I had often, cowled in the slumberous heavy air . . .'

Chubb knew the poem, of course, but nothing had prepared him for this performance of it, the strange and passionate waving of his free arm, the twisting of the head, the eyes rolled back like a blind man playing jazz piano. And the voice, which its original author had always imagined to be some variation of standard BBC English, was here so fierce and nasal, hoarse, ravaged by failure and regret. Chubb had heard a recording of Eliot reading and judged it as boring as a sermon, but this man was like a tethered beast, a wild man inside a cage.

I had often, cowled in the slumberous heavy air,
Closed my inanimate lids to find it real,
As I knew it would be, the colourful spires
And painted roofs, the high snows glimpsed at the back,
All reversed in the quiet reflecting waters –
Not knowing then that Durer perceived it too.
Now I find that once more I have shrunk
To an interloper, robber of dead men's dream,
I had read in books that art is not easy
But no one warned that the mind repeats
In its ignorance the vision of others. I am still
The black swan of trespass on alien waters.

This was and was not the poem Chubb had written. It had been conceived as a parody and the first key to the puzzle of the hoax, but this lunatic had somehow recast it without altering a word. What had been clever had now become true, the song of the autodidact, the colonial, the damaged beast of the antipodes.

My God, Chubb said. What did Weiss make of your recital?

He said I was a fake.

And what did you do? Chubb asked this with some considerable dread. A confession now seemed imminent, and he feared the consequence would be his own death.

I showed him the piece of scalp I had cut from Vogelesang.

And then?

He fled from me, the man said wearily. I followed him like you might go after a kitten that has escaped its basket. He was trying to climb out a sash window and I called that I meant him no harm, but he said I should cease tormenting him, that he had been tormented more than any man alive and I must leave off. And you too. He spoke your name and said I was your creation, that you'd put my parts together. All this time he was trying to get out the window. I swear I didn't go near him. I don't know why he would choose to climb out the top but the chair tipped and slid out from under him and he fell to the floor, giving his head a mighty crack against the wall as he did so.

And died.

I killed him, yes, the man said, and in his distress he once again released Chubb's hand.

In Room 604 of the Merlin Hotel, Christopher Chubb opened his own hands, whose lines of fate and love were highlighted by the oil of bicycles.

I was free, he said. I ran like a rabbit through the dark. I fell and rolled and came up running.

Next day, he said, I had a bruised face and a twisted ankle but I knew I had to go outstation. I dragged my old duffel bag into Spencer Street and spent three pounds on a second-class ticket to Sydney.

16

On that thundering day in Kuala Lumpur I could not guess what talent the remainder of the McCorkle manuscript might reveal. Thus far I had seen no more than the fantastical aura surrounding it, had glimpsed only the carapace; in other words, the story. To say I was intrigued by both is to understate it, but given Chubb's history of trickery I felt it unwise to proceed too eagerly. And that was how I became a fake myself, pretending that I would 'write him up', not for an instant imagining that thirteen years later I would sit down here in Antrim's gatehouse to do that very thing, and much more besides.

I had no understanding yet of what I was flirting with, no idea that Chubb's story would soon send me travelling to Singapore and from there to Sydney and Melbourne in a vain attempt to establish the true nature of this gigantic man who had emerged, so I assumed, from the darkest recesses of Chubb's disturbed imagination.

Three years later I would be in Australia again and, after I had driven those dreary six hundred miles that separate Melbourne from Sydney, I understood not a great deal more, only the vast distance Chubb had fled from his phantasm.

Chubb had been a sort of beloved boy in Sydney literature, respected not only for his precocious learning and the rigour of his arguments but for his ferociously high standards. The boy from Haberfield was known for the small number of poets he would allow into his library: Donne, Shakespeare, Rilke, Mallarmé. He had been born into a second-rate culture, or so he thought, and one can see in that austere bookshelf all the passion that later led to the birth of Bob McCorkle – a terror that he might be somehow tricked into admiring the second-rate, the derivative, the shallow, the provincial.

I heard about this bookshelf many times, but more often it was his affection for Jelly Roll Morton that his friends remembered, the long boozy nights when he played race music with a cigarette dangling from his mouth, a sweet private smile emerging from the shadowed corners of his lips. In this context, men never failed to mention his attractiveness to women. They came to him, they said, without him having to do a bloody thing. He played the piano and they rubbed his monkish head.

Yet when he returned home to Sydney after Weiss's death, he made no attempt to contact anyone he knew. He told me: I was a murderer, I had no face. I could not bear it, Mem, to feel such shame. He stayed away from Paddington and Darlinghurst and Kings Cross, places where he might run into fellow poets and artists.

Before long he got himself a job in advertising, writing fashion copy – a perfect hiding place for such a High Art character. He bought the first of many suits, a white shirt, a grey felt hat – Sydney was a sea of grey felt hats in those years. Then he rented a shabby semi in Chatswood, a lower-middle-class suburb which he had always thought hateful and life-denying. No-one here would give a damn for poetry or David Weiss.

That is where these were written, Mem. He did not say 'by McCorkle' and I did not ask. But it was clear I was to be given the parcel immediately. My throat was suddenly quite dry. I poured cold tea and drank it while he peeled off the black tape with his habitual care. Finally, from the two plastic bags he withdrew a thick sheaf of paper bound with a red rubber band which broke just as he removed it.

When he held out the bundle, I was frightened to display my greed.

Read, Mem, he insisted.

These pages were dry and dusty to the touch, typed on crumbling yellow paper of a variety once used for mimeographs.

Please, take your time.

But not one of these lines bore the vaguest resemblance to that single page which had so excited me. Are these by Bob McCorkle? I asked, speaking as if he were completely real.

Read, he said. That is, no.

I did read all forty-three poems, if only to hide my huge irritation from their author, whose stomach I could hear rumbling not three feet away. It is one thing to get this sort of drivel in the mail, another to judge it in the presence of such neediness. Though well accustomed to rejecting poets, I could not think of a single encouraging remark to offer him.

If this was his 'real' poetry, then I preferred the fake. True, these had none of the obfuscations that sometimes marred the 'McCorkle'. Nor did they have its life, its wildness, its nasal passion, the sense that nothing on earth can matter but a poem. Frankly, these dry yellow pages were priggish, self-serving, snobbish. The Poet in these verses was as a paragon of art, of learning. His enemies were Philistines and Trolls, and in particular there appeared and reappeared a strange little narrow-shouldered man with thin hairy wrists, white-speckled shoulders, a shining eggshell scalp. He was variously The Judge, The Executioner, The Spy. And in hopes of cloaking my disappointment with these dreary quatrains, I talked eagerly about these menacing phantoms, making much of their physicality.

He understood exactly what I was doing. Silently, he retrieved his pages, and without once looking at me, entombed them again inside their plastic bags. Seeing as you admired them, he said, let me tell you these personae are all based on old Blackhall.

Of course I had no idea who Blackhall was.

The Landlord. The Spy. Can you bear to listen? I do not wish to bore you.

Absolutely, I said. Of course. I picked up a pen I would rather have hurled across the room.

Mr Blackhall turned out to be not only Chubb's Chatswood landlord but also the local stationmaster. He was moreover, Chubb said, a compulsive and unapologetic snoop. Each night there would be a handwritten note in the kitchen. 'Mr Chubb, you left the tap dripping.' 'Mr Chubb, would you please mop up the bathroom floor?' What could I do, Mem? The rent was very low. But when I realised he was going through my verse, I was not happy-*lah*.

As Chubb described the little traps he set to prove the landlord's intrusions, his mood improved. Mischief showed fleeting smiles and his hands became precise, pincered thumbs and forefingers as he explained his various strata-gems. It was a gift, he said. For that whole year, it was my most intimate human dialogue, me and my voyeur.

I asked if he had been lonely. No, he was quite content. The job was easy, the money good. Also, he said, if I had not become a copywriter I would never have seen Noussette again.

Was that Weiss's girlfriend?

This, it seemed, was absolutely the wrong question, and having seen him cheer up I now had to suffer his irritation.

His brow furrowed as he fussed with his sarong. What a thing to say!

But this is the same woman John mentioned?

Obviously another bad question.

He shot me a hard glance. Slater was taunting me, yes or not?

I beg your pardon?

Saying how he wished to sleep with her.

How could that be taunting you?

Typically, he turned away from so direct a question.

There is an urge to always match people, no? We expect a couple to be *samah-samah*, equal in attractiveness, so I must tell you Noussette was much more attractive than I was. No contest-*lah*.

17

There could be no story without Noussette, he said. I would not be here, I promise you. I would be free.

How was he not free? He did not elaborate.

Noussette, he said, was only twenty-four, but she could paint-*lah*. Big reputation, believe me.

Indeed, as I would discover at the National Gallery of Australia, Chubb was not exaggerating. Though Noussette's later work turned out to be unbearably disingenuous, the early paintings were much steelier: small, completely abstract, owing something to the British and Russian constructivists. The gallery identifies her as Noussette Markson (Australian-Russian) but from the time she turned up in Collins Street she was a Polish Jew. Perhaps it is true, as the historian John Finch has recently written, that Noussette Markson was really Mary Morris from Wangaratta, yet when Chubb knew her it was generally accepted that she was European. Her accented English was sprinkled with French words and phrases, and she once won twenty pounds by reciting *Les Fleurs du mal* in its entirety.

She was one of those women who like to associate with the most daring males and push them to increasingly foolhardy acts. It was Noussette Markson who challenged Albert Tucker to climb onto the roof of the State Parliament, but only after she had performed the feat herself. She was also famous,

Chubb revealed, for having used the men's urinal at the Australia Hotel, not at a quiet hour either, and she'd had affairs with many well-known painters and critics including Gordon Featherstone and David Weiss.

Noussette had been a Marxist throughout the war. Chubb was therefore surprised to see her name show up on a pin board in an advertising agency. 'Photographer: Noussette Markson', written on a work order in the traffic manager's office.

Wah! I could not believe it, he said. Impossible.

Curiosity drew him to a studio in Kent Street, a grimy industrial site with tanneries and wool stores as its neighbours. And in a white-walled loft on the fourth floor he discovered the former Marxist confidently in control of a production which would eventually feature in the pages of *Vogue* magazine.

Two months before, in Melbourne, she had long auburn hair and a tiny waist, with peasant-like skirts that flared and flounced when she walked. She had very long legs, and though she often wore slippers in her studio she never ventured out into the street in anything but high heels. Now, in Sydney, her hair was cropped short in the manner of someone who had been caught in flagrante with the enemy, which, from her political point of view, was not inappropriate. The skirts were gone, replaced by pants and a long soft shirt whose colours were the sole reminder of her previous life, for they were all – right down to the single small black button at the neck – in the palette of her paintings.

This transmutation stirred Chubb excessively. At first it seems paradoxical that a man who put such weight on the truth should be so excited by a woman who cared so little about it. But Chubb was mired in his own history, and it is not difficult to imagine how attractive it must have been to see someone shed her past like an old skin.

How had she managed this transformation, not just of wardrobe, but of profession? There was no clear answer. On that first day Chubb was impressed by what appeared to be her complete mastery of the technical situation, the confidence with which she ordered the lights moved or the lens of the Hasselblad changed, and also the way she directed the model, which is not a skill a painter learns in life class. She was purposeful, even harsh, with everyone except the model, towards whom she exhibited an almost maternal warmth, constantly purring and stroking.

Noussette seemed not to notice Chubb's arrival and he remembered thinking that she moved like a dancer, with square shoulders and a straight back; even if her trousers revealed a bigger backside than he might have guessed in Melbourne, this did nothing to diminish her athleticism and grace. She moved continually back and forth between the camera and the model, and by the end of the shoot he could see the girl just hanging on her next instruction. Noussette whispered in her ear and made her laugh, creating a conspiracy which everyone else in the studio – the agency account executive, art-director, the two assistants, and certainly Chubb – felt excluded from and charmed by all at once.

There was no dressing room, nowhere to hide but a tiny lavatory with a stained bowl, and the model changed with a casual immodesty that would not be shocking to anyone who has been backstage at a fashion show. Chubb, however, was simultaneously startled and titillated to see the girl slip out of her suit and stand before the photographer in her underwear. At that moment he realised that he should not be there, an intuition that became a certainty when he saw Noussette place her hand behind the girl's long neck and draw her to her lips. They kissed, in front of everyone.

Such behaviour is almost expected in London these days, but this was post-war Sydney. The account executive was a sturdy, corseted woman in her early fifties, and the art-director a shy, wispy girl just past twenty. Two people could hardly have been more different yet they showed an almost identical tilt of the head as they smiled fixedly at the shocking sight before them.

Chubb began to retreat but Noussette, of course, had been aware of him all along. She came rushing at him and drew him to her and kissed him and hugged him and introduced him to the model and the others as a great poet and simply the most intelligent man she had ever met. Not once had she made this sort of fuss over him in Melbourne. He had not been fast enough, wild enough, handsome enough, his transgressions limited to playing boogie-woogie while smoking Craven A's. It did occur to him that the public attention of the McCorkle Hoax may have changed her mind about him, but in any case he was flattered to have her clinging to him. He could smell her slightly acrid sweat drying on her skin.

She demanded he write down his office telephone number and made him promise to call her. Two hours later it was she who called him.

Darling, Christopher, you must not tell *anyone* I am really a painter. Promise me, darling.

Noussette, they hired me *because* I was a poet. They'll love you for being a painter.

No, they cannot know. It would not fit. I told them other things.

What things?

Oh, photographic sort of things. Christopher, I can trust you, can't I? I know I can. After all, you are a fake yourself.

This offended him, of course. How could she say such a thing?

Darling, surely the McCorkle business –

How does that make me a fake? It was Weiss, he said, who was inauthentic. No offence, but he was a total fraud.

And what were you, darling?

The one who had made that clear.

Christopher, *cher*, listen to me. Promise you won't say that to anyone else. I doubt they'd understand.

And you do?

Of course. David was a total fraud, absolutely, in every department.

People think I killed him.

Oh, he killed himself, she said, and that was his decision. It was not the first time he was wrong.

Cheh, cried Chubb, staring down at the steam as it lifted off the surface of Jalan Treacher. That was a very hard way for the mortar to talk about the pestle. It really should have put me off her, except for one thing-*lah*.

Let me have the teensiest guess.

Guess. Guess away, Mem. You cannot know.

You wanted to fuck her.

The old hoaxer gave me a sudden fierce stare, then his lop-sided eyebrows dipped a degree or two and he smiled not unattractively.

We had barely touched, he said wistfully, but now I knew – I might tackle her.

Tackle?

This gorgeous animal within my reach. These huge dark eyes and a figure – I told you.

And she absolved you, didn't she?

Much *lagi*.

Lagi?

More, much more. He closed his eyes. Do you know, I was the most perfect man for her. I was raised for her. I was the only one. This is what I knew when she telephoned me that afternoon.

Chubb then began to talk – rather vaguely, as always when he touched on this subject – about his mother. Out of all his hesitations and qualifications, two things became very clear. First, the mother had been a strong character and this was why he was instinctively excited by a woman like Noussette. Second – and this was probably the same point – he felt himself invulnerable to her.

See, he said, I am not one of those *boh-doh* fools like Gordon Featherstone. Him she made climb buildings. Me she never could. And that would make it work, you see, she and I.

I don't see, no.

She could never make me be her dog.

Now you make me think that you were frightened of her.

Frightened? No. She had appetite for life-*lah*. What Slater said was true. She was *chili-padi*. Try anything. She could be who she wished. She could get what she wanted. It was always an adventure to be with Noussette. Not only the mortar and the pestle. Every aspect. Ups and downs. Her work was the same. Huge bungles on her shoots – product out of focus. But socially always a big success.

And you became lovers . . .

Oh, she had others, he said. She would bring the poor goats along to *makan*. If I had been in love she would've driven me mad. But she was not trustworthy enough to love.

And were you trustworthy, Mr Chubb?

You mean sexually? Most nights I wrote. He patted his manuscript and smiled. 'Therefore, dear Sir, love your solitude and bear with sweet-sounding lamentation the suffering it causes you.'

How well I knew that line of Rilke's, and how it disturbed me to hear it from his mouth. And so, I said, how did Noussette spend her nights?

Who knows? No phone-*lah*. She had to take a taxi if she wished to talk to me at home.

One night she broke in. Come, come, I must meet a fellow in a bar.

It was two in the morning! I was furious but she started to make a din and Blackhall probably had a glass pressed against the wall. I put on my shoes. Down the highway, over the Harbour Bridge, past Woolloomooloo and into Kings Cross. *Wah!* Very sleazy café. One man sitting at a table. He was bald, completely. Piercing dark eyes. Chin, brow, nose, all huge.

She asked me, Don't you recognise your playmate?

It was the madman, Mem. He had shaved his head.

This is my friend Bob McCorkle, she said. Soon she knew she had done a stupid thing, but first she was the joker.

You see, my darling, you are not a fake at all.

I should have walked away but did not wish to give offence. At another time I might not have been so timid, but Kings Cross at three in the morning? Crims and prostitutes – who knows what might happen? I stayed and drank my illegal cup of brandy. Noussette began to gabble *lagi*. She had used the madman in a photo shoot and the client went amok when he saw her proofs. For this I pay you? he had shouted at her. Two hundred pounds, that you should put this . . . this *thug* against my lovely frock?

She knew she was not amusing but still prattled on until the madman leaned across the smeary plastic table and circled my wrist as he had done in the cemetery.

I believe you have something of mine, he said.

I had no idea what it might be.

I applied for a passport, he said. Three months ago. They asked me for my birth certificate.

He was looking at me with such furious eyes, the stoutest heart would have been alarmed.

Tuan, I do not have your birth certificate.

At this he tightened his grip and I yelped with pain. And then he recited three lines from *Paradise Lost* in a voice which was very quiet, but terrifying: 'Did I request thee, Maker, from my clay / To mould me man, Did I solicit thee / From darkness to promote me?' Give me my bloody birth certificate, he said.

Is that all you want? Noussette said. A birth certificate?

All? he cried. Do you know what it is like to have no birth certificate?

Yes, said Noussette, I know exactly.

You're a liar!

No, darling, I am not a liar, and it would not be your

business if I was. She was very brisk now. You want a birth certificate? That is what is making you so tiresome?

Yes.

Do you know what a big baby you are?

You are very stupid to talk to me like that.

You come back here next Monday night at the same time. And don't be late, because we are not going to wait all night.

The creature was suddenly very quiet. He was a lamb. You'll bring the birth certificate?

You can go now, said Noussette. We will pay for the drinks.

She was amazing. I will say that for her. Who else could have brought that off? The madman rose, shook hands with us both, put on his hat, and walked – pranced really, his walk was most distinctive – right out into the rainy night.

Again Chubb looked out the window and shook his head. I thought she had the grace to apologise to me, but no. She would not be sorry.

He wants to be Bob McCorkle, she said, let him be Bob McCorkle.

I told her I thought he was dangerous.

Oh, darling, she said, all he wants is a birth certificate.

I can't do that.

Christopher, you are such a defeatist. People do this sort of business all the time. I'll get him a birth certificate. It can't be difficult.

How would you possibly do that?

I don't know, she said. I'll find someone. And she found John Slater, Mem, and then she worked him. I've never told him. This is how we know each other.

18

The very next night, Chubb had a 'vision'. He was not drunk; he'd taken a single glass of McWilliams burgundy. He was not overtired; the event occurred a little after nine o'clock on a spring evening. He had washed his plate and his knife and his fork, then carried his chrome and vinyl chair from the kitchen to his desk, an army trestle table he'd positioned in the bow window at the front of the living room. In daylight he might have looked out to where the jacarandas, although they never found a way into his poetry, dropped their loaded petals in a luminous, lilac carpet on the avenue. It was dark and he could see no more than his reflection. For a long while the scratching of his post-office pen was the only sound in the room.

He heard rustling in some leaves outside but the poem was one of his beloved double sestinas, a form in which the last words of each stanza are repeated though in a new order. It is never an easy endeavour, and as he proceeded the difficulty grew exponentially, a context in which he was not interested in rustling leaves.

Then came a loud rapping on the glass, and his immediate response was anger. *Cheh*! I imagined it was that little bugger Blackhall, nagging me to close the gate.

He flung open the window in some exasperation. There was no Blackhall.

Boys, he decided. Scabby-kneed boys, boys with erections in their pockets and heads filled with ignorant opinions. He returned to work, back to the beginning, like one of Mallarmé's sacred spiders whose web has been broken by a cow. Ten minutes later he was going very well and when he looked up again, in the eighth stanza, the last piece of the puzzle was hovering on the edges of his cerebrum.

It was then Chubb saw it. You must not laugh at me, he said.

I promise.

It was a *bloody horror*, he said in a voice turned suddenly hollow, his hooded eyes challenging me.

I felt the hairs rise on my neck. Boys?

No, no. A ghastly snotty *epidermis*, sticking to the glass, like a human squid in an aquarium. I will never forget it – whiskers on the lip, the red maw stretched wide open. You are laughing at me?

McCorkle was kissing you?

It was not funny. Besides, how had he found me?

Noussette . . .

Of course not.

He paused. It was not like that, he said, and with his fingertips he brushed away the dry white spittle in the corners of his mouth. I finally understood, he said quietly. I had brought him forth.

Imagined him?

Brought him forth.

From where?

Choy! How do I know from where? From hell, I suppose. How would I know where I brought him forth from? I imagined someone and he came into being.

I smiled, and saw him bristle.

Mr Chubb, I said hurriedly, there are certain great writers who attract the mad.

He raised a sarcastic eyebrow, and I was immediately sorry to have said 'great'.

For a certain period of time, I said, when I was very young, I was Auden's assistant.

Auden? Really?

You would not believe the things people sent to him – annotated maps, detailed confessions, love letters, photographs of themselves. One young man even tried to hang himself from a tree opposite the house.

Christopher Chubb clasped his papery hands together and fixed me with his pale eyes. How interesting, he said. It took me a moment to understand that he gave not a damn. Indeed, he was angry to have been interrupted.

What happened next, I asked him.

It was a threat, he said. That was how I took it.

What sort of threat?

A threat of what would happen if the birth certificate was not produced.

Did he say that?

Of course he didn't. The bastard was hiding in the dark.

I didn't need Chubb to remind me that the madman had once stood at Vogelesang's window observing him eat his supper before, finally, in his own good time, cutting the hank of hair and skin off that very strong policeman's head.

In Chatswood, Chubb turned off the light and quietly moved his chair to the middle of the empty living room, but he was not a coward and would no longer hide in his own house. So despite that numb terror he knew from the awful minutes before military engagement, he put on his hat and slipped on his suit coat and walked outside.

It was a moonlit night with a blustering westerly wind which tumbled the fallen jacaranda petals along the empty street. He kept clear of the hedges, heading up the centre of Victoria Avenue towards that long ridge road, the Pacific Highway. The wind here was even stronger, and all sorts of rubbish, wrappers, newspapers were blowing high above the verandahs of the milk bars and newsagents into the night sky, like the seagulls that swarm around the pylons of the Harbour Bridge.

He had nowhere to go but he was not about to scurry back to his house 'like a bunny', so hat in hand he began to walk along the Pacific Highway in the direction of the bridge.

In Kuala Lumpur there was a loud knocking on my door. Slater! I thought, and made to receive him in rather belligerent fashion, swinging open the door to discover no-one more offensive than a slim Malay maid who was delivering Chubb's suit in her extended arms. She had a slightly swollen mouth and lovely sloe eyes, a combination which has always been conflated, in my mind anyway, with desire.

Very sorry.

Not at all, I said. After all, this hardly seemed an excessive amount of time to revive a filthy old tweed suit, not in a hotel where one could easily wait thirty minutes for one's coffee. I held out my hand to receive the garment but she was determined to bring it inside.

As she did so, Chubb spoke to her in halting Malay. She answered – rather sharply, I thought – without looking at him. She laid the suit on the bed and lifted the skirt of plastic with her slender finger.

Too much old, she said to me. You see? I noticed only that the herringbone was green and white rather than black and grey, as previously. I could not think what to say. The lovely young woman's eyes then became fierce and accusatory, and I felt a familiar old disappointment. I had never been good with servants, not even when we had a dozen of them, and I had inherited from my mother a great passion not to upset them in case they gave their notice 'for no good reason'. I directed my gaze where the maid wished, at the same time searching desperately in my purse. I have always been awful with tipping. At Christmas I didn't mind it, because those sums had long ago been decided by my father, and it was more of a tradition than that American habit which is calculated to reduce all one's servants to the status of beggars.

You see! she said.

I held out a blue note, but could tell I had insulted her.

Chubb now came to my side, and I asked him how much should I give.

He did not answer but reached down to the suit, and I finally understood, watching him stroke the lapel, that the process of cleaning had so shocked the fabric that it was now broken on the creases, papery and crumbling in his hand like the wing of a dead butterfly.

It was very old, he said. He draped it across his arms. Excuse me. It was the catch in the voice that made me look directly into his welling eyes. He carried the suit into the bathroom – a strange, pathetic creature with his tattered shirt, his ulcerated legs, his shining female sarong. Neither the maid nor I knew exactly where to rest our eyes.

He is your father?

I shook my head.

Again I offered the blue note. She took my hand, closing it so gently around the currency. I could feel it then: this woman was not angry with me.

It is not our fault, she said. You understand, Memsahib? The suit was very old.

Yes, I understand.

When she departed, I sat down at the window, distressed not so much about the suit but by my sense that Chubb was coming undone. These days everyone seems very keen for men to weep, but to be quite honest I have always found it rather off-putting. I would not know what to do with him if he were crying. Then the bathroom door swung open and I saw that the sinews had been manfully stiffened. He had removed the plastic wrapping from the suit and, when he offered it for my inspection, his eyes were narrowed.

What a horrible thing to happen, I said. I am so sorry.

It was not an accident, he said grimly.

I noticed that the damage was not limited to the lapel but extended to the sleeves, one of which was frayed as dramatically as a beggar's costume at Sadler's Wells.

They have done this on purpose.

Oh no. I reached out my hand to touch him but he flinched from me.

They don't want me in the hotel. Don't you see, woman? Without my suit, I cannot enter. They tried to stop me with that stinking prawn-head Sikh, and when that didn't work they destroyed my suit.

I did not wish to challenge him directly, but as I have been told often enough, my face is not good at keeping secrets.

You think I'm mistaken? Then say it. I could not bear to make you lie.

He was in a fury with me now, and I was becoming rather sick of his delusions. Excuse me, I am a little weary.

He bowed his head, as formal as a waiter. I hope my life has not been boring.

Not at all, I said. I did not try to dissuade him from changing back into his suit, nor, when he emerged from the bathroom, did I try to mollify his injured pride. I watched in silence as he retrieved his manuscript. Only when he tucked the parcel under his arm did I see that the suit was truly ruined, tattered at the cuffs and knees, white lining showing at the lapels.

Goodbye, Miss Wode-Douglass.

Goodbye, Mr Chubb.

You can say it would not have hurt me to have taken one of his poems, but you would be wrong. You might even say it would've been politic to feign admiration in order to get at the McCorkle, which is what I really wanted. Still, I could not do anything but stand there as he left. I did feel sorry for him, although of course he could not know that.

I sat at the window watching the street through the rainslick sunshine and after a while he came limping quickly along Jalan Treacher, bearing his manuscript before him like a pudding on a silver tray.

19

When my father was almost seventy, he got it into his head that Barbara – his mistress, I suppose you would call her – was planning to kick him out, so he turned up at *The Modern Review*'s office in Charlotte Street wondering how much it might cost to rent a room in a pub in the Orkneys.

Boofy always was a hopeless romantic, but there was something very sad and pathetic about this, and no matter how frightful he had been in the past, he was my father. I told him I would see what I could find out.

Straight away I rallied everyone possible – my cousin Janet, my pompous brother, and the one or two other relatives who did not actually detest my father – and we got together enough for a deposit on a flat in Bayswater which we would sell when my father finally died. It was quite an undertaking really, not least because he had betrayed so many of us, and also because we were, with the exception of my brother, rather poor.

Once I succeeded in getting everyone's commitment I took my father to lunch at Simpson's, where I outlined our proposition. I don't think I was patronising or showed excessive pleasure in my charity. Boofy took it all very calmly. He sipped his burgundy, nodded his head and, when it was all laid out, thanked me rather formally and asked if it was all right if he 'got back to me'. Then, a week later, he phoned to say Barbara didn't intend to kick him out at all, that it had simply been his imagination.

The arrangements had all been such a stretch. And my heart, I suppose you could say, had been filled with love for him, a very little girl's love at that. I had thought it a selfless love, but in fact it could not have been, because when he rejected the offer without ever once thanking me I suddenly, silently but violently, washed my hands of him.

We may have spoken once or twice afterwards, but if so the conversations were cursory and I can't recall them. As it happened, I was in Portugal with Annabelle when he died, and I found out late and did not even get home in time for the funeral.

I don't feel sad about this so much as grimy, as if I am a lesser person than I would wish to be, and the sight of that lost man limping down Jalan Treacher brought these earlier emotions quickly to the surface.

I felt depressed all afternoon and finally decided I might take a constitutional. Perhaps I was flirting with the notion of visiting Jalan Campbell, but I got no farther than the foyer when I was waylaid by Slater, who called to me from the other side of the Highland Stream. I crossed the bridge and found him with his books and notebooks all spread out on a corner table, as if the bar were now his private office, where all the gorgeous waitresses were his friends and came instantly to see what the gawky white woman might have.

Well? he said when I finally sat down.

Well, what?

His eyes were twinkling in his sunburned cheeks, and he scooped a handful of his stinking little fish and ate one or two of them. He looked mischievous, as if he had indeed contrived to have the servants scrub at poor Chubb's suit with a pumice stone.

Stark raving! I saw him – and in such a blinding rage!

Don't you see how sad it is?

Let me tell you what you wouldn't hear before.

What does this concern?

What does this concern? You're starting to sound Australian, like a bloody policeman. He paused. He told you about Noussette, didn't he?

That they were lovers?

Slater raised his eyebrows. Surely not? Is that what he claimed?

Exactly that.

Really? Slater did look immensely disconcerted. Lovers? Well, it doesn't really affect things if they were.

20

The war was over by the time Slater was shifted from Malaya to Sydney as MI5's liaison with Australian security. He was so quickly in the social pages that his job was never secret, yet the local press never did grasp the fact that this jitterbugging Brit was, like his famous detractor Dylan Thomas, a popular and controversial figure.

It was Noussette who made the connection and then called Trish Lawson at Australian *Vogue*, purring in her very best 'European' style, all *cher* and *merde*. On the subject of poetry *Vogue* was not easily persuaded, and it was not until Noussette showed Lawson the twenty-year-old photograph of the intense young man in cricket whites that she agreed that he might be 'done' on spec. Of course Slater was no longer that golden youth, but in his middle thirties he retained his dazzling blue eyes and cleft chin and the hair then was still as yellow as autumn wheat.

It is very clear that he was not at all averse to being photographed, particularly by a young woman who had such an exalted opinion of *Dewsong*. On the day he visited the Kent Street studio he arranged to leave his afternoon quite free.

Obviously, from Noussette's perspective, this was a lot of complicated skiving just to get a phony birth certificate, yet she seems to have had a taste for it. The point was not the complication but that nothing was impossible.

She had opened the big loft door on the westerly wall of her studio, and there, four storeys above the wharves, she'd carefully positioned a rather unstable bentwood chair. Big banks of grey cloud were massing above the Parramatta River and the afternoon light was changeable, sometimes moody, whereas at other moments the steely water below was cut with diamonds and the light inside the studio was unflattering and harsh.

Sit, she told the famous poet.

Slater, already delighted to find that her sultry voice had not misrepresented her appearance, was by his own admission titillated by this 'little bossy boots'.

In the chair, she said.

Connoisseur that he was, he complied happily.

The assistant began to take meter readings of Slater's face.

Norman, you can go.

This was a slim, foppish boy with a thin nose and a disdainful manner. He shrugged his slender shoulders, and smirked as his employer squatted immediately in front of her subject, unsmilingly turning his handsome face left and right.

In all his life no woman had ever 'handled' him in quite this way. Though of course he must've been accustomed to being regarded as attractive, it seems that this particular appraisement was new. The photographer's large dark eyes gave away nothing except his own reflection, and when she failed to respond to his jokes he had no choice but to offer himself to someone else's intense and very private will.

Norman remained a moment, his eyebrows raised as he watched Noussette work.

Light, he reminded her.

She changed the aperture on the Hasselblad.

Would you like me to take a reading?

Go. Remember to lock the door on the street.

He placed the light meter on a small stool near the door, where it stayed for the remainder of the sitting.

Noussette had exposed no more than a single roll of film when the westerly wind began to blow, lifting her subject's hair.

There it is, she said.

Slater squinted uncomfortably into the light, his eyes crinkling, and she emitted a small purr of satisfaction.

You wanted the wind, he asked her.

Once again she took his chin and tilted it until the sunlight drilled directly into his eyes and a shadow fell, into his anger lines, those two fierce furrows above his nose. She was very close to him, near enough for Slater, like Chubb before him, to smell the slightly stale and musty odour of her body. The corners of her mouth lifted, ever so slightly. Smelling one thing, seeing the other, suddenly he knew exactly what her face would look like when he fucked her.

For the next hour he exposed himself to her enquiring gaze, as if the degree of his trust would ensure that the photograph was flattering. Naturally enough, the portrait itself turned out to be a disaster, but the evening proceeded as they both had wished, and by four in the morning photographer and subject were at Cremorne Point, asleep in each other's arms.

Some time before dawn, Slater told me, he was woken by his new lover stripping the sheet violently from the bed. It was still pitch-dark and rain was falling like six-inch nails against the metal roof. Above this din he could hear a violent knocking.

What is it?

Noussette wrapped the sheet around herself and ran from the room.

Slater's first thought was: *Husband!* He found the light switch, and dressed swiftly. By the time he discovered his socks, his shoes were already on his feet, so he slipped them into his pocket and waited. He heard a man's voice, not in full control of itself.

Finally, he told me, *I decided I might as well get it over with.*

In the unused neon-lit kitchen Slater discovered a very distraught and wet young man who was, he was relieved to see, several inches shorter and a good ten pounds lighter. That he had his head shorn like a Yank also seemed important, for in telling me the story he mentioned it three times.

The visitor wore a towel over his sodden trousers and another wrapped around his shoulders, and if he was not exactly crying he was certainly disturbed. As Slater watched, Noussette took a third towel and began to rub the close-cut hair with such tenderness he typically decided the young man must be 'a nancy boy'.

All conversation had ceased once Slater appeared. Noussette offered neither explanation nor introduction, so he wondered if he was meant to leave.

On the kitchen counter top, next to a dripping Akubra hat, was an advance copy of Slater's new book, from which he'd earlier read to the photographer to what seemed great effect. Had he been prepared to sacrifice it, he might have escaped much else. Instead, he removed the book from the pooling water and thus caught the visitor's attention.

That's your book? Christopher Chubb demanded. Meaning, as Slater needlessly pointed out to me: *Are you its owner?*

Indeed.

Any good?

Not bad, said Slater. *Pretty damn good, in fact.*

Good, you think? Chubb took the towel from Noussette and, having wiped it roughly across a face which still showed all the signs of upset, tossed it through the doorway into the hall, a gesture Slater interpreted as territorial, 'like a fox terrier pissing on a fence'. In that moment he changed, Slater said, from this abject thing into a little Aussie brawler. *You know the type, always looking for a fight, about a woman, a* painting, or Sigmund Freud, it doesn't matter. Of course there is something about their accent. We never expect a voice like that to talk about poetry.

What was his first book? Chubb said.

Dewsong.

Yes, *Dewsong*, Chubb said, that was an awful lot of tripe, you know, like overripe Dylan Thomas, if such a thing is possible. He stared at my new book and made a face. I seem to recall 'ulcered air', he said. God fucking save me.

Slater was always physically imposing, and no matter what he said about 'pub brawlers', he was quite capable of using his bulk to intimidate another man. I am John Slater, he announced. I wrote the book. So who in the hell are you?

A man who cannot understand 'ulcered air'.

Ah, you should read more poetry then.

Not 'ulcerated'? And if 'ulcerated', how?

Let me guess, you're a school teacher.

Slater saw then in the other man's narrowed eyes what he described to me as 'the most awful Irish pugnacity', and 'the vulgar certainty of the autodidact'.

Let me guess, said Chubb, you are a fraud.

This was pretty damn rich, Slater said in the Merlin's pub, but he had appointed himself the Constable Plod of modern verse, as we all now know. I might have knocked him down for his impertinence but Noussette suddenly spirited him away, got him into the shower and then to bed.

If it hadn't been raining I would have left, but instead I went out onto her porch, one of those huge sheltered porches they have in Sydney, and took to the hammock. By the time the light was coming into the sky Noussette had joined me with a very large tumbler of rough Aussie whisky. We lay side by side and watched this glorious storm move out through the harbour. It was such an odd, disrupted day, but do you know, Micks, it turned out to be one of the most lovely nights of my life.

At which point, to the amusement of the waitresses, he quoted Pound in full stentorian display.

And if she plays with me with her shirt off,
　We shall construct many Iliads.
And whatever she does or says
　We shall spin long yarns out of nothing.

21

God knows what her relationship was with Chubb, said Slater, but she was obviously very fond of the bitter little chap. Still, it's a stretch to believe that they were lovers. If they had been, she would not have done what she did on the verandah.

What was that?

I suppose he had a sort of elfin charm, he said, but he was also a very aggressive and opinionated little snot. This is not a generous man, Micks. You heard what he said to me the other day, repeating that garbage of Wystan's – which, by the bye, was about something altogether personal. And look what a narcissist he is. His suit wears out and the whole world is against him.

Not the whole world, John.

Slater's wild eyebrows shot up. He thinks I did it? No!

Thinks you *arranged* to have it done. Now, do be calm. He is a little nutty, as you've said from the moment you finally admitted knowing him.

Yes, but ask yourself what sort of personality would even *imagine* having a fucking suit attacked. A fucking *classicist* – who else? He imagines this because it's just the sort of dirty thing he'd play himself. That's what his hoax was like. It was mean-minded. It was *little*. I knew David Weiss, did I tell you that? Yes, yes, I remember. Well, he was just a boy, a very generous, clever boy, and he died because of Chubb's jealous bastardry. And as for being a little nutty, he's far more delusional than you realise. This is what I was going to tell you. He actually believed that Bob McCorkle had come to life and was intent on killing his creator. That's what Noussette told me out in the hammock. It's what all the upset had been about. There he was stumbling round the streets of Sydney, too frightened to sleep in his own bed. It was even more grotesque than that, though. He had it in his head that if only he could give him a birth certificate this beast would vanish. If there was some mad logic to this, I never got it.

Slater sipped his beer, then pushed the glass away. She was very, very beautiful, he said wistfully. She was ravishing, and cultured too.

Did she know you were in MI5?

Oh, I don't think she worried about all that. What she cared about was that I was a poet. She admired my work, I thought I mentioned that.

You fool, I thought. It would never occur to you that a woman might not love you. Look at the way you sit here, puffing your chest out for the bar girls. I was not angry with him, just very irritated.

She had my book! he said. Not easy to find in Sydney back then.

Yes, but you did supply her with a false birth certificate for Bob McCorkle?

That stopped him for a moment. What are you suggesting?

I raised my eyebrows.

You know this?

I do rather think you may have been selected.

No!

I think so, John.

His eyes turned acid-bright. He brooded. The bloody tart, he said at last. Are you sure? Now he was smiling. Christ, she must have loved the prig. How very strange.

Behind us, a band was setting up: three boys with silver-sequinned jackets and pomaded hair. Hearing them, Slater immediately began to pack up the snazzy bright-red Olivetti portable, far too mod-looking an object for a man of his age.

That was a hugely generous act, he said, but he had that same unsteady smile I'd seen at the Faber dinner. His pride was damaged badly.

In the hammock?

Don't be vulgar, Micks, it doesn't become you. I mean, here's a beautiful woman going to extraordinary lengths just to ease his pain with a bloody birth certificate. So she did love the neurasthenic little beast.

Slater had been set up and used, and I was uncharitable enough to relish the frown lines now deepening on his forehead.

Well, fuck *him*, he said as the drummer knocked his snare. You know what I am going to do? Lines of mischief appeared beside his eyes. I'll buy him a new suit.

Why?

He smiled. So he can sit and puzzle about what foul and devious plot I am hatching against him.

I thought: God save us from old men.

And by the way, he said, this has nothing to do with the certificate. I can see you think otherwise, but I was very happy to get it for her and still am.

I'd be very surprised if he accepted the gift, I said.

This irritated him immensely. For Christ's sake, why not? Oh, I see. Well, *you* give it to the little yoik. Say it's a present from you.

No, no. I won't play your games, John.

Micks, I am *trying* to give the silly cunt a decent suit. Is that really so evil?

I looked at him directly and his mouth quivered.

This is *very* boring, Sarah. Really, I am truly sick of it.

The band had begun a loud, discordant cover of 'Love Me

Do' but Slater was now reopening his trendy typewriter and rolling in a sheet of Merlin letterhead. I had never seen him type before and was surprised to see how lightly his large hands passed across the keys. A minute later he ripped the paper out, signed it, and slid it across the table to me. Read, he shouted.

Dear Mr. Chubb, we at the Merlin Hotel were most distressed to learn of the damage that our cleaners inflicted on your suit. The maid should have informed you that all our guests' apparel is insured against such loss and we will therefore be able to reimburse you for a new suit up to the value of M$500. Yours sincerely,
Rashid Ahbud,
Manager.

Who is Rashid Ahbud?

Doesn't matter, he said. Now it's just a suit, right? Does that make you happy? Is that nice enough for you?

But I saw that he had somehow made himself utterly miserable, and I was sorry for him.

Shall I take the letter to Jalan Campbell?

As I reached for the false document he latched on to my hand and squeezed it very hard. I know you think I'm a nasty piece of work, darling. You've always thought I killed her, haven't you?

For some insane reason, I thought he meant Noussette.

Your mother, he said softly. His eyes were watery. That's why you told me such a hurtful thing. You're furious with me. You've always hated me. You think it's all my fault.

Finally we had reached the conversation I had come to have, but I found it impossible to breathe.

I'll take the letter, I blurted. I fled into the street, umbrellaless.

22

When the foetid odours of gutters and ripe durian blossom in the dark – that is, in the very first minutes of the tropical night – I found an oily, ragged figure sitting on a low stool in the open doorway of the bicycle shop. It was the Ancient Mariner himself, doing violent battle with some piece of metal he had locked inside an old black vise. What the metal's purpose was, I still have no idea, but something in the way he worked it – his light and regular tap-tap, tap-tap – suggested a facility I should have anticipated. After all, the author of the McCorkle Hoax had been repairing bicycles on Jalan Campbell for over a decade.

The tough little Chinese woman sat behind a crammed display case counting rubber bands and packing them in cellophane bags. Seeing me, she called to Chubb. At the time I thought she was drawing his attention to a visitor. Actually she was ordering him not to speak to me.

In any case, Chubb did not directly acknowledge me. First he laid the hammer on the concrete floor, then rinsed his oversized hands in gasoline. As he dried himself on a filthy cloth, he really did look like the lowest sort of beggar. I was blind to the complicated nature of his defiance; in fact I thought him embarrassed by his poverty.

Holding out Slater's letter, I could not help staring at the suppurating ulcers on his sturdy peasant legs – so deep they seemed to go down to the bone. He caught me at it, and at the time I thought I saw his shame. As for Slater's little hoax, he accepted it with no enthusiasm. He had more dangerous games to play.

Can't talk now, Mem. Customers unhappy, he said, and not only customers-*lah*. He jerked his head towards the woman I assumed must be his wife. So sourface! He turned over the envelope absently.

Just open it, please.

By now we were outside in the busy colonnade which, like all such passageways in K.L., is exactly five feet wide, a specification stipulated by the great Stamford Raffles, who never seems to have anticipated the claustrophobia it might induce in members of the white races. I drew into myself like a tall pale-breasted bird while the crowds pressed in relentlessly about me and the bicycle-wallah with his crumpled envelope.

Of course I was waiting to enjoy his pleasure, to see his face at the moment he understood the generous nature of the gift. This was not to be.

Is something the matter?

They claim, he said, staring angrily into the envelope, they are giving me money. But there is no money, Mem. It has been stolen.

Here Slater's sarcastic plan began to show its shoddy construction, and I had no choice but to plug the leaks as they appeared. The insurance company will reimburse me, I said.

But what is my suit to do with you?

It had been identified by my room number. Thank heavens, I said, you can have a suit again.

Yes. He retreated deep into the oily tangle of the shop-house, leading me into a maze of old bicycles. But the suit was worth much less than what they are offering.

In answer to this I invented some nonsense about insurance companies' minimum payments. He raised an eyebrow, an expression I read more clearly when I learned that he, like Bob McCorkle, had worked in insurance. Still ignorant, however, I followed him back to a workbench set up as a Kim's Game of tiny metal parts.

With the letter in his right hand, he sifted through this miscellany with his left. How would they know the value-*lah*? You told them, isn't it?

Yes, I said miserably. I told them it was a very old suit.

He cocked his head and peered up at me. Damn the rascal. He was smiling. You are a very kind young woman, he said. Very, very kind.

I could feel blood flushing all the way into my tingling scalp.

Tomorrow is Monday, he said. Come early-*lah*. We will go to the tailor together. Perhaps I bring you a little poetry in return.

I was pleased, so very pleased that I kissed him on his poor dear grimy cheek.

Of course I would not reveal my literary ambition to Slater, who by eight o'clock that night had taken possession of a larger corner table which the flight crews had previously monopolised. Engaged, no doubt, with his fluff piece for *Nova*, he had his Olivetti Valentine open and a self-important mess of papers spread all around him. What a peacock. This was exactly how he had squandered his talent.

Good, he said, when I told him of the tailor's appointment on Monday morning. I feel happy for the poor chap.

Given his original spite, this magnanimous response should have surprised me.

Poor beggar, he said now, as if all he'd ever intended was an act of charity. What a miserable existence he must have, don't you think so, Micks?

We sat in silence a moment. I could see he had been brooding, though I misconstrued the reason until he asked, rather brusquely, what I was doing that evening.

Then I understood immediately. He wished, finally, to talk about my mother.

Perhaps we might have dinner, he suggested.

If you like.

Shall I call in half an hour?

Though this was the *only* thing I ever wanted from him, now I was suddenly almost ill with fright. He had, as far as I was concerned, simply killed her with his prick. I went to my room and waited, wondering what disgusting secrets I was about to hear.

Slater, it seems, was equally hesitant. In any case, the phone did not ring and I went to bed hungry but grateful just the same.

Monday morning Christopher Chubb was waiting for me. As I entered the shop he held out his arms and twisted his mouth in a rictus of embarrassment. He was dressed in the clothes of a far heftier man – a huge khaki shirt and a pair of shiny black trousers. Though well known for my lack of fashion sense, even I would have been embarrassed to be seen in this get-up.

Fortunately I had already passed two Chinese tailors, and the first was only two doors down. So this was where I rushed him, before he knew what I was doing.

The tailor was about Chubb's height, very thin, with pixie ears and freckles on a wizened jockey's face. He smiled at me politely but when he looked over my shoulder his countenance became less friendly. *Cheh.* Wha you want?

I told him I wished to look at fabrics.

He did not seem to hear me. No open, he said, scowling angrily. Closed today. Too busy now.

And then, somehow, the interview was over – Chubb retreating, me in the street, the tailor shuttering his store. Too busy now, he snapped. Very sorry.

This rudeness was so unexpected that I did not yet appreciate how colossal it had been. I will come back, I said.

No return, he said, pulling down the roller door and locking it. Very long time busy.

I turned to Chubb, who was standing on the ruptured pavement with his arms folded across his chest and a most unpuckish expression on his face.

These tailors no good-*lah*, he said. Too expensive. They cheat you. Batu Road much better.

I imagined our ejection to be caused solely by Chubb's peculiar choice of clothes. At the second tailor's, only a few doors from the first, I clarified this matter straight away.

My friend's good suit has been ruined, I explained. We need a new one rather quickly.

This fellow appeared much more reasonable, dressed in a splendid dark suit, a blue shirt, a white Eton collar, and something very like an old-school tie. But once he understood that I wished to have a suit made for his neighbour, who was hovering uncertainly at his door, I saw he was a frightful snob. He sighed and bowed his head.

I became rather head-girlish about the fabric, but my fierce forward action had not the least effect on him.

He waited for me to finish, pinching the brow of his nose between thumb and forefinger. Missus, I ask you a question? You know this man?

He is a very famous poet.

No. He is not.

He is my friend.

You are buying him a suit?

Yes.

Madam, please, you leave him.

I beg your pardon.

He not your friend. He not a person.

He is a poet.

Madam, when he first arrived in Jalan Campbell, the doctor saw him, Madam. Very late in night, he come along the centre of the road. No legs-*lah*.

I looked towards Chubb, but he had disappeared.

See, said the tailor. He gone. He very frightened now I tell you.

When you say he had no legs, do you mean he was drunk?

Not drunk. He come into street in the middle of night. Not human, Missus. No legs, see?

Was I meant to believe Christopher Chubb had somehow floated up Jalan Campbell like a figure from Chagall? The tailor – whose name was apparently Arthur Fatt – seemed in every respect an urbane, even sophisticated man.

This sort of ghost, so Mr Fatt informed me, was of the type that are like leeches: they will drink your blood until you grow weak and die. Did I understand this?

All I understood was that Christopher Chubb had seriously alienated his neighbours. And just now, as he re-appeared at the shop door, he was shown no more courtesy than a pariah dog.

Go, cried Fatt. We don't talk with you. Get out, get out.

More shocking than this abuse was how Chubb cowered in the face of it. As he crabbed back towards his shop in his big floppy ugly clothes he really was like some poor tormented thing.

You ask Mrs Lim, Fatt said, energetically rolling up a bolt of pale-blue linen. That man drains blood.

I beg your pardon.

Choy! Beg *his* pardon. You know bowl for soup. Drains blood into bowl and drinks it.

No.

No? Sorry to argue. You welcome anytime, Madam, but not for that one.

Then he too began to close his store, and I found Chubb sulking in the recesses of his shop. He was working on an upended bicycle and did not turn as I approached him. Instead he unclipped the chain and wound it carefully around his shaking hand. Not for you to stick your nose in, he said wearily.

I'm very sorry.

These people I know. Not you-*lah*.

I waited for him to say more, but he would not face me. The woman had come down the stairs and was standing in the shadow at the bottom, staring at me expectantly.

Then it was to Chubb she turned, speaking angrily, I thought.

He picked up a spanner and attempted to fit it on the axle nut, but there was such a tremor in his hand that he had to lay it down. You see what has become of me, Mem, he said.

I could not see how one might answer him. He seemed a soul in hell, like a prisoner turning the capstan in the drowning room, forever indentured to something to which he himself had given birth.

23

One minute I would be filled with pity and the next with such intense dislike that I could only shudder. In addition I felt guilty, for even after I recognised the complete awfulness of Chubb's situation, I never ceased plotting ways to pry that poetry away from him. You must really believe me – I was prepared to take it, using whatever cruel hook was required to rip it free. This is not appealing, of course, but I did not shock myself. From my first year at St Mary's Wantage I had known myself a nasty girl.

I returned to my musty refrigerated room and, after fidgeting and fretting for an hour or so, I began to snip at my hair. I first attacked the vile little tropical cockatoo crest and then, as always happens, I could not stop. Annabelle would have shrieked at me but she was home in the Slough of Despond, drinking gin and tonic and chewing her lovely little fingernails. Unchallenged, I was free to continue until I had made myself into a ragged mess. I then used Brylcream, which can give an art-student look, or something close to it. My linen trouser suit really needed pressing, but nothing else was available so I put it on and went down to The Pub. Slater was ensconced there, naturally, but I was feeling very jangly and not even he could deter me from a double Scotch.

So? he said, shifting papers away lest I wet them with my drink. Has the oaf from Porlock shoved off to Savile Row?

I could not bring myself to repeat what I had seen that morning in Jalan Campbell – not just the ragged creature hammering metal in his vise but that horrid vision of him crabbing along the shadows of the five-foot way. Blessedly, Slater was distracted by my hair.

Micks, sit next to me.

Do I look awful? I slid around the banquette to submit to his inspection.

My dear girl, you are so blessed you could never make yourself look awful. God, I'll never forget you when you came back from Wales that year you were kicked out of Lady Margaret Hall. You were like a little wild animal, smelling of goat and with burrs stuck in your hair, but still you did not look awful.

Slater could not say this sort of thing and stay in neutral gear, so I stared at him until he dropped his eyes.

Just the same, old girl, when you get back to London tomorrow, you might want to pop into Sassoon's. Molly always goes to Sassoon's, I'm sure she could get you an appointment straight away.

Tomorrow?

Tomorrow is the thirteenth. We leave on the thirteenth, arrive in London on the fourteenth. You could go there straight from the airport.

But we haven't even talked, I said – and suddenly, to my complete surprise, burst into tears. You hid from me all the time, I said. You left me alone. I don't understand you. Anyway, I can't go. I won't go. I have things to do in Kuala Lumpur.

What things, darling?

But of course he would have become hysterical if I had told him. I shook my head.

What things? He reached for my hand. I let him take it. Still, I could not stop crying.

Micks, he said, I've been rather busy. I'm sorry.

What have you been doing, John?

His mouth went odd, and I understood. He had been busy being Slater. Well please do not write it up in *Nova*, I said, because it's more than anyone needs to know.

Come, Sarah, don't cry. Why should you care what I do? You don't even like me. You never have.

I don't have to bloody *like* you.

I could feel the grief gurgling inside my chest like some dark and viscous thing I did not ever wish to see.

You promised we would talk, I said. It's why I came.

Slater put his arm around me and pulled me to my feet. Very well, he said. Shall we go?

No, no. We have to talk, John.

Yes, he said. Abandoning his typewriter and his papers, he led me out the door and did not release his hold of me until we were in a taxi.

It was Jalan Petaling he took me to, I realise now. At the time I knew only that it was a kind of night market and too crowded for me to hear what he was saying, so in the end he took me into a very rough-looking restaurant where the concrete floor was wet and the customers used a garden hose to wash their hands. He ordered beer and they brought a huge plate of crunchy shrimp. Slater tasted one or two but mostly watched me eat.

I suppose, he said, I can guess what you want to discuss. I'm sure you realise I want to talk about it too.

My mouth was filled with shrimp. I could not stop myself. I ate their heads and tails, coughing as their little beaks stuck in my throat.

What aspect of it seems most pressing to you?

I paused in my desperate feast. Sometimes, I said, I have imagined you were my father.

He laughed.

But I know I have Boofy's eyes.

You also have his hair – very good hair too, I would say, thick and dense. I wish you would not mutilate it so.

I don't know why she did it.

He was listening intensely. He did have the keenest, most demanding eyes. They were what the frown marks pointed to, the sexual focus of his face.

You dumped her, I demanded. That was it, wasn't it?

Dear Micks, how could I drop her? I never had her.

But he'd had everyone, all his life, even now. He was famous for it. He'd had my mother well and truly, cock and balls, I knew it, could see it in my mind forever. Oh, that's not true, John, and you know it. Even when I was nine years old I could see what was happening.

How could you know?

Do you think children are blind? I saw how she used to kiss you. You think a child wouldn't notice these things? Her father is away and her mother is kissing another man like she wants to eat him for her breakfast. I remember her kissing you like that in public, in front of bloody everyone. Neither of you gave a bugger who saw you.

Oh Jesus, he said, you poor baby.

That baby is long dead, John.

How many times do you think your mother kissed me?

I don't even want to think about it. It makes me sick. I really don't like sex, I wonder why!

You remember her always kissing me?

Yes.

It happened exactly once.

Don't make me laugh.

Once. That is the kiss you remember. It was at the garden party for the Hammonds. That's what you're remembering, isn't it? I don't know the names of all the guests. It was when Boofy was making a mess of being a film producer. The investor was Scots. Your mother said he was 'Edinburgh common'.

I'm not likely to forget it, am I? Christ! The day my mother committed suicide.

And your father had taken that young actor, it was Trevor Roberts, up to see the horses.

John, I do remember.

Then you would know that your pater was being rather naughty and your mother becoming most upset.

What exactly do you mean by that?

He hesitated. Think, he said.

And I thought, Christ, Slater, you have no bloody idea, do you? I could see that day in every detail, that lovely English summer sky, a watery haze, my mother's hallucinogenic flower beds. It was the last summer before the war. The martins had just returned and were swooping round the eaves of what we called The Gardener's Cottage, although no-one had lived there for many years.

Not all the guests had arrived and there was a small group – about six people in all – admiring the pond. A short, wide Scotsman in an expensive jacket – the investor, I suppose – skipped a stone across the pond. He got it to skip ten times and I was rather thrilled to see a grown-up do some- thing which was against my mother's rules. I turned to see if she had witnessed this outrage and there she was, directly in front of the tent, slobbering over John Slater, her hands pulling his face into her mouth.

Daddy was being rather naughty? I said, outraged. I had finished all the shrimp. Slater made a gesture and a fat woman in an apron took the plate away. He then had one of his conversations with her. I don't know what it was about. I did not care. I told him I didn't see how he could possibly dispute what I had seen.

You know, darling, do you really think it is sensible to involve yourself with matters behind your parents' bedroom door? Do you really want to know?

We never had any horses in the first place. We had no horses to show to anyone.

Is that yes or no?

I was more than a little nervous, but I would not be bullied. Please don't tell me lies, I said. I can bear whatever it is so long as I know it's the truth. You must swear.

I solemnly swear I will tell the truth, if that's what you really want.

I do.

Very well, darling. Let's just say your father had rather *catholic* tastes.

What does that mean?

It means he did not discriminate. He was very fond of women, as we all know, but he liked young men as well. Your mother knew this. She always thought I was doing it with him.

Hearing this, I did not imagine myself at all upset. Yet at the same time it was not a thing I had ever suspected. I asked John Slater if my mother's suspicion had been well founded.

Not my sort of thing, but your father did love me and she knew it. And when he took Roberts up to see the horses, I suppose she imagined that everyone knew what was going on. She was humiliated. That's why she kissed me, you see? And I failed her because I was embarrassed, and I should not have been. I should have participated – that is what I've thought ever since. But I freed myself, and she was completely furious.

You did no such thing.

Oh yes I did, dear girl. That you must believe, for it has stayed with me all these years. Do you know the last words she said to me? She said: You bastard, Jacko, you total cunt.

My mother never spoke like that.

She did that day, Micks.

24

We had been drinking, he said, which may explain why none of us were excessively concerned at first. In fact, I distinctly remember wondering how the Armstrong Siddeley's motor kept on turning. It was a large and eccentric beast, given to running rough and stalling on the sunniest day. But here, in the middle of the pond, it just kept blowing big fat bubbles out its exhaust pipe as if it never planned to stop.

I could see your mother through the narrow rear window. She was sitting behind the wheel. She didn't even move her head. Who could imagine what she was thinking? She had wound down the windows and rolled back the hatch in the roof, presumably to accelerate the sinking, but the car, while being pathetically underpowered, was very well made, and the damn thing floated. It seemed almost comic at first, this great tank of a motor floating in a lovely pond and all of us in our best tatt, champagne glasses in hand. But finally the engine stopped and the royal old beast began to list. I saw then that something unfortunate might occur. Yet even when I plunged in, I was rather more worried about my new plus fours than anything else. I swam out to get her but the weight of water against the door was too great and it simply would not budge.

Through all of this your mother clung to the wheel, staring straight ahead as if I weren't there. When I tried to get in through the window, my weight made the car list even more, so I headed for the hatch up on the roof, clambering over the radiator and walking along the bonnet. Then I saw she was crying and it began to dawn on me what a bad state she had got herself into. I climbed up on top and hauled her – a little brutally I fear – out through the roof. She did not like me, not at all, but she did not use those horrid words again.

Boofy, meanwhile, had been up at the stables with his friend and he looked down to see his beloved Armstrong Siddeley sinking in the middle of the pond. He quickly finished whatever he was doing and came striding down. He had a riding crop, I seem to remember, and was swishing it in what might have seemed a jaunty way. He did not know your mother was inside the car.

John, that's not right, I said to Slater.

You were not there, Micks. You had already run away.

But you cannot have pulled her out. She drowned.

He hesitated. Don't you remember where you were?

I was in the house, but I know she drowned. She was my mother, for God's sake.

Darling, the pond was too shallow. The water never rose above the door handle. Don't you remember where the car was next morning?

Actually, I did. The gypsies from below the Oxford Road came and pulled it out with a rusty old Ferguson tractor. They charged a lot of money and left horrible ruts and skid marks on the lawn my mother loved. She would have had it top-dressed and reseeded before the day was out, but she was lying in a funeral parlour and the house was so wretchedly empty without her. I don't know what the servants were doing, though I do recall that the flowers in the hall were left to die and that I was surprised they could've gone so quickly.

Yes, but where did you go when you ran into the house?

To my room, I suppose.

You were under the kitchen table, said Slater.

I had not the least memory of this.

You poor little thing, he said, you were shivering. You

must have been there for a very long time because it took a while to get your mother out through the roof and carry her onto the lawn. The pond had always looked absolutely gorgeous but it had a good foot of silt on the bottom and was filled with bright-green algae that now clung to both of us. Who can say what she really felt? Sheer mortification, I would guess. She stood so very straight and squared her lovely shoulders, but her clothes were sodden and her underwear was showing and there was weed clinging to her knees. She had lost her shoes in the mud and walked past her guests with bare feet and a rather terrifying smile. Boofy was in a total fright, but he did his best to help her through this humiliation.

My dear, he said. And he held out his arm, offering to escort her to the house. She seemed to consider this for a moment and then she pushed him very violently in the chest, so hard that he staggered backwards on his heels, and then she ran up to the house. Boofy lumbered after, but she'd ducked into the kitchen, a place he would never have thought to find her. And that was where she did it, darling. Not in the pond.

How?

Please, Micks. You don't want me to do this.

How?

Knife, I'm afraid.

Where?

Throat.

She cut her own throat?

I'm sorry.

So why did everyone lie to me? Why did they tell me she drowned inside the bloody car? She was my mother.

Who said this, do you imagine?

They all did, I cried. I was exceedingly angry. I slammed my glass down so hard that everyone in the sordid restaurant turned to look.

Darling, don't make a scene. Please. Would you like to take a walk?

No, I bloody well would not like to take a walk.

Who told you this story, darling? Was it poor old Boofy?

I couldn't remember who told me. It was just something I had always known.

But you see, dear old Micks, it makes no sense that they should lie to you.

On the contrary, it's so like my fucking father. He was such a coward about death.

He was not a coward, dear, but I think he was rather ashamed of the way he carried on at funerals.

He didn't have the spine to tell me the truth.

Micks, he would've thought you already *knew* the truth. After all, he did find you beside her body. She had fallen next to the table, and you'd crawled out and taken her hand and all that blood soaked the hem of your frilly white dress. It was so ghastly. I do not doubt that you have very properly forgotten it. I wrote a poem about it once, you know. 'Blood Poppy'.

I believed him then, not because I remembered the poem but because I recognised the fuzzy outlines of the event, as one might recall a childhood nightmare that contains no more than the dregs of terror. It was a horrid feeling, a kind of nausea. I saw John Slater watching me, his bright eyes dulled by his own distress.

I should never have told you, he said.

But all I could think was how wrong I had been in hating him almost all my life. When I rose from my chair I felt the whole noisy restaurant go quiet. I did not care. I squatted beside the great seducer, took his hand, and held it against my lips.

I'm so sorry, I said. I have been so unfair to you.

I laid my cheek against the hand.

Come now, Micks, he said, everyone is staring.

I don't give a bugger.

No, but I do.

I don't recall him paying, though of course he must have. I had no idea where we went walking, only that it was down by the river where there was a grand old mosque. Then we passed the cricket ground and that famous club the English called The Spotted Dog because its early members had included non-whites like Sultan Abdul Salad.

It was along this street beside The Spotted Dog – it was actually Jalan Raja – that we now continued, in a close, companionable way, joined by the awfulness of a past which by now had seeped into us so deeply, leaving us with a sadness which would always ache and never properly mend.

You know, Micks, for years and years I've had this rather pathetic notion that Malaysia is my home. In fact there are instructions in my will that my ashes should be scattered in the South China Sea off Kota Baru. But of course I don't know a soul here. Looking at mad old Chubb made me see how pathetic a gesture that would be. They can bury me in Highgate – I'll be happy enough there. But the women *are* so beautiful, don't you think? And I would have liked to fall in love just one more time. It was the only thing I was ever any good at, you know. No good at life at all.

Perhaps that is life.

No, it isn't.

We turned onto Batu Road and then up Jalan Campbell, past the shops that now, thirteen years on, are so familiar to me: the doctor with the photographs of haemorrhoids, the *kopi kedai*, the two tailors and, of course, the bicycle shop. Here Slater paused, producing first a fat envelope and then a pen with which to write on it.

The money for the suit, he said. I'm just sorry I won't be here to see the little prig looking dapper. I do not doubt that a good suit will make him appear even more insane.

This plan was frustrated by the shop's steel roller door, with no slot through which the envelope could be safely slipped inside.

We can send him a cheque, I suggested.

Instead Slater took my hand and led me first down a side

street, then into an alley filled with puddles and unsanitary smells.

Couldn't the hotel look after this for us?

Certainly not. He moved confidently through the maze of little lanes, then stopped and took me by the shoulder. We were looking down a passageway no more than three feet wide.

He pointed at a lighted window. That's it.

How could you know?

As we watched a second window lit up on the floor above and there, as clearly illuminated as on a stage, stood a young woman, perhaps twenty years old. Neither Chinese nor Malay, she may have been Indian, but not Tamil, for her skin was far too fair. She had very large eyes, wide lips, and was startlingly, achingly, beautiful.

Slater squeezed my shoulder far too hard. There it is, he said.

No.

Yes, that's it, he repeated. God damn it.

The girl was peering at the glass, studying her reflection.

It's Noussette, he said.

At that moment I was scarcely paying attention. I was filled with sadness, for many reasons, not least that I was leaving in the morning and would never get my hands on that poetry.

It's her *child*, Slater said. Micks, look at her. There must have been a child.

You mean this is Noussette's child?

Shush! Just look. God. It is her. Exactly.

The girl now began to brush her hair and the pair of us, side by side in the nasty little alley, watched her until she drew a curtain and left us alone in the night.

In Jalan Campbell we caught a cab. We did not speak. Slater seemed to have forgotten all about the money. He looked pale, exhausted, stricken. In the hotel lobby we said goodnight, arranging to meet for breakfast at six o'clock and depart for the airport an hour later.

25

I went to bed with the disconcerting knowledge that almost everything I had assumed about my life was incorrect, that I had been baptised in blood and raised on secrets and misconstructions which had, obviously, made me who I was.

Yet to finally glimpse my white dress dyed with my mother's blood was, quite honestly, not much worse than the horror I'd invented for myself. If my life had been shaped by my misunderstanding of John Slater, I was not unhappy with the shape itself. For no matter what crooked road I had travelled, it led me to the moment when I first opened 'The Waste Land' and found the laws all broken, and in those dazzling eruptions and disconcerting schisms I saw a world whose dreadful harmonies I never guessed existed. How I fed off it, puzzled at it, peered into it, scratched its scabby surfaces to uncover the coral reef below. I had read poetry before, of course, but nothing that prepared me for this – and no matter why I hated Slater or wished to prick the pretensions of his verse, I arrived at 'The Waste Land' and knew that to be both mysterious and true. It is very hard to wish things had happened any other way.

Actually, what had most startled me about the evening's revelations was my father's sexual nature. It was this that later stopped me from sleeping. Perhaps Slater had been correct – I should not have looked behind my parents' bedroom door, for not even three large glasses of Scotch could still the whirling pictures in my head. For hours and hours I put Boofy with all the men I recalled from childhood, one on one, together, getting accustomed to the idea. I mean I mated him. I put him with the Squire to see how that would fit or feel. I put him with our gardener – my father's moustache to the one side, Wilke's stubbly chin to the other – but of course it was already too late to learn the truth. Had Boofy prayed to God in Chapel to forgive him? Did he think it a stinky, beastly business the moment it was over? That is not at all what I would wish for him. No, I would prefer that he strolled up the hill with a blond-haired actor, just as casually as Slater had said. I wish for them to stroke the horse together, and for Lord Wode-Douglass to move his broad hand from the horse's flank to between the young man's legs.

Of course this desire for the happiness of a dead man is not really about him at all. Like my father, I have a secret.

I have said that I do not like sex, and if you say a thing like that clearly enough and manage to make yourself look suffi-ciently frightful people do tend to believe you. Fortunately or not, it is untrue. And while I had always imagined my secret nature as being perverse and original, I now began to wonder if I was nothing more unique than my father's daughter.

You must not think me promiscuous, because this is not the case. I live mostly like a monk inside a cell, surrounded by my mess, my manuscripts, cat food, kitty litter, gas fire, and a shilling in the meter. But I am not mild, would never be thought mild by anyone.

I told Slater about my jealous cat, but what I really had was Annabelle – by then my secret for over twenty-five years. We met at the disgusting boarding school they sent me to when Boofy had his breakdown. I was in a fury for years before she finally arrived. They could not control me. If I had not been The Honourable Sarah Wode-Douglass I am sure they would have sent me down, for I very quickly became a bad girl and was a very well-established bad girl when Annabelle turned up. She was fifteen when I first saw her, such a dazzling creature even then, with very pale skin, very black wavy hair, wide mouth, and the darkest, most mischievous almond eyes. I fell in love watching her play tennis the first week of term. She was really just a little thing but she had such grace and fight and she gave a little 'uh' every time she hit the ball. Dear Jesus. Of course she did not mean to set me off. She was not a bad girl at all, which made it particularly difficult for me to get her attention and for her to understand that she would finally like me very much indeed. I am not patient by nature but with Annabelle I had no choice. From the day I was smitten until the moment that we actually kissed was in fact an entire year, a year made lovely with so many tiny successes, and so much longing.

That summer her absent-minded mother let her come to stay at Allenhurst, so in the long days when Boofy was up in London, mostly occupied with not much more than lunch, I had my clever, pretty darling to myself. I shocked her often but delighted her all the more, and there was no part of her that was secret to me.

Annabelle now lives near Kew, where she is terribly respectable, but she does so love to go shopping in Kensington, twice a month if we are lucky. This part of my life is unknown to anyone. The Housewife and I will have a little lunch. She will tell me about the latest crisis with her children and I will complain to her about the magazine. We will shop a little. And some time in the middle of the afternoon I will take her back to Old Church Street.

We are very proper indeed, which is the point. Even when we get to my flat, even when the door is shut, there is not so much as a kiss. I live in a pig sty, it is true, and she cannot bear it. She tidies while I drink her in. She moves around my hovel as she once moved across a tennis court and now my mind is filled with sex and I lie on the sofa just watching. She does like how tall I am, the length of me, and I do stretch myself, point my toes, extend my arms back over my head, releasing myself from all the tension that comes from wishing to be small.

This makes her smile, but nothing can happen until she has taken me to wash my hair, and dried it, until she has put make-up on me, and it is as she does this that she begins telling me how well my face is made, how fine my nose, how she alone on earth can own me like this. She makes me look at myself in the mirror and it is true. I am beautiful, but only for her, only with her, in the secret part of my life.

That Monday night in Malaysia, I tossed and turned until somewhere around four o'clock. Finally I dealt with myself, and then I slept.

26

I suppose Slater had been lying to women all his life, but what he did the following morning still takes my breath away. Sleep in, he told me at six. The plane is broke. The flight is cancelled.

It would take all of five years, by which time we'd become much better friends, before he confessed that it was he, not the airline, who had cancelled our flight to London.

The effect of this vast untruth was to bring me rather violently awake. It was good news, of course – a second chance to get the poetry. On the other hand my board meeting was on the fourteenth, tomorrow. Lord Antrim was about to leave for Italy on the fifteenth. Without him present it was very likely that Mrs McKay would not bother coming down from Manchester and without her cheque book, there was, quite bluntly, no point in having a meeting.

Telephone them, darling, Slater said. Talk to London all day long if that is what you need to do. But of course I could not phone London then. I spent a completely wretched day waiting until I judged that Antrim would have finished breakfast.

I realise now my calculation was off, but desperation never makes one sensitive. Without preamble, I begged him to delay his departure.

Sarah, you might as well ask me to change the date of Christmas.

What would make you stay in London one more week?

Nothing.

A death?

Only my own, possibly not even that.

Bertie, I said, do you remember that night in Cheltenham when you made me cry?

Please, Sarah. This call must be costing the firm a fortune.

You said I had not published a single great poem in fifteen years.

Silence.

Bertie, I do know how you love to be in Italy *on time*, but if you will only stay in London just five more days I will bring you a really nice surprise.

This meant leaving on the eighteenth and going to the meeting straight from Heathrow.

If you are not there when I open the manuscript, I said, you will be exceedingly jealous of those who are.

There was a second silence, somehow rather warmer than the first. What I had laid so recklessly before Antrim was the very thing that kept him coming to our meetings – the thought that we might one day publish a work like 'The Waste Land'. I could hear the singing of the submarine phone cables.

Sarah, he said at last, are you smuggling *ganja*?

You know exactly what I am saying.

Well, certainly you haven't found a genius in Malaya.

It was my turn to be silent.

In Malaya? His voice had changed.

I now knew he would postpone his departure. Immediately I felt ill. It may take a little guts, I said.

That cheered him even further. Antrim was so easily bored, so mischievous. It was the best thing about him.

You will put the cat amongst the pigeons?

Bertie, I promise there will be feathers floating in the air all over Bloomsbury.

By the time I had rung off, he had given his agreement and I had not so much as a limerick to put before him.

27

While I was pacing the room, waiting to make my reckless call, Slater had been presenting himself not at the airline office, where he had promised to 'deal with this nonsense', but down on Jalan Campbell. What he wanted was the girl, although exactly what sort of 'want' was by no means clear, not even, I suspect, to him. He was responding instantly, as he had responded to the invitation to Kuala Kangsar, as he had responded to Noussette's touch in the hammock while the lightning sheeted across Sydney Harbour. He dressed himself in a rumpled white linen suit in which he managed to suggest a romantic, if elderly, incarnation of the English poet.

When he arrived at the bicycle shop Chubb was sitting on the concrete floor, searching for the leak in an injured inner tube. Can't talk now, he growled.

A less wilful man might have given up, but of course Slater didn't give a damn for Chubb's opinion and settled himself in a metal chair by the door like a Presbyterian cat with its paws tucked patiently underneath.

Soon the Chinese woman came down and set herself up behind the display case where she once again began sorting elastic bands.

When Slater raised his hat, she smiled, though he could not have known how unusual this was. In any case he felt himself to be at home. He had *kopi susu* brought in from the *kedai* at the corner. He smoked a clove cigarette. He thought about Noussette, arousing feelings so old and delicious that it is quite likely he'd forgotten all about Chubb's suit. But to Chubb, labouring in his filthy rags, the suit was at the very forefront of his mind. And this I know, because he told me so the following day.

But why was Slater in my shop, Mem? Why did he come? Because he loved me? No, I thought, he is involved in this silly prank to buy the suit. Then I am thinking, Why should he care I have a suit or no? Does he like me? Ha. It makes no sense-*ah*. Yet there he is, drinking his damn coffee like some maharoger, passing the time of day while all the natives swarm around him.

You would think I would ask him, What's your game, old man? But I held my tongue. I sandpapered the inner tube and vulcanised the patch. Mrs Lim came downstairs and started her idiotic business with the rubber bands. With this we will get rich? I inflated the tube, tested it in water, deflated it, fitted it inside the tyre, inflated it again, got the wheel back on the frame, and replaced the chain. For this we earn a few miserable shekels, God help us all. You will think me such a beggar but I could never afford another suit, not ever, and I was thinking, Without the suit I am trapped here until I die. I am K in *The Trial*, sitting outside the door. The door is for me. The suit is for me. I had intended to say nothing, but I could not bear it. I came right out to him.

What for you visit? My suit?

That startled him.

Why yes, he said, of course.

Why not say?

No hurry, no hurry.

I was suspicious. What for he do this for me? I thought. Get this over. If it is a cruel trick, then get it done with now.

One mo', I told him. Then I got togged up in what was left by the previous incumbent. How I hate to wear his clothes. Make my skin creep.

Come on, I said. We go now.

No hurry, old chap, he said. We have all day.

I saw I had caught him on the hop. No, now, I told him. The little battle-axe had seen me wearing her ex's suit. What an animal she is, you would not believe how bad. Come on, I said to Slater. Then I was off and he had no choice but to follow. Like you, he wanted to drag me to those Chinese bastards but I would not stop until we got to Batu Road. There is a Muslim Indian there, Hadji Ramesh, my customer. A decent man.

This tailor had his business set up in an alleyway between two gaudy department stores, and the bolts of fabric were racked so high up the walls that in order to fetch one it was necessary to send two small barefoot boys shinning up them like monkeys. When the fine grey wool was finally selected, Chubb stood on a wooden box and the tailor solemnly took his measurements and called them out for his older son to record in a leather-bound ledger.

I was waiting to see what trick it was, Mem. How badly I wanted that suit I am ashamed to tell you. I was standing on the box when Slater started off his questions.

How many are you, old man, in your little household?

What for I lie to him? I told him three.

Your wife has very remarkable eyes.

Not my wife, I told him, but why would he say such a flattering thing about her anyway? Her eyes are crazy. You've seen them? They would melt a pound of lead.

Then she has a child?

I have a daughter, I told him.

Where is she? Why have I not seen her?

So casual, Mem.

I'd like to meet her, he said.

Then I saw the trick. It was not the suit. He had me pimping for my daughter. No, I said, they don't like that.

What on earth do you mean, old chap?

Don't like to meet, no.

I did not want him near my daughter but I wanted the suit, so I begged the tailor full speed forward. He promised a second fitting – the suit itself – that very afternoon. I thought myself so very cagey, Mem. The time of the fitting was exactly when my daughter came home from college. But of course yesterday was Tuesday, and I had forgotten that she is let out early on Tuesdays.

She hesitated at the doorway, just a moment. With the light behind her she was outlined like an angel. Then Slater rose – he looked so old, Mem, but horribly powerful, I can't tell you. At that moment I saw the glory of her, young skin, fresh eyes. Slater was looking at her and I knew he saw her mother – who would not? Eyes, cheekbones, mouth, also the way of walking.

My daughter saw him but how would she know who he was? He looked like nothing she had seen in all her life. She returned his smile. And then he made the strangest bow, Mem.

I do believe, he said, I knew your mother.

My daughter ran away upstairs.

I had been soldering in the back of the shop, but I could not leave him with his filthy thoughts. You remember her-*lah*, I called. The mother? You mentioned her before. Noussette.

Oh yes, he said. So smugly, Mem. Such a Don Juan. But who was he to know a thing about her? Only his great arrogance.

One day, one night, I told him. Not much to know, isn't it?

I was angry, and he heard it, and came down through the bicycles to talk. Listen, old man, he said, is there something I ought to apologise to you for?

Something? *Cheh!* Of course, you slept with her. You think I don't know that? She was a bad woman.

Only one night, old man.

But when I said she was a bad woman, Mem, that is not what I meant. *Why* did she sleep with him? Slater was such a vain, romantic fool. He had no idea of how she used him. I thought it was time he learned who she really was.

Chubb then produced yet another of his parcels and, after his fussy unwrapping, handed me a plastic sleeve inside which a yellow sheet from a tabloid was protected. On the front of it was a photograph of a much younger Christopher Chubb dressed in his then pristine suit.

This is what you showed to Slater?

He shook his head. No point, he said. Turn over.

Through the plastic on the other side I saw the masthead of the *Sunday Telegraph* of July 4, 1952. FATHER OF 'MISSING BABY' TO BE CHARGED WITH MURDER.

Shit, I said.

Yes, Mem, exactly. Life is never what you think.

28

I do believe I mentioned my second trip to Australia in 1975, which is when I made a thorough attempt to locate Robert McCorkle in the Registry of Births, Deaths and Marriages. Three times I thought I had my man. Alas, not so. Finding Noussette Markson turned out to be almost as trying. She certainly knew I was looking for her but the only response I had was through her lawyer, a Kings Cross cock-sparrow named Bob Hamilton, who made it clear that I would be hurt in some way – legal or physical, he did not say – if I should 'muck-rake' Ms Markson's past. She was, Mr Hamilton pointed out, a public figure, the friend and confidante of well-known politicians and artists. Until the year before my visit, I discovered, she had been the owner of a very fashionable restaurant called Noussette, and this was about as near as I ever came to her. I found the walls still crowded with her *faux-naïf* self-portraits and through the grime of who knows how many years I could see her big eyes and wide mouth, and I strongly disliked the way she advertised her desirability.

The other woman in Chubb's life, his mother, had died in April 1960. I could discover almost nothing about her and in the end she must occupy this story like a fire that is known from the scars it leaves on the trees it has briefly engulfed.

I know she threw Chubb's father out of the house, although why she did this not even their son could tell me.

She worked as a saleswoman in the glove department of David Jones for thirty years and, at her death, had ten pounds and five shillings in the bank. Years later in Kuala Lumpur, Chubb was still passionately angry about her parsimony, forever referring to the little bowls of leftovers in the kerosene fridge. He seemed unaware of how he'd replicated the habits he despised, and when he described his ascetic life in Chatswood – the one chair, the single setting of cutlery – his lack of self-awareness was breathtaking.

How different Noussette must have seemed to him: beautiful, reckless, spendthrift, fearless. While insisting he did not love her he certainly did admire her and celebrated behaviour he would have judged fiercely in anyone else. She lied continually about her life, reinventing herself at will. Between 1945 and 1952 she changed her occupation five times and her nationality twice. By the time she started the restaurant she had decided she was French. She could not cook but she hired a Maori chef called Bibi and served snails and onion soup and steak au poivre.

Meanwhile Chubb was still writing brochures for the same undistinguished advertising agency. By 1952 this job had become part-time, for he had determined that just two afternoons of employment would provide income sufficient for his needs. He could write verse each day. Every morning he moved the single chair to his trestle desk where he laboured over his sestinas and villanelles.

They do seem an unlikely couple, yet when Noussette discovered she was pregnant it was to suburban Chatswood that she drove and Chubb's hand she placed upon her lovely stomach. Did this mean the poet was the father? Later this question would be of immense importance to him, but at the time he had the rather touching idea that it was not his business.

He does not seem to have made any plans to either care for or support the child, nor does Noussette appear to have expected it. In anticipation of motherhood, she was, as with everything, energetic. Once the pregnancy was certain, she spent her mornings creating a nursery in her cottage. She painted more of those naïve self-portraits on the walls and constructed mobiles to hang from the ceiling. She filled the cupboards and dressers with baby blankets and smocks, interviewed nannies, and drank countless glasses of champagne to celebrate her great good fortune.

Sydney has a reputation as a raffish sort of town, but this was 1952 and even her customers at Noussette were amazed to see their beautiful hostess making her putatively fatherless pregnancy a public event. It seemed, Chubb told me, that there was not a single patron who had not touched her stomach and felt the baby kick. The breaking of her waters was almost a performance. The supper crowd applauded her as she left for hospital.

But she was, when Chubb next saw her, dark and moody. The delivery had been by caesarean section and a brutal scar now marked that perfect stomach. She was tired. She hurt all over. The baby was small, just six pounds, agitated and fretful, having considerable difficulty in latching on to her mother's swollen breasts. She was starving, so Chubb thought. He had the ghastly sense that the child was panicked, gulping and gasping for its life.

And Noussette, who had always been so light and lively, was stiff and unyielding. Chubb thought, This woman does not want this child. It was the first time he had ever felt angry with her.

When he returned on the following day, however, the room was filled with people. Champagne had been opened and Noussette was once again her generous, reckless self. After the crowd had gone, he sat with her while she fed the baby. Perhaps the champagne had helped relax her, as now she nuzzled the little dark-haired head, and afterwards Chubb walked from Paddington to Chatswood, nine miles with a silky north-easterly blowing in his face.

The next day the wind swung to the south, but even if it rattled the windows of the Women's Hospital the room itself was sunny and bursting with flowers. The baby was asleep in the nursery. Joe Cahill, the Premier of New South Wales, had visited with more champagne, and plastic tumblers covered the windowsill and bedside table. It was in tidying these up that Chubb saw papers by the bed which he assumed were hospital bills. He slipped them in his pocket, but later, as the Wahroonga bus ground on its northern route across the bridge, he discovered they were adoption papers concerning the girl child of Noussette Markson and Father Unknown.

He left the bus at the next stop and took a taxi back to Paddington, where he found Noussette implacable and unflustered.

Christopher, she said, you should not snoop.

You know I wasn't snooping. I thought it was the bill.

Even if it was the bill, it is my bill. Please give it back to me.

Chubb was furious. You cannot give her away.

Well, darling, I certainly can't keep her.

You hired a nurse.

A nurse is not a mother, Christopher. How could I have her raised by a servant?

Then a very strange thing happened, Chubb told me. Suddenly I loathed her. Don't ask me why-*lah*. I told her I would adopt the child.

Every woman knows these big placid men can be the most terrifying and as a young man Chubb must have been formidable with his wide shoulders and great powerful thighs. But it was not Noussette's style to show fear and she began to laugh. Christopher, darling, how could you possibly care for her? You cannot even earn a proper living.

I don't know how, he said mulishly, but I will.

You think she's yours, don't you?

I don't care whose she is.

You know nothing about feeding babies.

Then I will bloody well learn.

It is likely that Chubb, at that moment, tangled in emotions which he could neither name nor recognise, imagined that Noussette would eventually assist him in caring for the child. He did not understand that he had come to that sudden, unexpected part of the journey where the road has simply ended at the edge of a cliff.

Starting that afternoon Noussette was extremely cool and no amount of detachment – always his strong suit with her – would rekindle her ardour. She acted rapidly. A week before the adoption was formally completed she was taking pills to dry her milk supply. She had hired a nanny and surely could have offered her help for a week or two, but she did not. She had blankets and clothes and books of helpful hints for new mothers, but none of these were given to Chubb, who three days after finding the adoption papers was alone with a fretful child in a house in Chatswood.

Nothing in his life had prepared him for this. He had been raised without brothers or sisters or even cousins, with never so much as a tadpole to care for, and now he was all alone with a wilful wailing new-born who could thrust her head back so violently as to almost throw herself onto the floor. She was a wild one, Mem, he told me. It is a horror to think what they must go through.

It was an odd choice of word, 'horror'. Doubtless he drew a great deal on his own feelings to explain the anguish that shaped that contorted little face, and yet it was her will, her need, her energy that touched his heart. When he held her in his arms it was as if he'd been given charge of Life itself, and in the draughty winter nights he would lie awake listening to her breathe. This breath, that breath, the next, the one after. When he should've been sleeping he was willing her to stay alive.

He was not expert, but what parent ever is? Fearful of her catching cold he baked her with blankets and electric radiators. She developed a heat rash, a nappy rash, a colic that arrived at four every afternoon and did not stop till nine.

Yet he coped, more or less, although how could he continue? He called into the office sick every morning, exhausted from the excursions of the night, the continual feeding, burping, washing, the long walks through the dark streets while the colic ran its course. You can imagine this caused no small scandal in his little street, a strange, unshaven, crew-cut bachelor carrying a baby to the shops for powdered milk. Having no pram or even a bunny rug, he wrapped her in a double-bed blanket which trailed behind him on the footpath.

Mr Blackhall saw his red-eyed tenant and, even while he judged him, took pity. He helped Chubb carry his shopping and so learned that he kept the bastard baby in a cardboard box, a little nest like you would set for a puppy or a kitten. Blackhall went home and returned with baby blankets.

So you have children, Mr Blackhall?

Grown up now. Grown up with families of their own.

I wonder you did not go mad, said Chubb.

Ha-ha, Mr Chubb, said Blackhall, but later he would have reason to remember this exchange, the bedraggled poet standing in his doorway saying, Quite honestly, Mr Blackhall, I don't know how long I can keep this up.

29

Chubb was young and fit. He would have thought nothing of walking thirty miles through the bush to Govett's Leap, half of it not even on a track, but this tiny, tiny girl with her mother's huge eyes and her little clinging pink-nailed fingers had got the better of him. Even in her first week of life she was delectably pretty, very clearly defined lips and a fine bird-bone chin, and when she slept he would sometimes sit and marvel at her. But for the most part he was just plain knackered, sleeping like a soldier in the trenches, never long enough or deep enough, the slightest murmur from the box being sufficient to set him wide awake and back on his feet.

Yet his hearing was obviously selective, for when the back door was jimmied open, so brutally that the wooden frame was later found split along the length of both its verticals, he continued sleeping, and it was not until he was spoken to that he raised his head and stared into the dark.

Noussette? he said happily, for he had convinced himself that she would finally relent. Is that you?

You bastard, said the hard, accusing voice he'd first heard in the Melbourne court and had expected to never hear again. You unmitigated cunt, said the so-called Bob McCorkle, standing at the foot of the bed.

Get up, the intruder said, and then the light switch, an old bakelite contrivance, clacked on. In the light of the bare hundred-watt bulb Chubb saw that the monster had captured his baby, and had it clutched to his chest with the yellow blanket spilling down below his knees.

Give me the baby, he said. I need to feed her. It was the best he could invent.

Then fetch her milk, the creature ordered. His appearance was again much altered, but no amount of drooping moustaches and old-fashioned starched collars could hide the cruel planes of his distinctive cheeks, the broad dark brow, the hugely modelled nose and chin. He now turned as Chubb rose naked from his bed and followed him into the kitchen.

Get the milk, the other said. Put it in the thing. He snapped his thick fingers. And that thing. There. Use that.

What thing?

The thing, damn you, the beast cried, pointing to a rubber teat floating in the steriliser. The tit.

The teat?

I am a poet who does not know the names of things, but whose fault is that? Tit, tight, teat, tote. What a great joke that is. Fee, fie, fo, fum.

Chubb would recall this odd conversation later, though at the time all of his considerable intelligence was focused on how he might rescue his baby. Excuse me, he said. He loped around the kitchen naked, making formula, pouring it into a bottle. Excuse me, he said as he lit the gas, boiled the water, heated the bottle in his single saucepan. All he could think of was saving her, yet his tormentor was almost seven feet in height and Chubb could not conceive of a way of injuring him sufficiently, not without risking damage to the baby who was sleeping peacefully against her kidnapper's breast. Once the formula was warm Chubb felt he had no choice but to relinquish the bottle to him, and though the babe had been fed an hour earlier she now began to suck again.

The creature gazed down on her, fury in his eyes. You never gave me a childhood, he said.

Chubb quickly pulled on his trousers.

Can you imagine what it is to be born at twenty-four?

But Chubb had no interest in entering into what he felt to be an unwinnable argument with a large and angry lunatic.

Can you even begin to imagine the cruelty of that? Answer.

It would be very puzzling, Chubb said, I am sure.

You made my life as a joke.

It was not the last time Chubb would be brought trembling to the abyss, where he might consider the blasphemous possibility that he had, with his own pen, created blood and bone and a beating heart.

Mr McCorkle, he said, I swear to you I regret the first time I ever wrote your name.

But you will regret it more, much more. It is far too big a thing to just say sorry. There are consequences. There must be justice. I have been thinking of justice for so very long.

And where have you been thinking?

Where? You think I would tell you that?

As you like, it doesn't matter.

You think I will tell you where I live? So you can send the coppers? Well I'm not frightened of police, as you must bloody well remember. But where I am, dear Father – and he spoke this last word so hatefully that Chubb felt the hairs rise on his neck – where I live I am not a joke at all, not a fake in any way. I am a Lord, in fact. You see, being a foreigner, no-one thinks it strange that I do not know the names of things. Sometimes they themselves do not know. Where I am, if you must understand, I sleep with the snakes and the spiders and often I have named them too. *Syzygium McCorklus*, he said, and when Chubb, not understanding, questioned him about the spelling he was happy enough to provide it for him.

It is a tree, he said, and in the slight compression of his lips revealed a pride which his eyes challenged the other to undo.

At that moment Chubb had the sudden intuition that this

dangerous fellow had invented himself as some Edwardian botanist. You are in Africa, he suggested.

Wherever I am, I have put myself outside your power. I have made myself a whole man, almost – except, when I hold this child, I feel the weight of everything you stole from me. This I had not expected, but now I know exactly what I want from you.

What is that?

This is a childhood, he said.

A child, Chubb corrected. A baby. Just one week old.

But all the parts of its brain are already growing. When he touches my finger, he learns something.

She, said Chubb, watching in horrified silence as the baby's white hand grasped the creature's index finger.

You must give her back to me, Mr McCorkle.

Of course, the other said. Just permit me to show the stars to her.

I doubt she can see that well.

The creature was wrapping the fallen blanket more securely around the child. He was not without tenderness. Indeed, he fashioned from the folds a little hood for her head. Just the same, he said, I will tell her their names.

What was Chubb to do? Even with no child to concern him, it is unlikely he could have overpowered this giant alone. It is cold, he said.

No it isn't, said the other.

Chubb held open the screen door and stepped out into the night behind him. He paused just a second to make sure the lock was snibbed open, but by the time he reached the front gate the creature was sprinting soundlessly up the middle of the road with the baby's blanket streaming behind like a piece of ghastly skin. Chubb began to run. The kidnapper swung into the shadow of a jacaranda and was swallowed by the night.

30

Mr Blackhall was not yet late for work. He was in the hallway, standing on Chubb's chair and – as the court record reveals – reading the electric meter, when his tenant unexpectedly dashed into the house and knocked him to the floor. Christopher Chubb had looked unwell for the past week but now, as he grasped the frightened landlord by his skinny shoulders, he appeared deranged.

Mr Blackhall, they have took my baby, or so Blackhall was quoted later. They have took my child.

Give me a shilling!

Chubb dug deep into his pockets and pulled out a fistful of pennies and threepences. Blackhall then hurried across the street to the phone box and called Chatswood police station. He was put through to Sergeant Bob Fennessey, who ordered him to stay with the father, and so he did.

I never met Mr Blackhall but imagine him rather like some sort of mouse in a stationmaster's uniform: the peaked cap, the blue serge trousers, the New South Wales Railways watch in his fob pocket, shadowing Chubb as he paced up the hallway and out into the street, along the verandah and down the side of the house by the blue hydrangeas. Five minutes later, a freshly washed black 1939 Chevrolet pulled into the kerb and from it emerged a tall, sharp-nosed man with deep-set grey eyes and the build of a champion wood-chopper.

As Sgt Fennessey approached, Mr Blackhall drew to one side, as one does when trying not to obscure a work of art. They took his baby, he said.

The policeman noted the way Chubb shied away from him, shaking his head like a heifer that does not wish to get into the truck. He noted too that Chubb wore no shoes and his yellow socks were worn through on the soles.

Mr Blackhall then led Fennessey into the house, which the latter discovered to be in an alarmingly neglected state, causing him to experience what he later described as 'a bad feeling'.

There was nowhere to sit in the kitchen, but the sergeant took out his notebook. Your missus left you, he suggested.

The father did not respond.

Who took the baby, Mr Chubb? Was it the mother?

Chubb opened his mouth but the reply was like a bird lost inside a house. It was a man, he said at last.

Was this man known to you?

Can I sit down?

Mr Blackhall consulted his watch and then fetched him the chair.

Chubb collapsed onto the seat. It's a little girl, he said, just one week old.

You chased the mongrel, did you?

He tricked me.

And he was known to you?

Here the policeman noted another significant hesitation.

I had seen him before, Chubb finally admitted, but I do not know him.

Could you describe him for me?

This Chubb could do very well. He might have supplied even more detail had not Mr Blackhall, who'd quietly retreated into the front room, now interrupted from the doorway. A word, Sergeant, he said.

On entering the front room the policeman saw the

landlord holding his left finger to his small moustached mouth while with his right hand he proffered a collection of yellowed newspapers. When Sgt Fennessey returned to the kitchen it was with an entirely new sense of purpose, all his natural sympathy now neatly packed away.

Have you ever been in trouble with the police before, Christopher?

Am I in trouble now?

Don't be a smart-arse, Christopher.

No, I haven't.

Not even in the state of Victoria?

No.

He produced the *Argus* of May 7, 1946. What about this, then?

Have you been going through my things? Chubb demanded, and then he saw his landlord in the doorway. You bloody dill, he cried. I was never in trouble with the police. It was Weiss they prosecuted.

Don't you worry about him, Christopher. You worry about me, because I am someone who is worth worrying about. Did you ever make a hoax, Christopher? I think you should know what a hoax is.

I do, yes.

It is when you try to make a mug out of someone. Would that be a fair definition, Christopher? Did you ever hear of Bob McCorkle? That would be a hoax, I reckon.

Having taken the paper from the policeman, Chubb looked down at the collage he had made so light-heartedly, so long ago, and only then did he understand what trouble he was in. For the moment he claimed he had breathed life into this image, he would be declared a lunatic, and once he was a lunatic he was as good as guilty. And while they were wasting time in the kitchen, the creature had his child. At this moment, somewhere in Sydney, she would be crying for her bottle and her captor knew not even the names of the things he needed in order to care for her. If he did not tell this police-man the truth, there was no chance in hell she would be brought back alive.

He sat there, silent, unable to move or speak.

31

Australia is the country where a woman named Chamberlain was very recently convicted of murdering her baby on the basis of no evidence other than her refusal to cry on television. Her crime, it seems, was being unwomanly, and in looking at Christopher Chubb, one might detect a corresponding unmanliness. After all, what normal man would want to adopt a baby to raise alone? To the tabloid press, there seemed one reason a male would adopt a child: to murder it.

By the time Chubb was found not guilty, his life had been effectively destroyed. He had lost his child, his mistress, his job, his house, and the last of his friends. Yet he was not convicted, as Mrs Chamberlain would later be on just as little evidence. In this sense he was lucky. And if many people believed he had smuggled the child out of the country simply to spite its mother, this damaged only his personal reputation, not his civil liberty.

Still, he felt no joy in his acquittal, only the most colossal and unexpected emptiness. Having been so exhausted by the child in a single week, why did he now seek her face in every pram? The man whose romantic relations had been distinguished by his profound lack of need could now be devastated by something as saccharine and sentimental as a knitted bootie abandoned on the smeary floor of the Bondi tram. Every little sign of life, even a powdery bogong moth captured inside the cup of his hand, somehow felt exactly like the child, the desperate beating of a life whose needs must be obeyed.

One might have expected this agony at least to nourish his writing, but at this moment of crisis all art seemed worthless to him and there was nothing else he had ever believed in.

The public scandal meant that even copywriting was now closed to him, and after trying a number of poorly paying jobs he finally settled into the occupation he had once invented for McCorkle, selling insurance door-to-door. Even here, inside the sixth circle of his own prank, he toiled as a mediocre salesman, always expecting that behind this door, in answer to that bell, he would discover his child. For the same reason there was not a bus he boarded or a railway platform he waited on where he was not looking for that great dark figure with its distinctive springy gait. He found himself hoping that the monster might not yet be satisfied with his revenge, so when forced to abandon his house for a flat, and that for a boarding-house, he left a forwarding address to ease his tormentor's search.

Chubb's slow slide towards the boarding-house took almost four years, during which, he told me, he was far too distressed to write or even read. Finally, in the spring of 1956, he received a forwarded parcel from the Australian painter Donald Defoe, once a casual acquaintance. Defoe now lived in Indonesia, which was presently most turbulent, and he seemed not to have heard of Chubb's difficulties. The artist was a graceful, thoughtful man who apologised for intruding on his privacy, but hoped the poet 'might like to hear of a wonderfully mad character who has just left my house today – a shadow of the hilarious avant-gardist you invented back in '46 . . .'

Defoe's visitor had been travelling with a little girl about four years old, and they'd fled to Bali from Yogyakarta, where 'the alleged McCorkle' had been busy learning the local language, an ambition foiled by his 'completely tragic inability to roll his r's'. The artist had found the pair of them wandering the streets during Ramadan and took them in so they would not be arrested by the religious police. That first night, he wrote, 'McCorkle recited "The Darkening Ecliptic" to great dramatic effect'.

He and the little girl had stayed two weeks, at the end of which the visitor, having drunk too much arak, declared his host a mediocrity and himself a great genius, but in spite of this Defoe had enjoyed his company. Though 'quite mad of course', he had great energy and a huge curiosity about everything he saw. The painter was sorry when he took the little girl off to live in the north of the island, at Singaraja. Accompanying the letter, Chubb told me, was a charcoal drawing Defoe had made of the man and child. It was only six inches by four inches, but very powerful: the great hulking, brooding figure with the delicate child snuggled into his lap.

This all occurring before the Xerox age, Chubb had photographic copies made of both the letter and the drawing and sent them to Noussette. I am sure you know who this is, he wrote, and asked her for money so he could go to Indonesia and fetch the child. If the mother recognised the man, she made no mention of him in her reply.

'Dear C' – and in being unable to spell out his name gave some unintended sign of the distress she felt.

It was cruel of you to send me the Defoe. It broke my heart all over again. I have every right to hate you, but instead I feel very sorry for you. For now you know, as I certainly do, what it feels like to have a child stolen from you. You hurt me very badly, and I wished you ill, but I can see the course of your life now and understand that you will finally be made to suffer even more than those of us who you have injured so carelessly. There is some justice, so it seems.

The letter was unsigned. She did, however, enclose a cheque for a considerable amount of money and Chubb was, as a result, able to buy a ticket to Bali, and from there he began the long and fruitless journey to the northern coast, and thence to Java and Yogyakarta, where he finally had some small amount of luck. That is, he discovered the Agam Hotel, where 'Mr Bob' had stayed during the year he doggedly pursued his studies in Javanese. The owners remembered him, and happily let his room to Chubb.

No reason to stay. No reason to go. I waited.

In those days Indonesia was under martial law and seems to have been rather free of tourists, but even in the middle of this particularly tumultuous year, a certain number of Europeans made the trip along the volcanic spine of Java to Yogyakarta, where they would put up at the Agam Hotel. In 1956 these travellers would have been shown Donald Defoe's charcoal sketch. One of them, a German botanist named Karl Burkhardt, recognised the subjects. The man and girl were living in a lodge on Lake Toba in Sumatra. The child had had very serious dysentery, and Burkhardt himself had cured her with rice water.

So, cried Chubb, he does not care for her.

Oh no, the German said, it is very touching to watch him with her, how he combs her hair and has her clean her teeth.

Chubb abruptly excused himself, went to his room, returned to the front desk, and settled his bill. He took a trishaw to the railway station and, seven hours later, at one in the morning, boarded a crowded train for Jakarta. Then began a long and difficult journey: small rebellions were erupting here and there, and soldiers were forever taking him aside to learn his business. But he persisted and finally was rowed across the eerie flat surface of Lake Toba. He came ashore on the island of Samosir, where the German said the lodge was situated.

Of course there was nothing there, or worse than nothing. He was shown the vacant lodge, and there, tucked up inside the low rafters, he found a collection of leaves and flowers all roughly glued to the brown paper pages of a hand-made scrapbook. Had his daughter made this with her abductor? It was painful to imagine.

Once more Chubb fell into a slump, which differed not in nature but in degree from those he'd suffered in both Sydney and Yogyakarta.

Lake Toba, according to Slater, is breathtaking and the people are famous for their good looks and beautiful voices, but Chubb's only memory of the place is of dreary water, interminable nights where he lay in darkness, his head aching, in a fug of burning cow dung.

What did you do there, I asked.

Black dog, Mem.

How long did you stay?

He shrugged. All he was certain of was that it was wet season when a small boy in a motor boat arrived with a letter addressed to him. The stamps were Malaysian, he said, the postmark Penang, and it was addressed in the beast's own hand: 'Mr Chubb, Samosir, Sumatra'.

But listen, Mem, to the note inside. 'Dear Chubb, the little girl has died. She contracted a fever. It did not take very long.'

How horrible!

No, Mem, no. It cheered me up. That's the point. Whatever blow he intended to deliver, it bounced right off me-*lah*. I knew she was alive, and that he now was frightened of me.

32

All through the hot morning, he had interrupted his story to preen at himself, smoothing his close-shorn head, buttoning and unbuttoning the jacket of his new suit, fussing with his trousers until they were suitably loose across his sturdy knees. This suit, at first a rather touching novelty – which indeed gained him entry to the hotel – soon turned into a time-wasting distraction as he continually interrupted himself to worry at the motives of his benefactor. Time, of course, was getting very short. Today was the fourteenth. My meeting in London was the evening of the nineteenth.

At lunch I took him out to eat beside the pool, but not even food could stop him fretting about John's gift.

If Slater thinks I am angry because he slept with Noussette, he's wrong.

You shouldn't worry.

He could have saved his money, Mem. I am not the jealous type.

Certainly you were when – I hesitated, not knowing what to call the kidnapper, if indeed there was a kidnapper – when 'McCorkle' stole your daughter.

That was not *jealousy*, Mem. Jealousy is a little thing. I had known this child for one awful week, but what I had seen was *life*.

His eyes – too big, too shiny – demanded my agreement.

I embarrass you, he said.

Of course not.

I must serve life, do you see?

But he did embarrass me, and irritate me too. I was stuck with transcribing this story when all I wanted was the rest of that damn poetry. Mr Chubb, I said. You remember the first day you came to the hotel, you brought McCorkle's manuscript.

I see through you! He was suddenly, inexplicably, delighted. You want to go straight to pudding. Look – you're blushing. You think I don't know what you want? Would you be listening to me now if you hadn't read McCorkle? Here, he said, your pen is running dry. Take mine.

He continued – maliciously, I thought: I came straight to Malaya from Sumatra.

And I had no choice. 'Sumatra, Malaya.' I wrote it down.

There was a steamer, he continued coolly, from North Sumatra to Penang. Horrid. *Lord Jim* or even worse – all of the Malays crowded below the decks in this filthy, sweaty dark. They were village people, very kind to me even though I was in a frantic hurry and kept pushing that charcoal drawing on them. At first they had no clue, but when I got through to them they were very affected. By the time we docked at Swettenham Pier they all came to say goodbye, fifty of them, just to wish me luck. But what could I do? Now that I saw Penang I understood what I was up against. Needle in a haystack. Hopeless. I ended up in a hotel – lovely old colonial place with the waves crashing against the sea-wall at the back. Tall palms, Chinese waiters – five hundred years old in stiff white jackets – and the famous Albert Yeoh playing 'Misty' in the Anchor Bar. Would have been a perfect place to bring a pretty woman. But it was not an adult I was in love with, and with her not there I had no peace. So I wrote, on a wrought-iron table in the garden. It was agony, like cutting words into your own chest, but finally I knew I was a poet.

I have been an editor long enough not to give a damn about how a poet looks or talks, but there was something weirdly persuasive about Christopher Chubb in full flight.

May I read those poems, I asked.

His head jerked up. Ha! You have already!

No, no, the ones you wrote in Penang.

You saw them.

What a horrid, twisted smile he gave me. So you *are* McCorkle, I said. You have hoaxed me!

This drew from him a strangled cry and then a queer convulsion – grabbing his head as if he wished to pull it down inside his ribs. Have you listened to *nothing*?

I began to speak but he rudely cut me off.

If I could write McCorkle's poem, do you think I would not claim it? No, you listen to me now. Do you imagine I would invent this pain? He thumped his chest. Who would want to feel like this?

I'm sorry, I must have been sitting here for rather too long.

Then you should understand, he said, and in his fury his mouth gave a nasty twitch. I am Chubb. He is McCorkle.

Frankly, that is a puzzle.

There is no bloody puzzle, can't you see? I could never, *ever*, have made that poem. Can't you imagine how hard that is to say?

So where else could I have read what you wrote in Penang?

Smirking, he took a letter from the inside pocket of his jacket and laid it on the table. Even from where I sat the handwriting was recognisably my own.

You rejected me in 1959. Perhaps you will reject McCorkle too?

I would hope, I said, not to miss my chance to judge.

Then you write down my story, Miss. And we will see.

What choice did I have but to uncap his nasty little pen?

And at that very damn moment I saw John Slater making his way down the steps from the Pool Bar. As he skirted the pool he waved some airline tickets.

Go away, I thought. He did not know what he was interrupting. He threw the tickets on my lap.

All set for the eighteenth.

This is exactly what I had demanded, but I did not thank him. I wished only that he would go away. It appears, I said, that I have previously read Mr Chubb. Thus I'd hoped to impress him that this was a private conversation. Nonetheless, he pulled up a cane chair and parked himself between us.

She marked up your stuff, old man? Oh, Miss Wode-Douglass began that business *very* young. He patted my knee. I pushed his hand away and glared at him while he ordered Singapore Slings for all of us.

Micks, my darling, what was the name of your vitriolic little friend? Was it Annette?

Go away, John.

Do you know, Christopher, these two girls began correcting their betters at the ripe age of fourteen.

Don't be a beast.

The mischief was making Slater's complexion a healthier colour. He took an angel on horseback from the table, grinning rather wickedly. Beast? I'm being a bloody dormouse, darling. They used to mark up my poems, Christopher. Girls, little slips of things. They would tear verses from my bloody books and send them to me covered with their comments.

Once, John.

At least ten times – and of course I forgave you, for all sorts of reasons. But I was bloody scared of you, Micks.

He gripped my hand and I was shocked to see, through the storm of my annoyance, that his eyes had suddenly filled with tears.

Chubb must have seen this too, and was already excusing himself. I took John's hand, in fact burrowed my own inside his. It was impossible not to be aware of the old goat's considerable affection, and it made me not embarrassed in the least, but somehow grubby and deceitful, to be carrying on this negotiation behind his back.

I never published a great poem, John.

He blinked. Where did that come from?

Nowhere. I've been thinking about it since we arrived.

Well, old darling, I'd have to say I never wrote a great poem.

Even now, when I think of this moment, I wish I could have brought myself to contradict him. Instead I kissed his hand. It was an awful thing to offer – sympathy.

33

It happened to slip out, after lunch, that Chubb's lovely hotel in Penang was none other than the Eastern and Oriental, and I had to wonder why an impecunious poet would even think of staying at the E&O, or 'Eat & Owe' as it was then known. I had not yet visited Penang, but the E&O was famous, like Raffles in Singapore, as a very pukka-sahib sort of place, once favoured by Residents, rajas, and those dreadful 'Twicken-ham Duchesses' who would gather on the lawn on Friday night to complain too loudly about their servants. While this type of establishment occasionally welcomes guests who arrive in something less than black tie – wealthy tin-miners, say, who have travelled by mule through the jungle in order to take tiffin in the long room – they are sure to have been perplexed by Chubb's rather down-at-heel appearance, so I asked him how he had been received.

I had Australian pounds, he said sharply. There was some fuss with the exchange rate.

Whatever that was code for, I do not know. Certainly he was almost broke, and checking into the E&O was self-defeating. Had he wished to run out of money and therefore be permitted to give up his search? I suggested this to him. Who, I offered, would not understand his dilemma?

Don't *tunjuk*, you, he snapped. Better you listen.

The morning after he arrived, he was shown to his

breakfast table by a shabby, felt-covered screen which did nothing to muffle the continual slap and screech of the swinging kitchen door. His dining companion was a very dark-skinned Tamil who seemed violently offended by the food he was being offered.

Of course, said Chubb, we were in Siberia, isn't it? I was beyond caring, Mem, but the Indian was in a state. They would not give him face. An educated man. Very sharp, clever tongue to him. He ticked off the waiters. Called in the maître d', a Scot with thorny ginger eyebrows. Ticked him off as well, declared the scrambled eggs so bad they might have been served at Eton. Well, the Scot's eyes looked like bloody murder. He snatched the dish away, so fierce that half the meal fell on the floor.

I asked the Tamil, was this so?

Was what bloody so?

Did you go to Eton, *Tuan*?

It was not a silly question but you should've seen his lip curl. *Cheh*! Was I some kind of moron? No, he was a *cikgu*, a schoolmaster. Chemistry and physics.

And you, he asked, bored rigid before I answered.

I told him I was attempting to find my kidnapped child.

The maître d' arrived with more eggs, same vintage as the last, but the Tamil's mood had changed completely. He pushed the plate aside and when he turned his head I saw his wall-eye – one eye on the pot, the other up the chimney, as the saying goes. He fixed the good eye on me, but perhaps it was the bad.

Glass falling on a rock, he said. You must be worried sick.

I had already been shown much sympathy but his injured beauty was particularly affecting, a badge of his own suffering. I liked him immediately, enormously.

When I placed the portrait of monster and child on the table, he stared at it, his brow twisted, nostril flared, then he placed a delicate hand upon my wrist. The rickshawallahs will help you, he said, much kindness in his voice. Talk to them, he said. A little tea money, that's all.

Tea money?

A few dollars, small payment.

He was dressed exactly like a school teacher – closed coat, silver buttons, an array of pens and pencils in his pocket – but all I understood was the big gold watch worn loose like a bracelet on his wrist. Who could know what his idea of small payment might be? I told him my daughter might be dead already.

He crossed himself. I was not to say such things. He was very fierce, very definite, like someone accustomed to giving orders, also like a small bird with fixed ideas. He took out a pen and rapped McCorkle's nose with it.

The rickshawallahs know every white man, he said, where they live, where they drink. They will be finding this fellow for you and we will get your daughter back. Take my word.

You see, Mem, I was being saved. But I did not dare believe my luck. Who was this man? His skin was black as coal. His eyes were crooked. My mother would have thought him marked by God, more wrong than just the eyes. Me, of course, she would have judged more harshly still. What blasphemy. I had made a life.

The Tamil poured himself a second cup of tea and as he squeezed the lemon he invited me to come and live with him. His mouth was very pink, a wicked edge to it. I thought, Whoa, Dobbin. Not for me, that business. But when I said no – my mother too, in chorus – his fine face appeared so hurt I felt a cad.

The house is free, he said, provided by the school. I am being at the E&O one night only, to let the roofers do their work.

Finally I understood he did not plan to bugger me.

We shall celebrate my new roof, he said.

When I did not immediately respond, he glared sideways

at me as fierce as any kookaburra with one eye on a worm. Gal iron-*ah*.

You may not understand, Mem, what a gal-iron roof means to an Australian. All my childhood I lived under galvanised iron. Such peace, the lovely din of rain at night, it was home to me. Also, although I had my hopes of funding in the future, the dough was running very low.

I asked Chubb to explain his 'funding' and he admitted he'd sent an E&O postcard to Noussette in which he had quoted from McCorkle's horrid correspondence and repeated his belief that the child was still alive. Five hundred pounds was what he asked for.

I can pay no rent, he said to the Tamil.

My name is Kanagaratnam Chomley, but you call me Mulaha or K.G. if you like. You must come with me and see your digs, and on the way I will talk to these rickshawallahs. Did you report the crime to the MPs?

Who?

Police.

No.

Good man, he said, but did not explain.

Chubb still did not know whether to trust him, but the two of them checked out of the E&O together, the diminutive K.G. Chomley all starch and spit and polish, Chubb slovenly in socks and sandals, short-sleeved shirt, pleated brown F.J. trousers made in Warrnambool, Victoria. *Seperti durian dengan mentimum,* Chubb told me, an unlikely pair, the durian and the cucumber.

On Farquhar Street they encountered the usual crowd of rickshawallahs, as loud and quarrelsome as seagulls in the off-season. This type of Asian scene had always alarmed Chubb, who now threw up his arms as if to shoo away the yellow hordes.

K.G. Chomley comfortably immersed himself in their sweaty, nicotine-stained midst and was soon talking in rough

Hokkien with two old men in white singlets and ink-blue shorts. Money was passed. Chubb saw this and fretted about how much he owed.

Don't worry, said Chomley, I spend you. Only tea money.

I wasn't sure what this meant, Mem. His treat, or the opposite?

They saw your man, said Chomley.

Chubb's pulse quickened.

Your daughter too, he said, taking the dazed Australian's sleeve and pulling him out of the path of a blue Hin bus, and then urgently forward across Farquhar Street, where outside the Morris dealers he settled his Craven A into a long ivory holder.

Please, what has happened?

They were staying at Batu Ferringi, but they are in the jungle now.

Why would they do that?

The Tamil shrugged. Perhaps they are communists?

Are we going there now? To the jungle?

No, I am sending you to inspect my new roof.

Please, Mr Chomley, do not tease me.

The Tamil again lay his unnervingly feminine hand upon Chubb's hairy wrist. Call me Mulaha, he said. Much friendlier.

Please call me Christopher

Christopher! So saying, Mulaha grabbed hold of a snazzy bright-red Vespa which Chubb had somehow connected with the Morris dealers. Christopher, he cried once more, and leapt athletically upon the kick pedal.

Christopher, he shouted, the cigarette holder clenched between his perfect white teeth, it is Saturday. No action now. On Monday morning we will address him an E.S. parcel. He twisted back the throttle. Hop on. Now we *cabut*.

Cabut, Mem, means to leave the scene, but I was thinking, What is an E.S. parcel, and how will it save my daughter?

I would have asked but was trapped on the only Vespa in Penang. Bloody thing flew off the footpath. We landed like a rock. Disaster imminent.

Mulaha, by Chubb's account, seems to have been in his element. He waved to the rickshawallahs, wobbled, lurched into second gear, and then most definitely *cabut* up towards North Beach with his passenger's arms tight around his narrow waist. Years later Chubb would recall the sweet air clinging to his sweating skin, the smells of fish, hawkers' fires, jasmine, the salty mud flats at the creeks, and all that coral-blue sea off the right side of the road. In 1956 Penang must have been like paradise. Some bungalows here and there, dusty casuarinas, but mostly the giddy smell of a still-unpolluted sea. The Vespa bounced across the bridge at Sungai Babi – Pig River – and passed the Chinese vegetable gardens where the air was thick with the unholy smell of human shit. Then there was a Malay village, and just beyond the last rust-roofed shack, at the foot of that distinctive lumpy hill named Bukit Zamrud, the driver eased the scooter off the road and, without dismounting, walked it slowly into a stand of tall yellow grass.

We leave it here, he said to Chubb. Our little secret.

What is E.S.? You said we would find my daughter with E.S.

Extra Size, said Mulaha, carefully arranging the grasses so as to hide the scooter more effectively. A parcel too big to deliver, he added, fastening the silver buttons on his coat and arranging his pens in a line along his pocket. Come, he said, no peep about the Vespa-*lah*.

Yes, but how will this E.S. help me?

Now is my day off.

They began walking up a dusty road which rose from the coastal plain and curved around the base of Bukit Zamrud, which from this perspective appeared to be covered in dense jungle.

Before long they came to an elaborate wrought-iron gate with a large enamelled sign: Bukit Zamrud English School.

This, Mulaha said as he unlocked the padlock and unwound the sturdy chain, is a disaster area. Free School is better, Xavier better still, and both are gratis. But here they are shanghaiing the princes from Thailand and Burma. Also any titled youngsters they can find between George Town and Kuala Kangsar.

Chubb looked down on a large wedge of playing field cut like a cucumber sandwich from the rugged landscape. Perched high above on a nubbly hill was a fine three-storeyed colonial building with arched windows and green wooden shutters.

You like it, Christopher?

Yes.

It is a bloody folly, man. The school board is so desperate to catch the sons of the rajas that the headmaster is making foolish discounts, so even though we now have the desired class of pupils, the school, between you and me, cannot keep up its payments to the *chettiars*. They'll foreclose anytime soon, so enjoy it while you can.

The road had now dwindled to twin tyre tracks which circled around until all view of the sea was lost. Here, at the back of Bukit Zamrud, there was no breeze. The jungle was very still: palms, vines, huge trees with buttressed roots pressing so insistently against the ten-foot barbed-wire fence that the concrete posts were tilting inwards.

There is a bright side, Mulaha said. They have no money to call in the thatchers. That is good, you see. I get a gal-iron roof. Much cheaper than the damn *attap*.

Now the double track became a muddy path and the two men walked in single file with grass brushing their trouser cuffs. Ahead of them, in a tight niche between the high cliff of the hill and the wall of jungle, was a blinding rectangle of silver – Chomley's new roof.

When we entered, Chubb told me, I thought I'd made

a big mistake in coming here. The front room! *Cheh.* Like an oven. No door or window open. No ceiling, just the blinding naked roof which stank of kerosene.

I am a modern man, said Mulaha.

There were great lumps of *attap* fallen on his sofa, Chubb said, bits of his old roof. You'd think a man like this would be offended by such a bloody mess, but he did not seem to notice.

See, he said, it is more modern! Here, I'll show you to your room.

I went, Mem. What choice-*lah*? It was an oven too, but I could not afford to leave him now.

34

No sooner had they arrived than Mulaha disappeared into a back room and there was nothing for Chubb to do but wait. His own room was unbearable so he returned to the living room and began to release the windows, but immediately found himself opposed by a wizened Chinese 'house boy' who followed behind him implacably shutting everything he opened. Chubb turned on the ceiling fan, the house boy switched it off. Chubb attempted a conversation but the man had no English. He sat down on the clear end of the sofa. No books. No food. No water in sight.

So did he rethink his decision to stay?

Who cares I am boiled alive, said the old contrarian. I had rickshaws and postmen. This E.S. I did not yet know how to work; I knew I must wait for it. Mulaha was also most *engagé*. No, Mem, I know I complained about the heat, but I was happy as a dog with two tails. Kerosene practically dripping from the boiling iron – not even that could disturb my equanimity.

'Equanimity', however, does seem *exactly* the wrong word. I imagine ants and luminescent insects, dispossessed of their thatch, crawling around his feet as he sat there worrying over his remaining currency. Twenty dollars, is this sufficient tea money? No matter what he claimed, it was surely frightening for a man so emotionally exhausted to give himself not so much to the toxic heat but to the buffetings of hope.

The house, he told me, had two bedrooms and a third room, distinguished by a brass padlock, now hanging open from a strong steel hasp. This was where Mulaha had gone, and Chubb now sought him out to ask if perhaps some windows could be opened. But the house boy picked up a bucket, tucked his sarong between his legs and, coming forward like a batsman facing a ferocious fast bowler, began to splash water aggressively towards him. Chubb retreated to the safety of the verandah and here he squatted, native style, with his back pressed against the clapboard wall. In the distance he heard the thwack of a willow bat hitting a leather-cased ball, the first sign that he was on the grounds of a peculiar English school. Staring down into the shadows of the rainforest he was reminded of New Guinea, and when he heard rustling amongst the vegetation he flinched only once, for what appeared before him was a tall man wearing an Australian slouch hat. With the man was a Scotch terrier. When Chubb stood and waved the terrier ran back to his master, yapping fearfully.

The man approached slowly through the scaly shadows, slapping a leash against his leg. He emerged in a patch of blinding sunlight which revealed a very large revolver in his hand.

The pistol did not really shock me, said Chubb. What I noticed was he had a great big schnozz, Mem, a totally Aussie schnozz, painted white like a parade-ground rock. It made me homesick, so homely and familiar.

Hello there, said the man.

Hello, said Chubb.

I'm David Grainger.

Christopher Chubb.

Yes, but I mean – I'm the headmaster.

Something in the way he spoke should've warned me, Mem, but on the other hand he was Australian. I had been so very pleased to hear the accent that now I made a try for one last joke. I asked him, You've been shooting rabbits?

Went down like a bag of warm sick, as they say at home. No response at all. Up the steps he came. The communists have just killed a Christian Brother on Penang Hill, he said, as if I were a shit for joking at such a time. They broke into his school and butchered him.

Is that near here?

He didn't bother answering. Do you have a weapon? he said.

No.

He stepped inside the house and talked to the house boy in Malay. Did not sound a friendly conversation. On and on he went, with the house boy only answering reluctantly. As for the interrogator, his language sounded like it had been learned in Ballarat.

Mulaha he did not speak to. Too polite, perhaps, to cross the threshold of his private room. But he's only too happy to grill me. Did I understand the country was in a state of emergency? Was I a friend of Cikgu Chomley?

I said we had just met at the E&O. Wrong thing to mention, it seems.

His eyebrows shot halfway up his forehead. No, he cried. Clapped his big freckled hand onto his head.

I tried to make a joke, said the eggs were so bad I would not return.

He gave me a hard look. You'd be surprised how small George Town is, he said. You do Mr Chomley no favour by taking him to the E&O. A reputation can be easily lost.

Only later did I understand that a Tamil would never go to the E&O, and what had happened that morning was generally thought impossible.

He asked me was I a university man.

Sydney.

B.A.?

Already I disliked him. *Kn'ua kuan bo kniua kair*, Mem.

Looks high, never looks low. A snob. I told him Ph.D., which was one year short of the truth.

Cricket?

A grade, I said. Like county cricket, Mem, for your information. This was a lie as well.

Grainger looked me up and down as if I were a horse he might buy when the price came low enough. Very good, he said. Please inform Mr Chomley to keep a sharp eye out. The police have shut down the train to Penang Hill. He whistled and his Scottie came running. From his pocket he took a greasy-looking lamb bone which he threw into the long grass. The dog took off with its master close behind him.

A moment later Mulaha emerged, no longer in his suit but dressed in a white shirt and white dhoti. He had bushy black hair all up his legs. Master Grainger, he said with a smirk. They call him Mad Mat.

He said there are communists.

Yes, of course. Shame you told him about the E&O.

Sorry.

Not to worry, but you must never let a dog into the house like that. Not your fault, old man, but best keep the door shut.

I don't like animals in the house either.

It's this, you see – what if he had died? More than my job is worth.

Why would he die?

Mulaha looked at me.

Take my word. They die.

I thought that a little strange, Mem. But pick up the pen. Gets better.

35

To reach this stage of his story had taken until Wednesday night – that is, just four days before I must leave for London with my treasure. We sat by the Merlin Pool all afternoon and took dinner there, but by midnight we had shifted inside to the Highland Stream, where I was still transcribing, no damned end in sight. On and on he went, often repeating himself and circling back to correct some imagined misunderstanding before, finally, continuing.

In Penang, he said, there is also a Campbell Street. The Chinese called it New Street: Sin Kay. But when you say that in Hokkien it can mean 'fresh prostitutes' as well. Mulaha told me this at least four times – his good eye glistening, his enthusiasms clear even before I detected his cologne amidst the flood of kerosene. The delicate little fellow was *kutu embun*, a dew beetle, coming home at dawn each Sunday. Singsong girls his weekly sport-*ah*. As for me, I never visited a brothel in my life. Once, perhaps, in Townsville. It was not the tarts that put me off. It was my fellow patients in the repat. Missing arms and legs, some of them, but they would hobble into town and then come swinging back into the ward boasting about their bloody gonorrhea. *Aiyo!* They had no face, Mem, showing their disease to one another, howling each morning when they peed.

Come, come, said Mulaha Chomley. Time for dancing.

No thank you, no Sin Kay for me.

Sin Kay? Sin Kay is finished since the war. But you must visit a certain place. A man in your position. Essential, isn't it?

His dead eye on me – horrible really, sucked dry of all emotion. This grim organ signified nothing but I supplied a horrid meaning. Made me hot all over.

I asked him what the hell he meant to imply.

Releks, man, he said. Steady on.

But I could not forget the stories from my sergeant who served in Egypt. He swore men had sex with kiddies.

Promise it is not her?

Pardon?

My girl? My girl is not in a brothel.

He might have laughed at my hysteria but he did not. They say Malaysians don't touch, but Mulaha took my sleeve. *Releks*, he said, and I took that kindness as my right. I had no idea, Mem, how much worse his own suffering was, could not begin to guess what his dead eye saw as he rode his Vespa around Penang. The blazing body of a Tamil merchant, sitting upright with a violent jerk. Flies crawling on Captain Suzuki's unwashed arm. The fluttering eyelids of a decapitated head. Blood spurting from a neck, rising as high as the roof of the Hong Aun Coffee Shop and Hotel. Yes, yes, Mem. I will explain in time.

In my ignorance I was the proprietor of all pain. He held on to my sleeve and guided me down the wobbly steps and along the muddy path. It was dark now and the lights of the school spilled over the queer-shaped hill and brushed the edges of the jungle. I did not have the sense to be afraid.

We let ourselves out the gate and soon were laying a blanket of blue smoke behind us on the road. Malay Village, Shit Stink Gardens, Chinese Cemetery, Rambutan Plantation, then a sign that had been hidden in the morning sunlight: The True Parrot, glowing green above the tops of the rambutans.

Cabaret only, said Mulaha.

What a lie that was, but never mind. We bounced down a dirt track, then navigated an untidy tangle of parked cars and Chinese trucks, walked past the biggest Sikh you ever saw, crossed Sungai Babi by a rickety footbridge. The air here smelled appropriately of beauty and corruption, foetid river-mud and salty sea. I could hear a woman singing 'Venus', and a lovely syncopated piano. And suddenly, without warning, we were on the edge of a dance floor. No roof at all, just a platform of polished concrete above the lapping sea. The moon was huge and mustard-yellow. Bass, drums, piano, this gorgeous Eurasian woman singing. 'Venus, Venus, if you will . . .'

Come, said Mulaha, I spend you.

I thought he meant a drink, but when he returned it was to press a roll of something into my hands.

Tickets for the taxi-girls, he said. I spend you.

Then I saw the so-called taxi-girls sitting in a row along the back, a numbered card held in every lap. One ticket per dance, that's how it worked at The True Parrot. Upstairs some rooms, just like Chusan and other nightclubs in those days.

Ipoh girls, Mulaha said. Jiggy-jiggy, isn't it?

Ipoh, Mem, is the city where these girls are said to come from. They had gorgeous legs showing through their long slit dresses.

Cannot, I said.

How cannot? But he was not interested in my answer for his good eye was already on a tall girl rising from her seat to greet him. Part Malay, lovely almond eyes, a head taller than my jet-black friend, who was in some exquisite way her equal. A lovely, lovely dancer. How I wished to spend my tickets, yet I could not break free of myself. I drank – what else to do-*lah*?

Believe me, the shy develop expert strategies, as complex as a molecule of haemoglobin. So when the band finished their set I seized the piano for myself and began 'In the Mood' with a few flashy runs, then a low boogie baseline. Shy, not shy, how can I explain it? A show-off. Repeat the baseline but never release the melody, so everyone is waiting for it.

It was Mulaha and his gorgeous taxi-girl, Chubb said, who came to me first. He laid his crisp white handkerchief on the piano and his whisky glass on top. They claim Bertie Limuco had once played that particular piano, but it was well past such polite treatment. Then he stretched out his delicate left hand, the one with the Rolex hanging so loosely from it, and played the single notes of the melody.

Taxi-girls came wanting business-*lah*. I could not look at them. I upped the tempo. Then Mulaha thinks to toy with me, playing the last note of each phrase after the beat. I can smell women's powder, perfume, the heat of their lovely foreign bodies. Mulaha's good eye is very bright. Two girls are dancing with a Chinese gangster in a huge white suit.

Then I put both hands to work. Gorgeous little taxi-girl with an ornate kimono – it would be worth a thousand quid these days – comes and holds a gin and tonic to my lips. I sucked on it as I played. Quinine and gin, they say it stops malaria.

I could go on, but no need. You are a woman of the world, Mem. I made the flowers in the melody and then the band returned and later I made quite different flowers on a narrow hospital bed upstairs. In the middle of my misery I was blessed. Spent all my tickets. First time in a long, long while that I was happy.

We delivered the girls back home to Armenian Street, four of us on a Vespa. Too drunk to fall. I completely forgot my child – but listen. I knew I had been lonely, Mem, yet I had no understanding of my desolation until my skin was finally touched.

36

It was almost four in the morning and I laboured on, in my room now, driven by a mixture of opportunism and curiosity while Chubb, showing no signs of fatigue, continued with his tale.

It had been at almost the same late hour, though many years before, of course, that Mulaha's red Vespa had become irretrievably jammed into a deep drain in Penang and, after doing their best to hide it beneath one of those heavy concrete slabs that dot the landscape of Malaysia, the two dew bugs set off on foot towards the Bukit Zamrud English School. They were very drunk indeed.

Coming into the neighbourhood of the E&O, Mulaha suddenly veered away, stabilising himself against the cyclone fence of St Xavier's School, where he insisted he'd been dux in 1938.

Come, I'll show you photos on the walls. See how pale they made me look. Special price, I bet you.

They negotiated the rusty latch, but had less success with the school doors, lighting match after match that fell blazing into the wet grass.

It was then that the dog appeared, barking.

This was one of those curs, Mem. You have seen them in K.L. – suppuration, distended teats, no harm in them really. But the Tamil – *wah*! Take this, he cried, and thrust his hand into his rumpled trousers. I told myself, he has a pistol too.

Hand still in pocket, Mulaha came directly at the dog, which bared its yellow teeth and backed itself up under the low branches of a poinciana.

Releks, I told him, may have rabies-*ah*. The Tamil gave me the dead eye and from his pocket removed – no pistol, thanks to God – something else, small and white. Then he made a gesture, like tossing deck quoits. Good form also. The dog skipped back before sneaking up to sniff the object. I thought it was a stone, but the dog swallowed it down, one gulp.

Watch, *Tuan*, cried Mulaha. He was the Cheshire bloody cat, teeth gleaming in the moonlight. Now, my friend, he said to me, both hands deep and happy in his pockets, kindly to observe what follows.

The dog had changed his attitude. No barking now. Ears cocked, head to one side.

Observe, my friend.

And Mem, the bloody mongrel fell. Like a pigeon from the sky. Good God, man! I said to Mulaha.

Sit, he demanded, not of the dog, but of me, patting a wooden bench where in daylight you can still see the Cantonese amahs waiting to pick up their charges after school.

Is it dead, I asked. I was not approving. Have you killed it?

You are going to live in my house? I am going to rescue your daughter? Then sit.

We sat side by side a while, the poor dog in the shadow not five feet from us.

You have an enemy, Mulaha said finally.

I was confused, somehow thinking he meant the dog.

I mean the bloody *hantu* who took your baby. McCorkle? Yes or not?

Yes.

Big head on him?

I told you.

Very strong . . . clever? Seven foot tall you said?

I told you – almost.

And cruel.

Yes.

And what will you do? You must have revenge, *Tuan*.

Had he killed the dog in revenge? All I could see was that lifeless eye. Mulaha, I said, you are drunk.

No, no, listen. Only our first day. You do not yet understand your luck. No-one better than me for you to have met. I will tell you how to solve your problem.

You told me already. We go to the rickshawallahs. Then we send the parcel.

That does not solve your problem, man. After that what will you do?

I will mail him the E.S. parcel, so you say.

Yes, yes, he will have to come to the P.O. to pick it up, but what will you do then? When you see the bastard, what will happen?

I shrugged.

You too half-past-six. You listen. I know.

Yes.

Do not worry about the bloody dog.

Very well.

You hear my little war story.

Now?

Yes, bloody now. This is why I am called Dato.

All right.

Do you know what Dato is?

No.

It is like Sir or Lord or O.B.E., that sort of thing.

Which one?

Any one. Don't worry. I am not Dato really. They gave me a medal instead – *Panglima*. Means bloody nothing. Do you know how old I was when the Japanese invaded? I will tell you, Christopher – twenty-one. I had two good eyes, not like this now. Both straight ahead, like the headlamps of my father's Humber. I had a very pretty clever wife, Rasathi, a sweet, juicy, slender-waisted girl, not from Jaffna – born on King Street in Penang. It was a *lauoo* marriage as they say. You cannot know how rare love marriages were before the war. Her parents never stopped being offended by the darkness of my skin. My mother-in-law was a light-skinned Jaffna Tamil, just like my father, but she was always drawing attention to her complexion, powdering it to make it even lighter. Also they were Hindu and I was what they call a Rice Christian, my Jaffna grandpa having converted in order to get his education. For all these reasons she thought her family above us, although in reality they owned a little spice shop on King Street while my father had a law degree from Oxford. Also we owned the mansion right on Queen Street, two pharmacies, a big rubber estate down in Segari.

The first Japanese bombers came in over George Town at ten in the morning. My beautiful Rasathi and her maid were packing our trunks for Trinity College, Dublin, where I was to study law. Two minutes later my father's chambers were bombed to dust, his clerk was dead, my steamer tickets shredded to confetti. He ran into the street to find our saviours and protectors, Australians and British, scattering like panicked chickens. Smoke, fire, awful looting all over George Town. They broke into our beautiful house – Chinese gangsters. Axe brand. That's what they called these goods when they were sold.

My father was a secretive man, always fearful of the worst. He had been collecting bicycles in preparation. Two hours after the bombing he and my younger brother delivered four of these precious machines to my in-laws' spice shop. He advised them to immediately set off for Segari. It was a hundred and twenty miles to the plantation.

I was not witness to this conversation, but my in-laws soon rushed into the house on Queen Street and we all began to strap jewellery to our bodies and slip banknotes into shoes. Soon we were prepared but my mother-in-law must first go to the Sri Mariamman Temple across the street. Here she spoke with a certain priest, a well-known supporter of the Indian National Army. She returned with a pamphlet for her husband to read. OUR FRIENDS WHO HAVE BEEN WEEPING UNDER THE WHITE TYRANNY! NOW THE DAY HAS COME WHEN YOU CAN BE FREE! HERE HAS COME YOUR SAVIOUR.

So, she asks, why we go to some cowboy town? No need-*ah*. These Japanese soldiers like us.

We were still in Penang three days later when our new saviours arrived. By noon the beheadings had begun. Then they were stealing bicycles and watches. Then they were raping women in the five-foot ways on King Street. Suddenly my mother-in-law wished to go to Segari, and a little after three we all set off, in the middle of a rain-storm, my wife with our pretty baby daughter swaddled to her chest.

It was the storm that saved us. By dusk we were at the waterfront without being stopped. We took a motorised sampan across to Butterworth. By ten we had covered the twenty miles to Bukit Tambun, where a client of my father's, a Mr Han, had a truck company. No more-*lah*! Japanese had commandeered the vehicles, Mr Han as well. The family weeping. Poor people. They let us sleep in the garage for the night.

My mother-in-law was in very poor shape for this journey. Her skin was chafed raw by her jewels and her lungs bad. We bicycled an hour next day, yet who could bear to listen to her pain? We came to Pantai Baru, a kind of Chinatown, but some Indian traders too. They had built their wooden houses on stilts along the banks of the river leading to the Strait of Malacca. It was a bustling sort of place, with a pharmacy owned by a cousin, and when he said our women might stay on, my father-in-law and I decided to strike out for Segari where we had a Land Rover.

When I left the next morning I was very proud to see my pretty wife asleep in bed with the baby at her breast.

I felt I was doing a good job of saving my family, but that very day the communists ambushed a patrol of Japanese and killed five of them. Very good, you would think. But nothing could be worse. That night the Japanese arrived in Pantai Baru. They ordered everyone into their wooden houses and then set the village on fire. Anyone who ran from their house was shot. Can't talk more.

Mulaha spat onto the grass.

Sorry, *Tuan*.

He stood and walked towards the road. I rose myself but he waved me back onto the bench. I turned my back and looked at the lump of dog lying in the moonlight.

When Mulaha sat down he spoke quietly. No point I tell you more, he said, except for this. I would have revenge, you see. That is the point. I would have my revenge and live to see it. I would kill the bastards and not die myself.

He faced me now. I could see the huge furrow of his brow, the one dead eye. See? He pointed at the dog. You thought I was just a Tamil slave.

I had thought no such thing, I said so.

Then I will tell you this: I am Dato Sri Tunku Poisoner, my friend. I am sent from heaven for you. I am the one that you need.

37

They were burned alive, I told you – *aigh*, the sea at Pantai Baru, blackened wood, bodies, all awash. It was then my left eye turned sideways, not until. Right eye weeping like a child, the other blind and dry with hate.

I had my father's Land Rover. They stole it and beat me with bamboo. I walked back north along the jungle paths. I could not spit. No, I wept my water.

My brothers had bicycles – not the sports models the Japanese preferred – these models were too tall for the murderers to reach the pedals. At Bukit Tambun my brothers caught up with me. When I would not return with them to Segari, they made me a black patch for my injured eye, but I tore it off, I would not cover up my hate. It was all that remained of love.

When he crossed at Butterworth, Mulaha learned how low he would have to bow to his conquerors. He did not care, or so he claimed years later, walking along North Beach in the moonlight.

I came back to George Town like a one-eyed worm, he told Christopher Chubb, a corkscrew jigger to burrow through their feet.

Municipal garbage collection was abandoned, so rubbish was piled high in the streets and the air was filled with huge mosquitoes. The house in Queen Street had been looted but he found clean clothes in his father's press and headed to the E&O. This was where the Japs had billeted their officers, he said. Where else-*ah*? The drains along Penang Road were covered with a thick black slime.

In Farquhar Street he stood directly in front of that exclusive door. Mulaha, the rickshawallahs whispered, circling him. Mulaha, you must go away, they hissed. Don't turn that eye on them. They will top you-*lah*.

But Mulaha means 'temper', Christopher. Have I told you that?

No.

Yes I did. Same nickname as my father. I was in a temper now, believe me. Then the rickshawallahs fell quiet, said Mulaha, and I immediately saw why. The beheader had come. He was already staring at me from the open door of the Eastern and Oriental Hotel, where you and I first met, where they thought I had no right to be, where my beautiful Tamil mother once danced with Mr Sarkis when he balanced Scotch whisky on his head.

A soldier?

This was a captain in the Japanese Army. He had a wild and straggly beard. His hair was long and filthy. Up his left arm were wristwatches, ten of them at least. His sword was not long but his legs were short and the scabbard scraped the pavement as he approached. I bowed, flopping down on the tarmacadam like a dying fish. I heard that sword skittering towards me, worse than fingernails on a blackboard. And then I smelt him, *Tuan*, and this is how I knew who he was. He stank. He stank like the lowest of the beggars who have ever lived. When I heard the sword drawn from its scabbard, my temper died, I pissed my pants.

Kepara poton, he asked.

He could not speak properly but I understood him. He meant *kepala poton*. Head cut. Would I like my head cut off.

No, *Tuan*.

He rested the point of his sword against my outstretched arm and drew a thin line of blood to underline my Rolex. I did not require to be instructed further. I removed the watch and offered it. I dared not look up at him, but it is clear he examined the casing closely for he read out the name and address my father insisted be engraved there. Lose your head, my father had said, if it was not screwed on.

Speak English?

Only a little, *Tuan*.

This your house, Rolex-san? Queen Street?

Yes, *Tuan*.

Very well. Chop-chop. We go. Now.

Christopher, there were flies crawling all over him, circling him, a swarm of them swimming inside his pool of stink. Later I heard many stories about him, that he had royal blood, that he had vowed not to wash his body or cut his hair until the war was won, who knows what was true, only that he was a notorious beheader.

Now he was in a rickshaw, his sword resting naked across his lap. He told me run in front of him to lead the way. At Queen Street I opened the door and he took the key and locked me out. I did not know he had taken possession of my home. I imagined he had gone to loot, the bastard. I would skin him alive, I would boil him like a chicken in a pot.

Take it easy please, said Chubb.

No, never. Never *releks*. Not now. Not ever. I know what these monsters do. I know what must be done. We permitted Tatsuki Suzuki to kill our wives and children.

That was his name?

This man, Christopher, this man who took my family's house, we permitted him to keep chopping off our neighbours' heads. Where were the English? Absent. The Australians? Gone. We let him do it. We watched him wipe his sword clean with a sheet of white paper. There was no-one better to kill than this filthy creature who slept in my own bed like a parasite inside my bowel. How to kill him, that was all I thought.

There was an old Chinese woman who lived on Queen Street, Christopher. The Chinese have too many babies, don't need all those girls. This one had been adopted by Hindus and now she made her living cooking *apom*, rice flour, coconut, sugar, Hindu breakfast, very nice. She made it in what we call an *ottu kada*, like a shell on a rock, a rough shack glued onto the wall behind. We never spoke to her before the day my house was taken. But she took me in, Christopher. I slept on the floor beside her in her tiny shed. From there I spied on my own front door, saw the demon come and go, plotted how I would destroy him.

Soon he had a red MG, confiscated from some North Beach *baba*, isn't it? On the other side of my front door was a man who had one of those papaya and banana stalls. Sundralingham he was called, a handsome fellow with a black moustache. Well, early one morning he accidentally scraped the MG with his trolley. Poor fellow. He was very frightened and when Captain Suzuki came out my front door Sundralingham immediately confessed what he had done. It was him, no-one else, his fault completely. He was offering his life, *Tuan*, so no-one else would suffer. I watched Suzuki rest his hand on the hilt of his sword but he did not draw it out.

You want *kepara poton*?

No, *Tuan*.

Then you get me musk melon.

What that?

Not monkey fruit. Not this. And he swept half the papayas from Sundralingham's stand. You get me musk melon. In season now.

Sundralingham knew he was *kepara poton*, for this request was quite impossible even before the war.

Yes, *Tuan*. Tomorrow, *Tuan*.

Next morning he was gone. Ran away or dead, which is

it? No-one would lay a finger on his stand. Bananas went black and fell. Papayas rotted and the flies were as thick as on Suzuki. For many, many hours I lay in the *ottu kada* smelling the sickly smell, thinking how stupid we had been to rely on foreigners to protect us. I now understood that it was Malaya we should have trusted. Our country was worth a million English soldiers. She is like those big poison fish that permit a tribe of little fish to swim within their gills. We are the baby fish, *Tuan*, safe in a place which is poison to the Japanese. Everywhere you look at nature you will see a secret way the country can destroy these monsters. There is a weapon in a tortoise or a frog or a toad. Death lives in a worm or grasshopper. See that bamboo over there – just there, Christopher. Touch it. It has silky hair like between a woman's legs, but I can make a poison from it which will leave you *mabok* like that dog.

I don't want to poison anyone, said Chubb.

Well, I got to thinking about a musk melon. Anyone could tell you it was impossible, no chance at all. Everything rationed, one *guntang* of rice for every man, that is all. But also there were large Japanese transports landed at the airport and much corruption, and lastly I knew the Chinese gangster Yeoh Huan Choo, known as Potato. A very tough negotiator, but I borrowed English pounds and three weeks later was the owner of three perfect musk melons, value three hundred pounds, a fortune, but not too much for something impossible.

The next morning, when Suzuki opened my front door he looked down on Sundralingham's stall. Everything scrubbed, shining, and three musk melons sitting in a field of silver. His eyes popped out.

Surely, Mulaha, he was suspicious?

Of course. If he had not been suspicious it would've been a waste of time. He had stolen my house. I hated him. He had not asked me for musk melon, he had asked Sundralingham, but Sundralingham had run away or perhaps was killed or jailed. In any case Suzuki had three perfect musk melons. He shook his finger at me, as if warning me. I looked into his two black eyes and was afraid.

We will share, he said at last. We eat melon together, Rolex-san.

My hands were trembling. I selected a melon but he chose another, with a tiny green blemish. I picked up the knife, cut it, handed him one half. Then he called out to his ugly sergeant, who ran into my house and came out with two of my mother's best silver spoons. We ate side by side sitting on low metal stools in Queen Street, the smelly beast with his sword resting in the dirt – an insect with a dragging stinger.

Very good, he said. But I could see that he was unsettled. I will come back tomorrow, Rolex-san. We will eat again.

Then he got into his MG and drove away.

The following morning, his sergeant found him in my parents' bed. He had bloomed in the night, like a chrysanthemum, petals of blood thrusting through his skin.

In the moonlight Chubb saw how bright and excited his friend's good eye shone. This man, he thought, is too dangerous for me.

Mulaha, all I want is my child.

Yes, you are lucky. She is alive.

I do not want to kill anyone.

Oh, and are you not wondering how this one died?

I suppose you had injected poison into one side of the melon.

But which melon – all three? And what would stop the poison flowing all through the fruit? No, you see, I used the Malay tradition. I prepared the knife. I will show you how to do the same. Can?

I don't need to know.

In any case, I will show you. For this and fifty-six similar services in defence of my people, the Governor of Penang gave me the bloody *Panglima*. I had lost our house to the *chettiars* – long story . . . I am back to being a *cikgu*, one more poor Tamil teacher, like my grandfather.

They had by now reached the front gate of the school and they walked in silence around the dark and airless wall of jungle to Mulaha's house. Here the host immediately unlocked the heavy padlock – a strange and intimate moment, as if some deep and dreadful knowledge waited inside the locked room, as if they were about to commit a crime or sleep together.

Come in, he said.

38

Dry bunches of vegetable matter were hanging from the ceiling and stacked in corners. Beneath the window was a grey metal desk, its surface completely covered by books, loose papers, scales, knives, and pieces of native pottery. Shelves filled every wall, crammed with glass jars which had formerly held peanut butter or honey but now bore white laboratory labels of identical size. The odour was overpowering, a smell like that of fermenting tea.

My little hobby, Christopher.

Chubb could recall only a few labels: 'Cat Fish Gall', 'Sting Ray Spine', 'Dendang Beetle', 'Grasshopper Pesan'.

But he had hundreds of them, Mem, can you imagine? Ants and frogs, and dried-up fish slime. At the time I thought it mumbo-jumbo, but I was wrong. I have read the literature in K.L. Most of these substances would kill you or make you very sick. The powders are the worst – powdered millipede, for instance. A puff of air and you are dead. This was why he would never have a window open. *Cheh*! What sort of maniac was this? You could die of his good will.

He had decided for me that I would murder McCorkle. No consultation on this issue. No need to thank him. He would kindly teach me how to do it properly. His point was that I was lucky to have met him, but at five in the morning it hardly felt like luck. He wished to find a dog and show me how to deal with it.

Tired, I said.

Forget the dog then. He would demonstrate how he had killed Suzuki only. I did not wish to know, not then or ever. He showed me the very knife he used on the musk melon. It had been soaked in urine so the poison would adhere. Then he mixed some powder with oil and began to coat one side of it. That was the trick, you see: poison on one side of the knife. Good eye, bad eye. Good side, bad side. He coated the bad side with four different poisons. The smell in the room was very strong and I had a strange taste in my throat. All I was thinking was I must depart.

The following afternoon, Mad Dogs and Englishmen. I walked all the way into George Town and there, *oy-oy-oy*, a long raving letter from Noussette. Page one: I was a leech. She would give me nothing, ever. Page two: I was a liar. She said I had brought McCorkle on myself. Page three was even better: the creature did not exist. She would sue me if I ever claimed that she'd met him in Kings Cross.

What could I say? I was now trapped at the Bukit Zamrud English School and when the headmaster finally struck I was in no position to refuse his pitiful wages. Mathematics and physics. Two hundred and fifty dollars a month less board. Chubb here looked down at his dry old hands. No more True Parrot for me – or maybe once. Each night I had to learn the maths I taught the following day.

For almost three months, until the end of the monsoon, Chubb continued at the poison house. He was twice excited by reports of McCorkle and his daughter, but nothing came of them and he quickly gave up hope. For Mulaha it was different: he would lose too much face if his promise was not honoured.

He made me prepare the damned E.S. parcel even though nothing more was forthcoming from the rickshawallahs. I was to kill him this way – no, no, that way. Whenever he changed his mind he must test the poison on some poor dog or chicken and have me watch it die. I hated to see the suffering. More than once he poisoned himself and then there were great scenes of retching and shuddering in the middle of the night. Never sure if some were not intentional. Three times he got out of taking the cricket team to Kuala Kangsar – severe vomiting at six a.m. – and each time I had to take his place and then I was trapped in the company of the headmaster. David Grainger from Ballan. Must sit next to him. No reading permitted, must listen to the moron talk. 'The Malay Character' was his hobby-horse.

Zinc cream all over his stupid nose, Mem, like a bloody sunburned ostrich. He knew nothing of Malaya but had a great terror of *amok*. On and on until the bus stopped unexpectedly. What's this? What's this? His first thought, of course, was terrorists.

Nothing, I said. A car broken down.

But Grainger was now standing in the aisle poking his bright white nose over the driver's shoulder.

A large silver car was stopped at an angle across the road. Surrounding it was a mob of Malays in colourful dress.

Nothing, dear chap? Nothing? It's an Orang Kaya Kaya!

The thing was this, Chubb explained to me, an Orang Kaya Kaya is not royalty, but almost as good. The title means he's bloody rich. Grainger immediately roared at the driver. His proper name was Kee Guat Eng but Grainger called him Ah Kee, as if he was a dog.

Ah Kee, door open.

Then the fool went hopping out onto the road like a scavenger that has found something nice and dead to eat.

The crowd opened like a gorgeous poppy and in its centre Chubb saw a tall light-skinned man whose grey hair and white moustache did nothing to hinder an expression of extreme hauteur. His tartan jacket combined many violent colours, and his loose white silk trousers were fastened by many yards of scarlet waist-cloth. All this he set off with sky-blue canvas shoes.

Before this luminous individual the sheep-coloured Grainger all but prostrated himself. The Kaya Kaya allowed himself a few words in reply before turning to speak to an equerry, thus leaving the headmaster uncertain of whether he should stay or go. Finally he bowed to the Kaya Kaya's back and boarded the bus. Chubb sighed and put his book away.

I offered him a ride, the headmaster said, but do you know what he told me? 'I have my own mechanist.' Ha-ha. That's good, isn't it? Mechanist. But imagine the piles of dough these fellows have. Travels with his bloody mechanist. Look, there he is.

The bus was pushing slowly through the crowd and as they passed the car – an Austin Sheerline – the great hulking body of the mechanic emerged slowly from underneath and a white face blinked up at them.

Good grief, cried Grainger, a bally Englishman!

It was Bob McCorkle. When Chubb saw him, he cared not a damn about the first eleven or David Grainger either. He rose from his seat and made his way forward.

Stop the bus, he demanded.

You sit, said Kee Guat Eng. Too late already.

Gostan, please. Meaning: Back up.

But then Grainger clapped a hand on his shoulder. Come, old chap, don't panic. You must sit down.

Chubb does not seem to have been a violent man, but the bus was now picking up speed and no-one was about to *gostan* for him. So he pushed the headmaster in the chest, just at the moment Kee Guat Eng accelerated, and Grainger followed the laws of first-form physics ($M = m \times v$), tottering backwards down the aisle with his hands held high and his freckled face contorted in a rictus of alarm.

Sorry, Chubb cried.

For a moment it seemed the headmaster would maintain

his dance all the way to the back seat, but suddenly he fell hard upon his tailbone.

Stop the bus, cried Chubb.

Get him, boys, Grainger shouted. Get the cad.

Both orders were obeyed and, as the bus came to a halt, fourteen doe-eyed princes descended on their maths teacher in a wave of soap and garlic, banging his forehead and scratching his face and arms and pounding his body with their bony knees and elbows. Chubb could not bring himself to strike back and so was held prisoner for the headmaster to inspect.

Get up, man.

All Chubb knew was he had to get out of that bus.

In your seat, said David Grainger.

I must get out.

Sir, be seated.

In a display of ingenuity that he was still proud of years later, Chubb doubled over and began to retch.

Open the door, cried the headmaster.

With one bound Chubb sprang out and began sprinting up the dusty Ipoh Road. In so doing he abandoned a notebook full of poetry, three shirts, two pairs of trousers, and his copy of Mallarmé, all of which were in Mulaha's cottage.

They had only travelled a mile or two past the Austin Sheerline but in reverse it was all uphill and severely rutted from the wet season, with the result that Chubb's sprint soon became a limping walk and when he arrived at the place where McCorkle had lain so short a time before, all he found was a large black oil stain in the dirt. This might have made another man regret his actions, but Chubb reckoned that so many people could not have been accommodated inside the Austin and as no-one was visible on the road ahead they must therefore have come from a settlement nearby. There was a large river not far distant, and so he reasoned the Kaya Kaya's palace was most likely on its bank. Further, there must be a path from here to there. Of course there was no guarantee that McCorkle would be with them, only that so oil-stained a man was unlikely to be welcome inside so grand a motor car.

He found a track which started out smoothly enough but soon became, Chubb told me, a succession of holes filled with mud and water, pretty much what you might expect if you knew it had been constructed and maintained by elephants for their own convenience.

He set off in cricket whites. Six hours later, towards the end of the afternoon, he emerged from the jungle covered with red mud and bitten beyond endurance. In spite of this, he was gratified to find himself looking across a wide, clear river, on the banks of which he could make out, beneath the foliage, houses and orchards and rice fields. It was a splendid view, made all the more so by the crimson streak in the sky above the last spur of a picturesque range of mountains. On the flats stood a number of large palm-thatched houses on stilts, and off by itself, a bright-yellow palace with high-pitched tile roofs and a cross-hatched gingerbread appearance. In the shadow of the palace was the Austin Sheerline.

I closed my notebook, and the extraordinary fellow looked at me with surprise.

It is not the end, he said. There is more to tell.

Mr Chubb, you have talked all day and almost half the night. I need a little rest.

Of course, he said. I will come back at noon.

I did not wait for him to go, but went to the bathroom to scrub the ink stains from my aching hands.

39

Years later the girl could remember the day of Chubb's arrival at the palace. First, the Kaya Kaya had seen the *ber-hantu*, a pillar of red fire in the evening sky, but he had not become ill until a second bad omen appeared, a very large bird which flew directly in through the open door. It was amongst her most vivid memories, how this bird had caused the grey-haired Kaya Kaya to collapse onto his big teak bed, all his family scattering like frightened chickens.

Before this happened he had been, as usual, very civilised. He had sat with her bapa inside the car and her bapa had shown him the part which was broken and explained the method of repair. Then they were invited to sit with him in his house, but on that day she had only one sip of her sweet red drink before there was a rush of air and a creature with heavy dark wings and a huge head and a pair of horns flew around the room moaning horribly. Then it sailed off into the dusk, gliding between the feathery leaves of palms. Then everyone ran away, leaving the Kaya Kaya alone on his bed with his blue shoes still upon his feet.

When people drifted nervously back to the big house, her bapa asked questions but they were too distressed to understand. Soon an old woman entered and this turned out to be the *pawang*. Dressed like a man in a short-sleeved jacket, trousers, and a sarong, she placed bowls of fluid and candles on the floor all around the bed. Soon afterwards came five young women with skin drums, and then her bapa took the little girl to sit with him beside the open door. The women went into the farthest corner and began to play the drums softly, stroking them with those lovely long fingers the undersides of which were as pale and pretty as a seashell. Then the *pawang* covered her face with a yellow silk cloth and sang a strange song.

What is happening, Bapa?

I reckon she is going to get the demon from him.

The little girl wanted very much to see the bad spirit emerge. She wondered would it be a lizard, for she had almost seen this sort of demon once before, in another place. There was a witch who had been casting spells and killing babies so they tied her arms and legs and took her to the river and held her beneath the muddy water with a long, forked stick. When she was dead a lizard climbed out her nose and the women caught and killed it and then put it in a bottle and buried the bottle in the dirt by the bananas where it would not hurt anybody ever again. None of this had she been allowed to see. This time she had a ringside seat.

Then they were being asked to leave the room – she could not even bring her red drink with her – and her bapa took her out into the bananas and here they squatted on the bare red earth until the big sun sank into the river, turning the water the same orange-gold colour as the silk across the *pawang*'s face.

In Kuala Lumpur, when she was no longer a little girl, she told me how she complained to her bapa about the abandoned drink, and one could guess that she was used to having her way. In any case, she was exceedingly surprised when he suddenly clamped his big oily smelling hand across her mouth.

There it is, he whispered in her ear, his breath smelling of peppermint and oranges. Look – the *hantu*. They have drawn him out.

And there it was, pulled down the hill by the *pawang*'s insistent song. Large and clumsy, the *hantu* stumbled and rolled down the steep hill behind the house.

Shit! it cried out angrily. It was white all over like a ghost but had disguised itself with mud and filth. And she was now sorry to be watching for she knew it would hurt her if it could. Her bapa wrapped his arms around her and pressed her face against his shoulder so the *hantu* could not see her. She was safe as she could be, but who knew what a *hantu* might do?

It walked around the house, calling out in its great croaking voice, and then three of the Kaya Kaya's sons ran down the steps. Two had krises drawn and one had a big fat gun and they leapt upon the *hantu* and soon had it tied up with rope. It cried and moaned, begging them to let it go, but the Kaya Kaya's sons dragged it to the car and lashed it to the wheel so there was no hope of escape.

Then the *hantu* saw her and cried horribly, pleading for her to come to it, but the Kaya Kaya's sons kicked the *hantu* until it stopped.

Once it was dark, she and her bapa went with everyone down to the river and soon the Kaya Kaya came too and they had a feast inside a floating house with walls of bamboo and everyone was happy. She wondered what would happen to the *hantu*, fearing that it would come and get her in the night, so her bapa took a burning stick and together they saw that the *hantu* was bound very tightly with a great deal of rattan.

Her bapa spoke directly to it. They know exactly what you are, he said.

You are a kidnapper, said the *hantu*, and I will catch you. Then you will go to prison for what you have done.

This frightened the girl terribly and she had to sleep next to her bapa all night long, but in the morning he showed her why there was nothing to fear. The *hantu* had been taken to a raft down on the river and sat there alone in its centre while men in boats guided it into the current and soon they let out a great cry as the river swept the raft away, carrying the *hantu* down to the sea where it would surely be destroyed and never again disturb the dreams of Kaya Kayas or little girls. Then her bapa picked her up and held her high and she looked down into his strong face and felt that lovely calm that only a child can feel, that you are perfectly loved, invincibly protected, and now she did not care what happened to the *hantu*, knowing only that the river would drag it to a place where the lizards would flee, running out of its ugly nose to meet their certain death.

40

On Thursday Chubb arrived far earlier than we had agreed and I therefore made him wait until lunch. As I was the one who had just three days remaining, this was perverse of me indeed, and not fully explicable even to myself. Quite likely I could not own to my growing involvement in his history, and was somehow embarrassed to see myself now making such detailed notes, cross-examining him so rigorously, and more often. I had become his collaborator, a role which made me, to say the least, uncomfortable.

This in turn invigorated him and when I met him in the lobby he presented me with a huge oil-stained map of Japanese-occupied Malaya. As we spread it across the table of the hotel's Chinese restaurant I began to imagine a whopping big issue of *The Modern Review*, one which would set Chubb's narrative against McCorkle's poem, a treasure which I was now so confident of obtaining that by five o'clock that afternoon, having drunk nothing more potent than tea, I sent a wire to Antrim: GREAT TREASURES LOOTED FROM THE EAST. I signed ELGIN.

Slater I did not see at all, and if you had told me he was robbing banks or bonking little boys I doubt I would have cared. I was racing for the finish line.

Early in the evening Chubb invited me to stroll with him through the soupy air to Jalan Campbell. Never once did I put my notebook away, and as we walked I questioned him about the various names and phrases that had poured from him. Malaysia, once so alien to me, was coming to feel more and more familiar.

We arrived soon enough at the bicycle shop and there, at the very front of the store, behind the glass display case with its violently tangled contents, was Mrs Lim, a large box of chocolates on her lap. At her side was a Chinese boy I had never seen before. Chubb spoke to them in his laboured Malay, and as he did so Mrs Lim unwrapped a chocolate. It was only then, it seems, that Chubb noticed what she was eating, and the sight of this extravagance somehow enraged him.

As he rushed around the display case Mrs Lim's astonishment was obvious, and it certainly did not diminish when Chubb snatched the box, turned it upside down, and violently shook its contents onto her lap and across the concrete floor.

Chubb spoke a single word. She curled her lip defiantly. The boy began to gather up the chocolates.

Chubb spoke again, much more sharply, and the woman stilled the boy. Perhaps it was the suit that gave Chubb this new authority, or perhaps it had always been like this.

Chubb now barked a question and she glanced towards the back of the store.

Come, he ordered me, and we pressed our way through a tangle of old bicycles into an open space where there was a tap and basin and a rather cruel-looking iron bed, beneath which I spotted an English edition of *The Duino Elegies*.

Not here, he said, and led me around the corner and up an echoing wooden staircase and there, on the top floor, we stepped into a room the nature of which one could never have predicted from the floor below. It was clean, uncluttered, with a high ceiling and oiled floorboards at least twelve inches wide. The walls were lined with books, not poems or novels or biographies but volumes the size of telephone directories whose spines were marked with Arabic script.

By the window sat John Slater, posing as Somerset Maugham in an artfully woven rattan chair, and at his feet was the girl we had both seen through the window on Monday night. Though I knew she was twenty, in Slater's company she looked shockingly young, almost a child.

Hello, old chap. Slater and his companion had been looking at a book but now he stood up, rather too quickly, and brought me the volume, as if it were proof of his innocent occupation.

Hello, Sarah. The pages held pressed flowers and leaves, all of them densely annotated. But although I would later regret not having taken the opportunity to study their very particular beauty, all I could think of in that moment was that Slater had thoroughly deceived us. I was not only angry but rather sick at heart to see him paying court to a child, and he all old and yellowish, with wrinkling folds of flesh above his collar.

She says her father made this, he said.

I saw not the book but his slack, sensual mouth and shifty eyes. I was so very sorry he had soiled our new-born friendship, rescuing and betraying me within three days.

There are fifty more just like it, he said.

You bastard, I said. I should slap your face.

He took me by the arm, as he would a pretty woman at a cocktail party, and led me quietly to one side. I'm truly sorry, Micks, he whispered, but in a moment you will understand.

It's pretty bloody clear already.

Shut up. You have no inkling of what this is. Micks, this entire room is a bloody *shrine* to Bob McCorkle. He rolled his eyes, but this was more likely a habit of his reflexive mockery and I am sure he did not mean to undercut the notion, for there was something rather excited in his tone. Look, he whispered.

I found myself confronting a peculiar little altar where a thin line of fragrant smoke was rising from a pale-pink joss stick. Beside it were three small ceramic objects – idols, I suppose one would call them – and, in a gaudy frame, a newspaper photograph of a severe and handsome white man whose long black hair was swept back from a high forehead.

This is him?

I picked up the frame and for the first time looked into Bob McCorkle's eyes, staring at me from under a veil of fifty-five-screen dots. I would prefer it, said its creator, if you did not whisper.

I was explaining to Sarah, Slater said, that this is Tina's father.

He isn't, said Chubb.

'Bapa', said Slater, means 'father', as we both know.

Chubb looked to the girl and she, now seated in the large rattan chair, smirked at him. Even thus contorted her features were extraordinarily beautiful, with limpid brown eyes and clear olive skin. It was really impossible to say what race she might be.

Chubb snatched the framed photograph from me, and the girl stiffened.

This is not your father, said Chubb, as you damn well know.

Are *you* her father, old man?

Chubb hesitated, slipping his right hand in his jacket pocket. If I was, he said, I would not want you courting her like some debauched old toad in a Beardsley print.

Now, steady on.

No, *you* steady on-*lah*. At the airlines, is it! But you cannot have her even if she wants you to. You own us all, is that it? Suit, chocolates, God knows what else you paid for. *Ada gula, ada semut.* Where there is sugar, there are ants. One more old white man come to Asia buying sex.

Sarah, Slater appealed to me.

But as seduction had really been his life and art, I did not see what I could honestly offer in his defence.

Chubb turned back to the girl. You trust him, is it?

The girl stared back implacably.

Chubb threw up his hands. I'm tired, he said, sick and tired of my *boh-doh* bloody life.

Again she smirked. She was a bad girl, that was clear, but who could know if she understood what he was getting at.

You realise how I work, yes or no? You see me with the stupid bloody bicycle. I am a scholar, isn't it? First-class honours. First-class. Then why am I here? For who? For what? You think I'm Chua Chen Bok? Buy you a bloody mansion with my bicycles?

Now listen, old man.

Chubb wheeled around. You defend her, Slater?

Yes, exactly.

Then buy her, he said abruptly. Good price.

Whatever was happening, it was terrible to see: a man crumbling to dust before my eyes.

Buy them all, he shrieked. One price-*lah*. Very cheap. The garbage of my life – women, bicycles, vulcaniser, everything.

He looked around wildly, as if searching for something or someone to smash and hurt. He was not yet old – just on fifty, I would reckon – and now he spun around and snatched a single volume from the shelf behind him.

I knew what it was. When I saw the cover, grey and wrinkled like the bark of a tree, a thrill ran through my body. Then I heard a howl of outrage from the girl, saw a rictus of triumph on Chubb's face.

There now entered a new ingredient into this chaos – the scarred woman appeared at the top of the stairs, crouched low, a rusty machete in her hand.

Jesus, I said.

As Chubb turned to confront her, the girl rushed to take possession of the book – but the papery sweep of her slippers betrayed her and he flung her brutally aside. There was a loud clatter as a silver kris fell to the floor.

I say, said Slater.

The girl darted for her weapon, but Chubb kicked it from her hand. The girl cried out and the kris skittered like a puck across the floor and clattered down the stairs. At the same time the queerly twisted little warrior advanced into the room, swishing the rusty blade in front of her.

I was a complete and utter coward, but John Slater, to his great credit, calmly stepped into her path.

Give it to me, nanny, won't you? There's a darling.

The blade was swishing fast as a propeller yet he offered a hand to her.

The woman paused, her eyes dangerously bright. I swear I saw her calculating whether it might be worth it just to kill us all.

There we are, nanny, Slater cooed.

She lowered her weapon but did not relinquish it or abandon her sense of readiness. Slater never took his eye off her but he spoke to Chubb, who was holding the book against his chest like a missal.

Give her back the book, Christopher.

This is not your business, Slater.

Put it back. Do as I say.

They don't understand a word of it, said Chubb, neither of them. He jutted his round chin like a stubborn boy. Try them on your own stuff. I wish you luck.

Just lay it down, Chris.

Chubb then cast a sharp look in my direction as if to say, Look how thick it is! So much poetry! I could not tell if he was celebrating or taunting me. You wish, he said to me, that I should leave this here to rot?

I dared not speak.

One could tell he was afraid of the Chinese woman but it was also clear that she was losing some of her resolve, for when Chubb rushed past she did not slash at him.

If the murderous kris and the machete had not indicated the value of that single volume, the triumphant look in

Chubb's eyes now left no doubt. As he clattered down the stairs, I thought: Fucking hell, what an issue I will have! For I knew that what he was escaping with was the life's work of the creature known as Bob McCorkle, although had his name been revealed as Rumpelstiltskin I doubt I would have cared.

He will burn the bloody thing!

This was the first time I heard the girl's speaking voice, and what a surprise it was, this rather rough Australian accent coming from her lovely face.

You bastard, she shouted, we will have you killed. And then she also dashed towards the stairs, where Slater, I am pleased to say, obstructed her.

Now, now, my sweet, he said, patting her slender shoulder. Mr Chubb is a man of letters. He will not burn a single couplet, I promise you. My friend Sarah is going to make sure of it.

He already killed my bapa.

Slater turned back to me. In his eyes there was an odd, excited light. You do understand, don't you?

I know. It is Bob McCorkle.

Hearing this name, the girl for once looked at me directly. You knew Mr Bob, Mem?

Behind her back, Slater was making dramatic signals which I could not understand.

I have read some of his poetry, I told the girl. I would like to read more. I would like to see it published in a book.

Yes, she said firmly, that is what we want. He was a genius.

Good, I thought. This was moving far better than the krises and machetes might have predicted.

Please show Miss Wode-Douglass the journals, Slater said quickly. You really must see them, Sarah, they're truly extraordinary. That's what I've been doing. It's not what you think at all.

He was a genius, Tina said, as if daring me to disagree.

Yes, but I must find Mr Chubb.

It is dark, the girl said. He could be anywhere. How would you find him now?

He can only be in one place, I said, and I will go and see him there.

It was Thursday at eight o'clock. Suddenly it seemed I had all the time in the world.

41

The stolen book was fat with poetry, pulpy, puffy, interleaved with small blue markers. I found it laid enticingly before me in exactly the place the reader will have already predicted: on a coffee table in the foyer of the Merlin. Yet even as Chubb lifted a napkin to reveal his treasure, I knew I might not yet possess it, not until I had recorded every remaining detail of his damn history.

The man is not the poems, he said, sliding his hand across the wrinkled, almost iridescent binding. Who can say what sort of being he was, Mem? Not me. He was the joke, and the joke cannot love its maker. So when he had me in his power he showed no mercy. He persuaded the Kaya Kaya I was a *hantu*!

Obediently, I uncapped my pen.

The Kaya Kaya was a good enough fellow, he said, but McCorkle filled his ear with poison. Tie him up, lock him up. And so they put me beneath one of the thatched houses where they kept the chickens in their baskets. The baskets were lifted up beneath the floor so the pythons could not reach them in the dark. No such privilege for me. They tied me to a foundation post. Mosquitoes. Sand flies. That was not the worst of it. Since the war I had a fear of jungles in the night.

One day I was a chalk-wallah in Penang. Next morning I woke to find myself shamed by my own piss. I was bruised, broken, covered with red soil, swollen up from my bites. It was the villagers who came for me, but it was that bastard in his *mechanist's* overalls who was their supervisor. Did I say he had shaved his head again? He was so hard and shiny, Mem, like bone, and if he was a figment of my imagination he was a nastier thought than any I'd ever had.

They set me on a large *lanchut*, a miner's wash box, and bound me to it with rattan. *Alamak*! I thought they meant to drown me in the river like a witch! I pleaded with him as a fellow poet, Australian, Christian. He was deaf to me.

And my dear child was at his side. And she *was* my child, Mem, I saw the proof of it in that grey and misty light, not in her beauty – all that was from Noussette – but in two tiny freckles, just here, and here, on her upper lip. See, I have the same. My mother also.

This I tried to tell her, that she was my blood. Yet when I pointed at my lip she became frightened, pushing her face against McCorkle and wrapping her arms around his great hairy fencepost of a leg. I begged him set her free. The request amused him.

Malays are geniuses with rattan and these lads did a thorough job of binding me to the *lanchut*. So firmly was I held that they could now turn me upside down. They slid two thick bamboo poles through rattan loops and carried me down to the river like a shrieking, shitting pig. There I saw what they had planned for me – 'raft' was too fine a name for this tangle of sticks. Flotsam! As likely as not populated by water snakes and rats and starving fire ants still stranded from the monsoon. This pile of debris they had moored to their bathing box with a length of rattan and now they carried me out through the shallows and lashed me and my box on top of it, and once that was done they pushed me out, no word of warning, no bye-bye, no curse, or trial, or sentence. Two of the young men waded out beside me until my craft began to spin in the current.

I twisted my head towards the bastard.

God help me, man, I called.

The mongrel did not move a muscle of his cruel and handsome face.

At my feet I had seen a little *chee-chuk* scuttling around the branches. While the current took us with a lurch, the lizard and I, the young men waded back to the pretty little village where my daughter had already turned her back on me. I rotated like a leaf. Mist lay across the water and lapped the edges of the jungle. It was a beautiful sight, except I was on my way to death. It was a case of *telur di hujung tanduk*, an egg teetering on the tip of a horn. I had no clue of how far away the ocean was, but it did not matter. My raft was breaking up. A large branch drifted loose. This was minutes from the start. My chair tilted. I am not a brave man, Mem, but it was not myself I cared for now, it was my darling little girl. What purpose would she serve for him when I was not alive to torture?

How I did love her, love her without relent or hope of return. What is Auden's line? 'If equal affection cannot be, / let the more loving one be me'?

Christopher Chubb coughed, perhaps in embarrassment.

I asked him did he not, just sometimes, hate her a little.

Instead of answering he chose to tell me how the mist burned away, how the sun tormented him. He had no doubt that he would die.

I tried to rock my box, he said, and I would happily have tipped myself into the river and drowned if I could have. The thought of the cool yellow water was much to be desired. Then a single bee came to torment me. This was not one of those black-and-yellow bees like you have in England. It had pale-blue stripes. Cruel and beautiful, isn't it? Once he had circled me a time or two he settled on my face, where he began to drink my sweat. The bee was very small and my body was working very hard, producing as much sweat as he might need. Why would he ever leave me? My hands were bound. I could do nothing more than bat my lashes and blow through my nose, none of which annoyed him very much. If they had, of course, he would have bitten me.

I will not bore you with self-pity, Mem. Some time, a little after noon, I fainted.

I awoke with a blinding headache to see the river was flying at a fantastic rate. It was nearing dusk, and there was no heat in the sun, not that it mattered, for I had so much still in my own body. The banks were crowded with casuarinas, mangle groves, nipa palms, and another palm – don't know its name – which towered over them all. Noisy as a market place with screeching birds, and behind this I could hear the pounding of the sea in which, I supposed, my end would come.

Seagulls came to look at me and I feared they would peck my eyes, but they let me off. The raft was floating lower now and my shoes were shipping water. I was travelling backwards and could not see how far I had to go when all of a sudden I was brought to a violent stop by what appeared to be a picket fence.

42

It was the year before Malayan independence, said Chubb, the modern age. Who could believe the squabbling that still went on amongst the aristocracy? How they fought-*lah*. So many of them! But it was exactly this situation that saved me. This Raja Kecil Bongsu had driven fat bamboo poles across the width of the river and was exacting a tax from the communists and smugglers and others who used it for business of their own. There were gateways made with floating logs and these were guarded by his men. I do not understand what the Raja Kecil Bongsu was doing in such a place, if he had fallen out with the Sultan or simply liked the scenery. No way of me knowing. But he had built a fort out on the mud flats between two rivers and here his young soldiers lived in a hut whose walls were six feet thick and eight feet high. They carried krises in their silver sashes. No-one to tax? No worry-*lah*. They would fight each other. They slept tucked in along the walls for at high tide the floors were two feet under.

They had built a watchtower, but the ladder had been burned so it was no longer used. I don't know how long I was bumping against the pickets before they spied me. A great shouting mob of them came splashing through the river just on dusk. They gave not a bugger for my sunburn or my headache. They pushed and pulled me and when I would not come from my box they took out their krises and cut me free. Not such a favour, Mem, for it was clear they meant to tax me blind.

There I was, a white man floating on a pile of sticks. Were they interested in how I got there? No-one asked a question until I had been taken across the mud flats to the village and here, after I had vomited, I was presented to the Raja Kecil Bongsu, who surveyed me very sniffily from his *selang*. You know *selang*? It was a kind of bridge that joined two parts of his rather humble house, nothing like the Kaya Kaya's palace. He was a young man, very delicate. He had long lashes and limpid eyes and a way of speaking Malay which might have made him seem effeminate had I not seen the authority he held over his men. To me he spoke coldly, in a very posh sort of English. Later I heard he had a first from Cambridge.

Where do you come from?

I am Australian.

Where have you travelled from on my river?

I was a Penang school teacher who had run away and been captured in a village whose name I did not know. All I could think might identify the place I had come from was the Austin Sheerline.

The young raja's eyebrows raised and he cocked his head and then burst into high-pitched laughter. An Austin Sheerline?

I am positive.

And this Austin Sheerline–wallah, what did you do to him?

This man was like liquid mercury, Mem, one moment whooping like a schoolboy, now narrowing his eyes as if preparing to slit my throat. So I *Tuan*'d him, believe me.

Tuan, I said, I did nothing to the Austin Sheerline–wallah. They have kidnapped my little girl, *Tuan*, and I came to rescue her.

He has kidnapped your daughter? No! He slapped his side and laughed again, this time at a pitch even higher than before. Oh, he is a fool, he said, a perfect fool. He is no better than a pirate and will not live as long as one. Excuse me, I am not laughing at your cruel loss, but at the ridiculous damned Orang Kaya Kaya. Come, come. You cannot stand down there amongst the hoi polloi.

He now spoke to his men and again I had the sensation of a different personality, clearly authoritative but exquisitely polite.

They will bring you to my house.

My handsome young robbers now returned their krises to their sheaths. What a change in them. This way, *Tuan*. They led me straight underneath the house, which was supported on high thin stilts, and delivered me to the front steps where, with great ceremony, witnessed by his family and his soldiers, the Raja Kecil Bongsu formally offered me his protection. Could not have said it better if he was the Archbishop of Canterbury.

I was sick and dirty as a pariah dog but I limped up the steps, and the raja personally showed me to a room. You will sleep here, he said. I did not know that I had been given the *rumah ibu*. This term you will not know. It is a room, of course, a bedroom, living room, and chapel all at once. Because I had been given the *rumah ibu* the raja and his family must sleep on the verandah. That's very nice, I said, and may I have a glass of water? I had not the least bloody idea of the extravagance of his gift.

I wanted water? No problem-*lah*. A very old Tamil woman was sent off and soon brought me not only a glass and pitcher and a large bowl of warm water to wash with, but also a butter box containing some stuff to rub on my injuries. This medicine stank of rotten fish and mango but I applied it as she demonstrated.

My own clothes were very dirty, and when I joined the family in the little dining room it was in a sarong and clean white shirt the most senior wife had provided me.

I had no appetite for their food, so the raja called his youngest wife. Get this man baked beans. Words to that effect. After dinner we retired to the verandah. Not a decent chair, of course. Crossed legs, aching bum. Then what a recital followed: the sins of the Sheerline-wallah. What a rotten egg was this Orang Kaya Kaya, wicked, foolish, a liar and a cheat.

I felt like death, of course, but must pay attention as he recited the crimes of our mutual foe. The Kaya Kaya, so he told me, kept a concubine.

Oh, I said, how terrible.

No, that was not offensive, but he publicly neglected his wife in her favour.

I clucked my tongue.

No, that might have been permissible, but his wife was of royal blood and that was why her humiliation could not be forgiven. It takes a great deal to lose the common people's love, but this one had done a damn good job of it. Even his own children had lost their respect for him and could be observed walking with their little toes curled up in mocking imitation of his waddle.

You see, said the raja, the people always wish to obey their betters. My men will stay on guard all night for me, but they also know I will not disgrace their good name. That fellow, on the other hand – a famous liar. His people know that. He does not pay his debts. He saw the Austin Sheerline in a showroom in George Town. What a scoundrel. He said he would take it out to give it a test and then he never brought it back. It was a Chinaman he robbed like this. The Chinaman took him to court and as it happens I was in Kuala Kangsar for a polo match, so I stayed on to see what lies he would tell in his defence. It was worse than even I imagined, Mr Chubb. No, he told the magistrate, he had never seen this Chinaman. No, he never took an Austin. He did not even know what an Austin was. Perhaps an Austin was a British Lord? No? A car? He detested cars. If he wished to move anywhere he had people who would carry him, and so on. Well, the sad truth is you can never win a case against a raja and the judge, being a Malay, naturally found against the Chinaman. But there was some justice, Mr Chubb, for very soon afterwards the Austin broke down and of course the Orang Kaya Kaya dare not ask anyone to repair it, certainly not the Chinaman. So the car stayed mouldering by the river through the wet season, at the end of which there was, so I'm told, lawyer vine growing all over it. There it would have rusted into the earth had not the big white mechanic arrived. This white man may not yet know what he has stepped into but he has as much chance of freedom as a crab eating happily inside a trap.

Christopher Chubb then apprised the raja of his daughter's kidnapping by this same mechanic. He was very forthright, so he says, not withholding any details, and the raja responded exactly as he wished, passionately slapping his leg and saying that the girl must be returned. It was a matter of honour. Also much dishonour for the Kaya Kaya to have his criminality so exposed to those in higher places.

Isolated by both language and his continuing illness, Chubb had no idea of the effect his story had upon the villagers. Though to him they showed no sign of it, they took his sorrow to their hearts. But all he saw the next morning was that shoals of a fish like mullet had just arrived in the river and everybody, women and children too, had been involved first in the harvest and then in the business of laying the catch on racks to dry.

Not until two or three days had passed, by which time the stench of drying fish was carried on the sea breeze through the *rumah ibu*, did the convalescing Australian stir himself sufficiently to walk down to the mud flats. There he observed two canoes setting off against the tide. Naturally it did not occur to him that their voyage could have anything to do with him, and that night he was mildly surprised to learn that one of the rowers had been the raja himself. Two days later a beaming

Kecil Bongsu returned to the village with the news that the kidnapper had been found living in the dense forest about a mile downstream from his shameful master's palace. Initially they assumed he had run away, but now it appeared that was not true. The girl was with him, as well as a Chinese woman from Sumatra whose husband had been murdered by Ambonese pirates within months of the couple's arrival in Perak. This woman was clinging to the white man like a leech. They had seen her climbing like a monkey in the tree. As everyone knew women did not climb, they had thought it the most comical event and made many crude jokes about her thighs clamping tightly around the smooth bark, etc. When it was discovered she was bringing nothing down but flowers, this amusement spread up and down the river and people who had never seen the mechanic and his entourage still knew this monkey woman.

Now it seems likely that even as the Raja Kecil Bongsu was telling this story so happily his wives were already disenchanted with their foreign visitor. A Malay would have known not to accept the offer of the *rumah ibu*; it may be offered, of course, but obviously must be declined. Chubb had no inkling of what he had done and it would be years before he would understand what an outrage it must have been to these wives, who normally regarded this part of the house as their own.

Perhaps, he told me, this is why the men undertook to fetch my daughter. Just to get rid of me, no? But who can say, Mem.

On the seventh morning of his stay, Chubb woke to a dreadful shrieking. Monkeys, he thought, and paid no particular attention. Once dressed, he opened a can of Spam and, in the absence of silverware, ate it with his fingers. The screams continued as he washed his hands. Perhaps it was a pig, but his hosts were Muslims so this could not be. He then descended to the sandy compound which was, to his surprise, completely deserted. Now the screams seemed to augur something ill. He hurried towards their source, down to the river, where he found what appeared to be the entire population of the village crammed onto the mud flats with the tide washing around their ankles. Thinking it some religious ceremony, he kept himself respectfully on the outskirts, but once his presence was noted the mob parted and he saw a large cane basket set upon the flats, perhaps two inches of water running through it. The basket was a larger, stouter version of the ones the Orang Kaya Kaya used to keep his chickens safe beneath his house.

To the reader the nature of this animal may be obvious, but it was a dreadful shock for Christopher Chubb to understand that the beast screaming inside this cage was his own beloved child.

He could not bear to hear her terror and so squatted down, moving slowly towards her through the mud.

It's okay, he said. Everything is fine.

But of course it was not fine at all. When the child saw the *hantu* stretching out his hands towards her, she froze. And the *hantu*, taking the silence for acquiescence, reached between the canes to stroke her hair.

The villagers watched the hand reach inside the cage, then heard a cry of pain, and saw the hand jerked back. The child began to shriek in earnest, the basket rocking on the mud flats like a distressed sea creature pulled up from the depths. The villagers stood there still as stones. Only their raja moved, and not very much, although Chubb was chilled by the way in which he stroked his fine moustache.

The raja then spoke briefly – to no-one in particular, it seemed. Then, without so much as glancing at his guest, he and his retainers started back towards the compound.

Once he had gone, Christopher Chubb could not induce a soul to look his way, in spite of which their collective disapproval was as palpable as the cloying heat. Of course their reaction is no mystery. Most of us would feel the same, and the Malays, who are such gentle souls with their own children, had already decided who the kidnapper really was.

They watched miserably as their young men slid cane poles carefully through the basket and then lifted the white girl to their shoulders. Chubb walked beside her as one might accompany a coffin to the grave while by his side the little creature shrieked in outrage at her situation.

At the raja's house she was first taken to the *rumah ibu* but then, at the insistence of the wives, was moved onto the verandah. Judging her too fierce to release, they brought a small bowl of black rice pudding and two bananas to set beside her cage.

All this Chubb watched from an awkward distance, keenly feeling the force of the wives' disapproval, but having no language to communicate the complications of his position. He watched how the women edged towards the cage and how one held out a plastic spoon of the pudding, making small cooing noises until a dirty little hand shot out and snatched the food away. So melancholy was his frame of mind, Chubb told me, that for a moment he was insensible to the presence of the raja at his side.

I have lost face with the idiot Kaya Kaya, his benefactor said in his soft, sibilant way, and if you had not looked into his eyes you could never have gauged his fury.

I am sorry.

You must take her back.

I will not.

For answer, Mem, he gave me the most awful slap across the face. I looked at him then, this man I had once thought effeminate, and understood he might kill me. I am not a brave man, but now there was no choice. I told him I would never give my daughter away. It was a very restless night that followed.

43

The argument over the child's return was rendered moot next morning when McCorkle himself strode into the compound, trailed by a jostling mob of excited tax collectors. They accompanied him, not in the bullying, sullen way they had escorted Chubb, but as an admiring crowd around a gladiator, jealously elbowing one another in order to be closest to their hero and his monkey woman, both of whom were carrying great canvas bags upon their heads.

The young men ushered the giant to Raja Kecil Bongsu's front steps and there he threw his heavy bag down on the ground.

Tina, he cried. It was the first time Chubb ever heard his daughter's name.

The child had been sucking on a can of *susu* but she responded immediately to the call and came running out onto the verandah, the can still clutched in both her hands. The wives had dressed her as a tiny princess in a purple sarong shot through with silver and her tangled hair had been oiled and combed and pulled back in a braid to show off her perfect little ears. At the top of the steps she hesitated, then smiled. But running down the steps she was already shuddering, and as her poise collapsed she buried her face in that massive shoulder and wept while his hands wrapped her shaking shoulder blades.

Like a villain in a village melodrama, her father watched the reunion from behind the verandah shutters. What he saw was intolerable, beyond belief. He had been sustained, until this moment, by his will to save his child from harm, but in defeat his mouth curved downwards, thin as the blade of a kris.

He was hauled out to stand before his rival, whose cold eyes glittered behind slitted lids.

If I see you one more time, said Bob McCorkle, I will destroy you.

You have destroyed me already.

He smiled, Mem, he smiled with pleasure, and at that moment I could have ripped his heart out. Oh, I imagined it – my hand deep inside his chest, his vital organs like warm mud in my fist.

If I could create you, I said, did you never fear I might unmake you too?

He did not answer, but put out his great leg and tripped me up. As I tried to rise he kicked me in the backside and sent me sprawling in the mud. This caused everyone to laugh, my child as well.

I was covered in filth, squealing like a hunted pig. I thought, I will kill him for this moment. I will see him die like a chicken or a dog dragging its legs into the dark.

Chubb now touched the book which had sat there on the table these last three hours. Its binding was both disfigured and beautiful, like the bark of a birch, but also wrinkled and tropical, like a Morton Bay fig. It was mottled, striated, and when he lay his square hand on it and his cracked nails and liver spots made contact with its weathered skin, both book and hand seemed to be related parts of the same creature.

I had been writing so rapidly that my hands were cramping, and therefore was pleased to take the opportunity to lay my thin biro on the table. As I did so he moved the book an inch or two towards me. It was an oddly flirtatious gesture, like a woman teasing with the buttons of her blouse. He began to slide the book back and forth, perhaps taunting me, or merely acting out his indecision – I could not tell – but he passed it through a little spill of tea.

Careful, I said. The tea.

Oh, he said, smiling, it has been through worse than that.

I would change my mind so often on this issue, but at that particular moment I again suspected that he was the author of this poem, and when I saw how gently he took the volume in his hand, I was completely certain.

You liked the little that you read, he asked.

So exactly like a poet, I thought.

He now placed the book directly in front of me, and I frankly told him I hadn't been able to get it out of my mind.

You were hooked, eh?

Well, yes.

Not always so obvious, a great work. You know what I am saying, Mem? What is this mumbo-jumbo? No head, no tail. Very bad-*lah*. But it has got its claws into you just the same.

He gave the book a sudden push and it was square in front of me. My heart was pounding.

I will leave it with you, he said abruptly.

It was much heavier than I had expected, and very strange to touch – a peculiar texture, slightly oily in places, scaly in others.

I can trust you, no? His emotion was obvious.

Yes, I said, you can trust me.

Then we will meet here in the morning.

I forced myself to wait until the Sikh opened the door for him respectfully, and only when he'd rounded the corner did I hold the poems of Bob McCorkle against my breast.

I opened the volume not at the beginning but somewhere in the middle. It was a curiously old-fashioned hand, very beautiful, with long austere ascenders and descenders and curiously ornate S's and G's.

— she's burning, our dew-lap beebee

That was all I read before Slater dropped companionably beside me, his arm immediately extending along the sofa behind my back.

Ah, Micks!

Furious, I closed the book.

Micks, darling, you're blushing. He looked at me quizzically, then began searching the empty foyer for a waiter. At least he had not seen the book, or so I thought.

In any case, you have her book back. Well done, darling.

He picked it up, and I confess I loathed the sight of it in his hands.

John, we have no idea whose book this is.

Did old Chubby say it was his?

No, but surely he wrote it. He certainly acts as if he did.

Slater now had found a waitress and was engaged in conversation about his order. Though I waited for him to relinquish the book, his hand was firmly clamped around its spine.

Have you read any of it, John?

Do you recall the photograph, in the little shrine? I showed you. That was Bob McCorkle.

You believe that?

Yes.

You're not being delusional?

This made him rather irritated. Well, how about this: we can say that the man in that photograph is Tina's father.

John, I don't think that's true.

Not only is he the father, but the girl was with him when he wrote the bloody poetry. Don't make faces, Micks. The book is hers, darling, no matter how you quibble. It is certainly not yours or mine. We have to give it back, even though you obviously don't wish to. Remember what you said when you left her?

That I would find Chubb.

You know what she understood, that you were rescuing her book.

Oh, John, don't be a beast. Please. I reached for the book but he moved it beyond my reach.

Sarah, you are behaving as if you are going to publish this work. Have you been sending wires to Antrim?

How do you know that?

Let's say you were going to publish it, or some of it. You would have to deal with the estate, don't you think?

Tina?

That's her name, yes.

Do you think she would permit it to be published?

Would she permit it? Darling, you're bonkers. Of course she would. Did you not see how proud those two women are of Mr Bob?

Whoever he is.

Yes, whatever.

Why didn't they do it before?

They are hardly intellectuals. How could they know where to begin?

Just like Bob McCorkle's sister.

What are you talking about?

I picked up my notebook and was able to quote him Beatrice McCorkle's actual words: 'I am not a literary person myself', I read, 'and I do not feel I understand what he wrote, but I feel that I ought to do something about them'. That is what Beatrice McCorkle wrote to Weiss.

What are you saying – that it's a fake and therefore public property? If you want it, Sarah, you have got to ask permission. You can't just steal it for the glory of the empire.

You did read my telegram.

I don't give a fuck about your telegrams. You have to pay them the courtesy of making an offer.

Yes, but first I must read it.

I reached for the book, but he would not relinquish it.

Micks, listen. They are poor people in a bloody bicycle shop. You cannot treat them this way.

All right, I said, standing up. Come on.

Come on what?

Let's do the business.

Now? They'll have their door shut.

Then we'll knock on it, I said.

And so, with Slater finally granting me possession of the book, we marched out into the night.

44

Of course I did not come to Jalan Campbell with the slightest intention of surrendering the poetry. I did not know how I would manage to retain it, only that I was an editor and that finally it must be mine. On entering the Moorish colonnade from the west end, I could see that the bicycle shop, far from being closed to me, was open wide, bright white neon flooding the footpath where the mad Mrs Lim and Tina sat sucking down their bowls of soup.

It will always feel far too familiar to call the girl Tina, for that would suggest an intimacy we will never share and a fondness I am very far from feeling. It is simply that I do not know her by any other name, not even now.

When I extended my hand to shake, she abandoned her soup to Mrs Lim and deftly, without a word yet spoken, snatched the volume from my grasp.

Jesus, I cried.

Slater immediately set a warning hand upon my shoulder, but when I turned to him for support he was completely passive, grinning like an idiot.

The hard-eyed thief – she was wearing the same white blouse and grey skirt which had earlier given such a girlish cast to her beauty – placed her booty on the top of the dusty glass display case and slowly checked each page – for what? Jam spots?

I asked her was anything missing.

She was solemn in return. Your *orang puteh* friend, she began. My what?

She means Chubb, old girl. White man.

Yes, she said to me, your friend Mr Chubb stole a page last week.

She held out the book and I could see the butt of the missing page, presumably the 'sample' he had brought to the hotel.

You have *bisnis* with me, she said. Not him.

This at least was encouraging. I tried to smile, though I am not very good at that sort of thing and doubtless I looked as grotesque as a de Kooning. Well, I said, I am the editor of a poetry magazine.

Yes. Her eyes were dark, unblinking. But first, she said, I roll down the door. Please be quiet-*lah*. Better the old man stay asleep. Too angry otherwise.

Slater and I waited amongst the tangled bicycles while the two women rolled down the door and padlocked it. Then, without my having had a chance even to whisper my outrage to Slater, they switched off the long neon light and shepherded us through to the back of the store where a reedy breathing told me Christopher Chubb was asleep in that hard bed. The air was alive with oil and petrol, but as they led us to the stairs up which Mrs Lim had made her machete charge the smells began to change. Inside the shrine the air was once more scented with pine and sandalwood and that other lovely smell, the aroma of libraries in country houses, thousands of spinster books with their pages chastely jammed together.

Slater and I waited in the foreign darkness while the two women closed off the stairwell with what seemed to be a heavy trapdoor. I had a moment of claustrophobic panic and wondered where the machete was. But then they turned on the light and Mrs Lim set up two folding metal chairs, one in front of the other like on a bus.

You sit now.

I sat behind Slater as Tina stood before us holding the book against her breast. Mrs Lim stood a little to one side. She was unarmed. We have *bisnis* now, she said, making it sound actually threatening.

Slater turned around in his chair, rolling his eyes like a naughty schoolboy. *Bisnis*, he said to me.

Tina meanwhile gestured to the walls of books. This is our family, she said.

Oh dear, I thought. Please, no. This sort of reverence really makes me sick.

Our ancestor, Mrs Lim explained.

I was beginning to understand how tiresome this negotiation might prove to be. I wished there were someone I could roll my eyes at, but Tina had me pinned.

Bob McCorkle had his country stolen, she said. He came here, knew no names, nothing. Our job has been to gather all the names for him.

All the names, said Slater, how extraordinary. Do you really mean that, Tina? The mind boggles.

Of course Slater was making fun for my benefit, but at the same time he was succeeding in flattering her.

Bob McCorkle is the tree-*ah*, she said, we are the roots. These poems are the flowers. You know what I am saying? When that old man steals this book, he has broken the flowers from the tree. You understand?

I could have done without the metaphors but was very interested to note that Chubb was not thought to have written anything at all.

Slater was obviously noticing the same thing. So the poetry is yours, he said, to sell or not to sell?

We will never sell this book, she bristled, not ever. We would die first.

I was speechless, literally. How in the world could one deal with such an ignorant and stubborn little girl?

Yes, said Slater, but I am sure you would sell the right to publish the words in a book?

For answer she turned to me. Memsahib, you brought your magazine here. *The Modern Review*, isn't it? When Mrs Lim gave it to me she said a lady wished to do some *bisnis* with me. Then you start to do *bisnis* with the old man. Maybe you thought you get it cheaper. *Cheh*! It is never his to sell.

Well, first I would like to actually read the poetry. I can't talk about it before I know exactly what it is.

Bob McCorkle is a genius, don't worry.

Don't you think that's for me to decide?

Oh no, but you will be able to read soon. Mrs Lim and I have seen your magazine. What we could not know from that: how much money you would pay us?

I laughed. Tina, I'm afraid that poets don't make very much money, nor their editors.

Yes. She smiled impatiently. But Bob McCorkle is a genius, isn't it?

Even geniuses don't make a lot of money.

She stared accusingly at John Slater. But you are rich.

Oh no, not at all.

I saw your hotel. You bought a suit, chocolates, nice clothes for me.

Nice clothes?

Well you see, dear, I have made some money writing novels. Bob McCorkle would not think well of me.

A genius would sell even more! She was close to tears.

Tina, I said, please. We must all relax. I will read the poems.

No, not please. You do not understand. Please, Mr Slater, she said, please turn around. Close your eyes.

Slater turned in his chair to face me, his face now rather pale and serious as he hissed, What is she *doing*?

I had thought she wanted privacy in which to weep but I was completely off the track for now, without a single word of excuse or explanation, with nothing more than the quiet rush of cotton brushing naked skin, the girl shed her skirt and blouse. My first thought was what a splendid, perfect body, sturdy yet refined, narrow waist but robust hips, nothing weak about her. But then I saw what she was showing me was not the mound of her pubis but the nature of her skin, which was mottled with scars as dense and as widely distributed as those on a rubber tree. It was not in the least disgusting, only strange, so strange in fact that it has never left my mind and I have spent considerable time since with books of tropical dermatology, examining gruesome photographs of trichophyton and miliaria and all the wood allergies for which the Malay Peninsula is famous. Most of these tend to present themselves as red and raw and ugly, whereas Tina's skin appeared thickened, callused in places like the sole of a foot. The insides of her thighs showed a grey lace-like pattern that was alien and beautiful at once, as if not only her mind but also her body had been singed by the poet's extraordinary will.

Slater was staring over my shoulder and I knew that he was looking at her reflection in the window.

Don't, I said.

But then she was dressing, still speaking to me: We helped him make his poetry. We gave everything. Now we must have money.

How could I not be moved by that body – and angered by it too, to see it so abused and used by her protector. You must let me read the work, I said. I have to judge myself.

You will not be disappointed.

Without reading it I cannot discuss money with you.

She stared at me, not so much hostile as stubborn. Here, she said suddenly, thrusting the book upon me.

My hands once again responded to the disturbing organic softness of the thing.

You can read it now, she said.

Now?

In this room.

I can no more read under supervision than a dog can eat while being watched.

You see? Tina said.

At the best of times my attention flickers and fades, and in order to pay proper attention I require not only solitude and silence, but also a pen to help fix my skittering mind onto the page. And now, at what I hoped would be the most important reading of my life, I had to contend with Tina's constant interruption, pacing feet, insects in my hair and ears, a tangled and eccentric handwriting and, not least, the panicked feeling that this might be my only chance to judge the work. It was like standing on a New York window ledge far above the street, the wind blowing, pages rattling.

But even here, in these appalling conditions, it was clear that this work was outside the law of taste and poesy. Whoever he was or had been, Bob McCorkle was indeed a genius. He had ripped up history and nailed it back together with its viscera on the outside, all that glistening green truth showing in the rip marks.

What a bloody battle it has been, and all through the combat the personae of the poet rage like a Hindu hero, many-limbed, a swirling figure, at once God and Fool. 'Not a word was known to him and twenty four years gone.' To say that the poet had attempted to create a country may sound simply glib, until you understand that this is exactly what he has done, and so deeply, and in such breadth that he sends you, as Pound will, back to the library of Babel, deep into the histories and theologies and dictionaries, like *Hobson-Jobson* with its treasury of *jamboo, jumboo, lac,* and *kyfe*. It was so far beyond what I had promised Antrim, 'beyond' in that it was previously unimaginable. This was worth being born for, this single giddy glimpse, on this high place, with the sound of my own blood singing in my ears.

It was with great reluctance that I gave up the volume to its custodians, who wished me not only to assess the financial value of the work but to listen to their own versions of the history. They were anxious to correct false impressions I may have gained from Chubb. Thus I was torn from the presence of this great book and transported back to the Kaya Kaya and the jungles of Perak. Not for the first time, I judged it politic to uncap my pen.

45

Mr Lim, of course, had been the one who had been killed by pirates. Hearing this story from Chubb, I had assumed that the jagged scars that marked Mrs Lim's cheek and neck were the consequence of that same assault, but that night on Jalan Campbell I learned this was not true.

The murder of her husband was a total horror, and when his screams had finally ceased and she emerged from the bathing hut where she had hidden from the Ambonese, she discovered that they'd hacked his head and limbs from his body. There are more disgusting details. You will forgive me for omitting them.

The newlyweds had been mining for tin in the upper reaches of the Perak River and as they spoke only Hokkien they had very little communication with the Malays. After the murder, of which she was for a considerable time a suspect, she survived alone for almost two years, living here and there in temporary shelters. She became adept in fashioning the more substantial parts of these structures from nipa palm and rattan, and they were light enough for her to carry from place to place. Though people mostly seem to have been kind, she shrank from society, and at the Orang Kaya Kaya's compound, for instance, would wait at the edge of the jungle until someone sent a boy out with a banana-leaf parcel of rice or some other food.

Then Mr Bob and Tina arrived and the two of them were almost immediately in the jungle, collecting leaves and flowers, and peeling bark and fibre to make paper for the journals.

They often came across Mrs Lim's shelters, and Mr Bob would leave food for her. How long this went on for, I don't know. Some weeks, I imagine.

Mrs Lim had meanwhile been observing the strange white man closely. Naturally she did not understand why he was hunting such inedible things, but she was determined to repay his kindness and therefore secured a gigantic orchid and left it for him in the middle of a path. The orchid's petals were a dull purple streaked with red, but its peculiar character derived from the strange fat rhizome with which it had grasped the tree, giving the orchid the appearance of a flower-headed snake. That it was also foul smelling did not diminish its appeal to the poet.

Later the same evening, with the stinking flower already in the press, the Orang Kaya Kaya and the priest provided Mr Bob and Tina the four different names by which the tree is known. The Muslim priest, who had considerable botanical knowledge, admitted that he had known the species only from its legendary smell, for the flower itself grows in the very crown, two hundred feet above the jungle floor. This was the first indication of Mrs Lim's climbing ability, although to call it 'ability' is to underplay the role of her extraordinary will.

We might imagine how the pair of them drew closer and ultimately became, unlikely as it might have seemed, a couple. Even before she was so cruelly disfigured, Mrs Lim was never comely. She was short and compact. She had strong stout legs, a rather thick waist, and crooked lower teeth. Mr Bob, we have seen sufficient of – a tall man, handsome in a slightly wild and angry way. That this pair would become lovers might seem unthinkable, and yet it is so.

We can assume the child was jealous at first, but by the

time she was rescued from the raja's compound she and Mrs Lim were fiercely attached to each other. How this came about, I do not know.

Although the eccentric threesome was often fed and sheltered by villagers, for years they lived in the jungle and communicated in a private patois, woven together from English, Hokkien, and Bahasa Melayu. It was during this peripatetic period that they perfected the manufacture of the paper for the journals which would later line the walls of the musty smelling shrine at Jalan Campbell.

Based on the single volume I saw that evening – there were fifty of them altogether – it was immediately clear that the scope and ambition of the work far outweighed the 'nature notes' of any poet who ever lived. They were also clearly superior to the nineteenth-century accounts of Raffles and even of Wallace, and one can therefore rightly claim that Tina and Mrs Lim had been partners in one of the great projects of Malaysian natural history.

Leafing through that gorgeous volume, with its pressed flowers and leaves and, with greater frequency as the work develops, Tina's lovely detailed drawings, I found it was apparent that McCorkle's desire to learn the names of things had developed into a full-blown mania, though it is perhaps unfair to give the name of a disease to such a voracious and enquiring mind.

That these books had travelled through the humid fungal rainforests of Malaya is hard to credit, for the jungle rots and discolours paper as brutally as it does human skin. These volumes, however, showed no signs of the incredible treks McCorkle had led from Kuala Trengganu in the north to Borneo in the south. No razor thorns or cassowary spurs here, no mention of the skin diseases or the event which left its dreadful marks on Mrs Lim.

This, it seems, occurred in November of 1960, by which time Malaya had won independence. Chin Peng and his comrades were still fighting their own revolution, however – reason enough to stay away from the densely forested valleys near the Thai border. But the strange little family had come here in search of the flowers of the casatta tree and that odd wire-barked shrub with the ugly name of 'hustt', both of which were blooming by the rivers at this season. There was a stream not half a mile away from their campsite, though because its banks were walled with a tangle of rattans and other spiny creepers, they had not yet penetrated to the base of the casatta.

Early one morning, when the river mists still blanketed the jungle, a slight and long-faced Chinese man arrived in the clearing, offering to sell them a chicken. What sort of fool would bushwhack through this wild country and then try to sell a chicken? They were miles from any human habitation.

The man had an oddly belligerent quality, shaking the chicken at Mr Bob as if he was very angry with it.

Mr Bob thanked the man politely and declined his offer. Hearing this, the visitor looked even more displeased. He threw his chicken to the ground and squatted down, curling his long toes in the soft mud. Shortly he was joined by two Chinese and three Malays, much younger men who, like him, were outfitted with machetes, empty bandoliers, and army fatigues.

Huddled with the women inside their little shelter, Mr Bob sharpened his machete.

The six men did nothing. They squatted on the edge of the clearing. One of the Malay boys had a cough.

Ah well, said Mr Bob. He yawned and stretched as he stepped out into the dappled light, machete in hand.

Apa nark? he said. In other words: What do you want?

The long-faced man smiled and held up the chicken. *Minta orang mat saleh.* I wish to be free of foreigners. Once he had spoken the other men rose to their feet and Mrs Lim, like a hawk escaping from a chicken egg, rushed forth and, just as their machetes were about to strike, threw herself on her protector from behind. Though only five feet tall she tackled him so hard that they landed together in the mud.

Get the fuck off of me, cried Mr Bob, thrashing violently about as she wrapped her compact body around his neck and head.

The assailants were, if possible, even more upset. They shrieked and kicked and struck her with machetes, slashing at her arms and back and face. Then the long-faced man barked an order for the others to withdraw and raised his weapon high above his head, as if to administer the *coup de grâce*.

Seeing this, the *child* threw herself on her exemplar's head, with the result that the three of them formed a strange, shrieking ball on the muddy earth. The attackers began to argue whether or not to kill the girl and in the middle of this debate Mr Bob rose with a great roar and, having roughly shed his adopted daughter and mistress, knocked the first assassin to the ground. He'd lost his own machete but now captured a new one and, taking advantage of his surprising reach, slashed the long-faced man's throat. McCorkle roared again, and cleaved the next man down the chest. For a moment the other boys stood still, looking with astonishment at the man's green innards glistening in the sudden sunlight.

Now, said Mr Bob, you can piss off.

Two of them took the body of the long-faced man while the remaining pair lifted their wounded companion, whose horrible howls echoed for some time through the jungle.

Neither Mr Bob nor Tina felt any pity in their hearts for they had discovered Mrs Lim's injuries. She was already in that dazed and weakened state which indicates a considerable loss of blood. They had little water to wash her wounds, so Mr Bob removed her sarong and Tina helped him plaster the gashes with handfuls of mud. Mrs Lim did not once flinch. She lay naked on her stomach, her eyes wide open, staring sideways without expression.

The soil of rainforests is filled with the spores of countless fungi and there are a multitude of horrid diseases waiting to enter the bloodstream, but what else were they to do? McCorkle quickly made a bamboo frame on which to lash the naked, mud-caked woman. She was a tiny thing but dense as a bulldog, and her weight upon his shoulders was considerable. Five hours later he and the eight-year-old girl, the latter now weeping with fatigue, stumbled out of the jungle and onto the main highway to Ipoh. By mid-afternoon Mrs Lim was in a military hospital in Taiping where, though her life was saved, her wounds were badly sutured. The ridged lines across her face would remain, sometimes livid, other times an angry pink, for all her life.

This story was one of many that she and Tina related to John Slater and myself in the middle of that long Thursday night at Jalan Campbell.

46

Having slept very late on Friday I did not come downstairs until it was already noon. By then I was hungry and had a headache and was not at all pleased to be confronted by Christopher Chubb, who must have been waiting outside the lift doors all morning.

A very foolish act, he announced. He had clearly discovered that the book had been returned. I got you the damn thing, he shouted, entangling himself in a big party of shiny Singapore Chinese – grandmother, grandfather, toddlers. Impossible, he cried. You gave it back to them! He knocked over the smaller toddler but did not appear to notice. He was oblivious of the attention he drew to himself, his big untidy walk, his flailing hands, the space he occupied. Have you any idea, he demanded, of the risk you took? The old bitch could have hacked your arm off.

Let me at least have my cup of tea.

He managed to shut up then, for just a moment, but he did follow me to the dining room, plonk himself down at the banquette, and glare at me, all his old obsequiousness quite burned away. He had become a wild dog, a drunken butler.

You don't understand them, he insisted.

Put a sock in it, I thought.

These are hard people. He leaned across the table and I understood that he would whine and wheedle and hammer against my resistance until he had bent me to his cause. Mem, you cannot know this type.

I thought, You don't know who you're talking to. You have not the foggiest idea.

They are slaves to that damned creature, he continued. What a great egotist McCorkle was. All for art! He drove them through thorns. Thorns three inches long, sharp as bloody razors. You think I am exaggerating. Cuts, calluses. Mauled by a wild pig, I am not joking, my daughter nearly died. Not just her, the pair of them. The bastard bent them, twisted them. They served him and even now that he's dead and buried they serve him still. Every night, they burn their incense and dust off his memory. And the book, that is the heart of it. They have not the least idea of what it is they guard, but they set its value very high.

Yes, and I plan to make an offer.

They will spit on you.

Wouldn't it be more sensible to ask me how much?

Everybody knows how much you pay. Twenty guineas, isn't it?

Mr Chubb, I said nothing about twenty guineas.

But you already had the manuscript in your bloody *hand*. Do you see what a stupid thing you did? You had it for nothing and gave it *back*!

I was very posh and frosty with him but of course he made me feel an utter fool. The book was lost and it was my fault completely. How could I have let Slater influence me like that?

They guard that book, you see, he said more gently. Don't you see, Mem, it will take a lot of talk to get it. We will negotiate, back and forth, forever. You go to market with Mrs Lim and you'll see what you are up against.

I have only until Sunday morning.

Then you have lost it, simple as that. Everyone has lost.

Give me a figure, I said. What would make them sell?

Oh, twenty thousand pounds.

Of course that number was unthinkable, but even as I began to tell him so, I recognised how stupid this was. Nothing is unthinkable for poetry. I might pay Slater twenty pounds if I liked his effort well enough, but what price would I put on a Shakespeare sonnet? How much for Milton, Donne, Coleridge, Yeats? Why does a grand and wealthy man like Antrim waste his time on a very plain little magazine, postpone his holiday in Italy, come to dinner with wretched snobs in hopes they might give money to a publication they never heard of? Because he is a civilised man, and for a civilised man great poetry is beyond diamonds, and as long as one publishes four times a year there is always a chance of finding it. As I sat there with Chubb it was, by my calculation, ten o'clock at night in London. Antrim was certainly not a night owl, but I could still politely call him now.

Please order something, I told Chubb.

I abandoned him without explanation and strode to the reception desk where I waited two agonising minutes to attract the attention of the Indian clerk. Finally I was able to give him the London number, and then it was too late to change my mind. I would get the twenty thousand pounds. I was pleased, reckless. The house phone was behind The Pub and the air was already rank with cigarettes and whisky. The instrument was ringing before I reached it.

Seeing me set off on this course, a sober reader might predict the extent of my misjudgement. Let me tell you, it was worse – I had made a complete mess of calculating the time difference. But that was not the least of it. Antrim is meticulous. If you wish to deal with him you must know exactly what you want and why you want it. While he might respect my judgement, he would despise any scent of indecision, what he might call woolliness. As I picked up the receiver I felt myself naked, with nothing to offer except my excitement and anxiety.

Are you all right, he asked.

Bertie, have I woken you?

Sarah, please tell me that you are all right.

What time is it?

Not quite dawn yet.

Oh, Bertie, I am so . . .

What is it, Sarah? Have you hurt yourself?

Bertie, I have made an extraordinary find. A really, really serious piece of work. When you read it you will not be angry with me.

He immediately became a great deal cooler. Sarah, I did receive your amusing telegrams.

I heard a man cough. Oh Jesus, he has a lover!

Do you think you might have waited to discuss it later?

Bertie, you know I would never do this unless it was absolutely essential.

As I launched into my exegesis of McCorkle's work, I knew I was ill-prepared for the task. I had only read it once, and in stressful circumstances. I began to flannel and then founder and in the end I could not even be explicit about the money I would need. I said nothing of twenty thousand pounds, only 'a great deal of money'.

Antrim let me say my piece, and when I finally tailed away he allowed a little silence to follow after.

How very wonderful for you, he said.

Yes, I said, we are about to commence negotiations.

Well, it will be an exceptional board meeting. I'll be so sorry to miss it.

No, no, everything's on schedule. I can be in London on Monday, as we agreed.

You know, Sarah, I'm just so very tired. I'm sure the meeting will go perfectly without me.

But you'll be there. I'll be on time.

I'm sorry, Micks, really.

There was no point in pleading. I was being punished: I had broken into his personal life, forced my way into his bedroom.

I am truly sorry. I should never have called.

Nonsense. Boofy was such a dear friend, and I am immensely fond of you, and you know how much fun I have had working with you.

I knew he would resign from my board. As I said goodbye I was really on the brink of tears, and although I would not cry I returned to the table with that sick, dead feeling in my gut. It seemed, at that moment, as if I had lost everything: not only Antrim and McCorkle's poem, but *The Modern Review* itself.

And there was one more middle-aged man waiting for me, a spider or an angel, with a napkin tucked into his shirt collar and a cucumber sandwich set before him.

Seeing me, he pushed his plate immediately aside and reached across the table to squeeze my hand. There was no precedent for this behaviour.

I will get you the book, Mem. I will bloody well steal it for you.

No, I am not a thief.

Cheh! Do you wish it to rot there? Imagine how you would feel, all your life! This book rotting in Jalan Campbell and no-one in K.L., certainly not in London, knows it is here.

His face was hard and passionate and for a moment I did think it strange that he should be so fervently committed to his Nemesis. But in truth my thoughts were of myself, for if Christopher Chubb did deliver the poetry I could put together an issue so extraordinary that all the problems would be solved. This strange story, the one I am now telling, would be part of it. As for the poetry, I would not tamper with it. I would not try to civilise it, or argue with it, or straighten out the shocking disconnected bits.

When might you do this, I asked him.

Soon. I cannot know.

This afternoon?

No, later. First I will have to tell you the worst of it.

Worst of what?

My story. The depths I sank to.

47

Three days after being evicted by the raja I arrived at K.G. Chomley's house at two in the morning – cut, bruised, muddy, broken, my brain in a boil of murder. The creature had poisoned my daughter's natural love for me. For that crime I would take his life away as lightly as I had given it in the first place. I knew to send his E.S. parcel in care of the Orang Kaya Kaya, and that this would draw him to the George Town P.O., where I would consign him to the fiery pit.

In the meantime, Mulaha constructed the weapon I would use. It was the plainest, most honest box you ever saw, Mem, stamped with the name of an orchard in Stanthorpe, Queensland. Even when he displayed it, I could not understand its mechanism. Since I did not wish to touch the thing, he pushed it at me and then I felt it sting my arm – his secret weapon, a nail protruding from the box. This caused me no more damage than a little scratch but Mulaha had yet to treat the nail, first with urine, then with millipede powder, arsenic, datura, and finally a simple coat of coconut oil. This same mixture he applied to a dagger with which he pricked a chicken. Just a prick, no blood drawn, but death was immediate.

He is a big man, I said, almost seven foot. Much bigger than this bloody chook.

Christopher, this little nail will bring down an elephant.

Then all we could do was wait. As the headmaster had diagnosed me 'troppo' and dismissed me in my absence, I was banned from the school and forced to hide all day in the locked room. Nothing to do but think about the bastard's face when he humiliated me before my girl. Drip, drip, drip, poison in her ear. He must have stolen her from me a little every day. He was the great genius. By this logic he should thank me, his bloody maker, but not so. One way only. He made her hate me-*lah*.

Waiting to kill him, fearing the nail would not hold sufficient poison, I prepared another dagger in secret. I found one not much thicker than a hatpin. As it had no sheath I fitted it inside a length of rubber hose which, once I had corked it at each end, I could keep safely in my pocket.

I was like a brumby at the Darwin Races. When the morning came I almost tripped with my box of fruit as I boarded the Hin bus. There was a temporary post office in Light Street in those years and here I sat on a bench inside the door, for all of one long day, never missing a face. Who could imagine I would come to this when I got my first-class honours at Fort Street High School.

The second day was raining early and I worried the poison might wash from the nail, but this was when he chose to come – that odd springing step of his, a pink chit in his hand. I stepped immediately behind him and, as he reached the counter, drove the nail into his thigh.

He gave a cry and turned. What contempt he showed, even then. He took my left arm and twisted it. I was weak as a child against him. The box spilled, fruit rolling across the floor. And when my dagger fell from its rubber hose, he forced me nearly on top of it. Thus it was with his assistance that I grasped the weapon and drove it into his buttock.

At about that time I was removed from him. Naturally they took me away to a cell in the Carnarvon Street police station, where I was very soon visited by the idiot Grainger and an English doctor who asked me ridiculous questions such as was I mad or not. I really did not care. What distressed me was that the creature had not died. My surprise at this seemed further proof of insanity, that I had believed it possible to kill a man by stabbing him in the buttock.

So there was one more court case, Mem, and I was deported to Australia. I understood I was to be sent to hospital but when the ship docked there was no-one to meet me and I simply walked away.

Sydney people are always bragging about this beautiful place they live in, but there were no pretty vistas in my life. I found a flat in a hot, bare street in Randwick and a job in the traffic department of an ad agency. Endless bus rides every day. A hateful job, nagging and whining, threatening and pushing, like a parking cop – brown bombers, we used to call them. The clever snot-nosed copywriters would not give me face. If I had not hated them, I would have had no passion at all. My girl was gone forever and now this horrid job provided my only society. Each night I drank two beers in a bar and then went home to work at my whisky. One more, one more – *satu lagi*, as we say.

You might think I would now feel free at least. I could lie in bed without fear the monster was about to creep into the room, yet in truth he had become part of me. After all, he had shaped my life, stolen my heart, cramped my fingers, made me a homeless traveller when I had never wished to leave my street.

Need not have worried-*ah*. Twelve months later his letter found me at the advertising agency. So you miss me also, I thought, for he was the type that always has to win the argument. *Kiasu*, they say here. Scared to lose. It is meant to be the Malaysian disease. And in his ten pages I felt the head of steam he had. What a triumph he now was. How he had overcome me. I had brought him forth ignorant into the world but now he knew six languages, five of which I never heard of. So learned now. He knew the holy books of Buddha and Mohammed. He knew the name of everything that lived on the Malaysian earth. He was the greatest writer ever born. Much tiresome bombast, such as had always marked him, the same sort of rant Donald Defoe had heard in Bali. Yet even as I read I had no inkling of what was to come. It was not until the last page, Mem, I found what was eating him.

'It is thanks to you', he wrote, 'thanks exactly to what you planned for me, that I am now dying of Graves' disease and will leave my family alone and penniless. When you stabbed me in the bum I almost felt sorry for you. How pitiful you seemed that day. But here you finally show your power. How you must hate my little girl to take her father from her. I hear you are an ad man still. I hope you enjoy your corruption and your wealth while you leave my child a starving orphan.'

But of course I did not mean the child to be abandoned. Never. Graves' disease, Mem, had been a joke, a pun, the disease of Robert Graves and T.S. Eliot, all the mumbo-jumbo men. 'Garlic and sapphires in the mud', what will that ever mean? But still I rushed to the dictionary: 'Disease characterised by the enlarged thyroid, rapid pulse, and increased metabolism due to excessive thyroid secretion'.

I called my doctor. Friend is sick et cetera. He told me not to fret and that Graves' disease was easily treated. But although he happily wrote me scripts for calmer-downers he could not write me one for this. Just the same, Sydney is a crooked town. I made enquiries.

Do you see what was happening, Mem? I was thinking, Will I go back to Malaysia? No harm to get a nice new passport with no sign of my deportation. Would they have my name on a list? A risk, of course. I finally met a greyhound trainer. Yes, mate, he could get me the medicine, no worries. From him I learned it could not be simply put in the post. Must be coddled, packed in dry ice. Hah, how perfect! I would have to take it myself.

My life in Sydney, so boring. I am sure you have not the

least idea of how a life can pass like this, leaking away like a dripping tap. Monday–Friday, Saturday–Sunday, sleep and drink the only luxury. It is how my mother lived. Work, eat, sherry flagon, sleep.

But now I was alive at last. I burned my bridges, resigned my job, broke my Randwick lease. How could I be sorry? My daughter would see me save the bastard's life. She could not hate me then.

Chubb paused here as if to appeal to me, and looking into those grey eyes I wondered what in his nature would permit him to shift from murder to nursing without so much as a change in breath. It was only here, so late in the story, that I considered the possibility of him being truly psychotic.

48

The minute my telegram had been delivered to Jalan Campbell both Tina and Mrs Lim were up and down the road. The *hantu* is coming. The *hantu* is coming. You have seen them together, Mem, so you can imagine the prance, the rage. Soon all the morons in the street were in a state about the ghost. *Cheh*! Peering out like aunties from behind their blinds.

The drug for Graves' disease was propylthiouracil – which Chubb duly spelt out for me. Got it through customs, he said, without an eye being raised. Passport stamped. Free to go. Everything was first-rate until the taxi pulled up outside the shophouse and I jammed the bloody box inside its sliding door. *Wah*! Suddenly great clouds of carbon dioxide all around me – not a man but a walking factory, a brewery. A dramatic entrance, Mem, but very tame compared to what the neighbours claimed to see. A creature with no body. Entrails flashing blue.

I stepped inside and was greeted by my child. Five foot six at least and almost prettier than her mother. But she had those two tiny freckles on her upper lip and was alight with foolish love for the creature. Luminous, she stung me.

Of course she was frightened and not only of the steaming box. She thought I was the devil. I asked, Where is the patient?

Atas. So saying she set off up the stairs, her bare feet

whispering against the polished teak. Is that not a sound a man will remember all his life – a woman's feet brushing across a wooden floor?

I followed with my dry ice billowing in the dark. There were lamps upstairs, no electricity. The room was not like now, Mem. It was ruled by the living creature in his giant teak bed. I beheld the wretch – the miserable monster whom I had created. He held up the curtain of the bed; and his eyes – *wah!* what eyes – were fixed on me. In the lamplight he was a grub in its cocoon, swathed in mosquito net. All around me, on the floor, stacked against the walls, were the journals his slaves had made for him.

He lay in the darkness like a raja. Beside him I could make out his little Chinese soldier. You've seen her. Hard to look at all those scars-*lah*. Her flat face shivered when she saw me, but I was her master's maker and she pulled back the mosquito net.

Tuan Bob, she announced.

And there he lay, the thing that I had brought to life, the brutish genius, glistening in the dark. His sweaty eyelids had retracted and the eyes were bulging from his shining face. He had become disgusting – gaunt, emaciated, the ribs nearly breaking through his wet and slippery skin. The old doctor in Randwick had prepared me for the jerky and spasmodic movements of the eyes, but not for the power of this disease to topple such a giant.

Seeing me, the tyrant made a choked-off phlegmy noise, presumably a laugh. What was the joke? That I had needed him? That he was my life? Yet the more damn vile he was, the better it suited me. 'Lo though I were despised and spat upon.' For now my daughter would finally see what sort of man I was.

I asked the name of his doctor so I could deliver him the drug.

No doctor, he said. It is the disease you invented for me. It has always been here waiting. Cure it if you can.

By this stage I did not doubt I had invented his disease. I set to work, Mem, straight away. Must unmake my joke, you see. There was a large bowl of soapy water on the floor and much of it was spilled. I placed my box where it was dry, and unpacked the bottle and pipette. The propylthiouracil was a tincture. My daughter brought the water so I might dilute it and, though frightened, she met my gaze. I could look directly through the iris and see her courage, as I named it. Silently she pleaded that I would not hurt him, and with more tenderness than she had shown when I was tripped and kicked into the mud.

I prepared the medicine and poured it into a little china cup as the females attempted to sit my genius up. They *Bapa*'d and *Tuan*'d and whispered in his ear but could not budge him. Finally he made it clear that I was the one he designated to touch his skin, to slip my hand beneath his sweating back and raise him so he might sip his tincture like a damned lover in my arms, a dying Jesus in a Roman church.

There was a strange metallic odour like copper about his skin. And his breath, Mem, dust and garlic. But what I felt most was his animus against me, the tremor of his hatred even as I ministered to him.

No sooner was the drug ingested than he vomited, and all the putrid contents of his stomach flooded down his chest and across his hairy stomach and my daughter began to weep convulsively.

You lift! Mrs Lim barked. Yes-Mem-no-Mem. I was her bloody coolie, so she thought. Lift now, she cried, and I carried her great *Tuan* and she was a little soldier beetle scurrying around the room, floating clean sheets into the air, fluffing pillows.

Tina watched, sniffling. God knows what she thought.

I held her bapa, all the while feeling his malevolent breath upon my cheek. To be so intimate with Bob McCorkle was disgusting, as unnatural and frightening as holding one's own vital organs in one's hands. His shaven head lolled back, and when I drew away he leered at me and sought my eyes. This behaviour I could put down to his disease. Nervousness, irritability, emotional lability, every symptom in the book. I held him for as long as it takes a two-gallon kettle to boil and only when his bath was ready could I be released.

To nurse a beloved friend is one thing, Mem, but a tapeworm who has tortured you so long? My daughter knew this. She must have known. I had made myself his nurse, his servant, his doctor. This was how the weeks passed for me. I slept on the hard floor beside him. I had no desire to lessen my pain.

Neither of the women would speak to me. They brought me soup and noodles but I always ate alone, squatting beside the great dark bed, one of them always watching over me.

I was so confident about the treatment, said Chubb, so certain of the cure, so slow to notice that my patient now weighed even less. His mind was wandering also. And his eyes – *wah!* Jellyfish about to burst. The weaker he grew, the more polite he became. Twice he smiled. From time to time he thanked me. He was dying. He knew that well before I did, and he was fretting, you see, about the woman and the child. What he needed now he could not steal or extract with violent threats against my person. He wanted me to promise to care for his dependants, and to do that he must charm me or make me pity him.

As my wishes were almost exactly the same as his, you might think I would immediately put his mind to rest? But by now I had known him for fifteen years and had lost my life because of him. I had good reason to be wary of his cunning. So while my heart could not help but be torn by his agony I did not dare let myself soften.

Tell me yes, he cried, or tell me no.

But I would do neither, and finally he could bear my recalcitrance no more and had a kind of seizure, thrashing and twisting on the bed as if he could rip himself apart. He roared.

His huge eyes were terrible to see. It seemed the skull could not contain them long. He fell from the bed and cracked his head against the floor. Even this I withstood, but his upset escalated and as it caused such distress to the women I finally allowed myself to offer the thing I craved the most.

I gave him my word that I would care for my daughter, the other one as well.

Hearing this, he collapsed back on his pillow. Everything in his hard, handsome face was sunken, everything except the eyes. *Wah*! So big now I could see my upside-down reflection when I spoke to him.

Come here, he said, patting the bed.

What was there to be afraid of? He took my hand and his own was soft and feeble, boneless as a ghost's.

I am easy now, he said. We are one, you and I.

It was a lovely morning in the dry season, Mem. Now their patient had grown so calm, they left on separate errands, Mrs Lim for Chow Kit, Tina to fetch a bowl of hot *tow too fah*, which was all the creature could hold down.

We were alone. The early sun was streaming through the windows and the mynah birds were in the mulberry tree out the back. In the street a cracked voice called for people to bring out their old newspapers – *paper lama, paper lama*.

What a shitty thing it is, Christopher, to come to this.

I said death comes to all of us.

No, no. I labour all my bloody life to make a work of art. And now the end is here, there is only you to give it to. My old enemy.

He twisted away and when he turned back I saw the volume which you held last night. Not the least idea of what it was. It felt as feverish and slippery as his skin.

What is this?

Swear you won't destroy it, he said.

There on the title page I read that fierce sarcastic title, *My Life as a Fake*.

Swear you will not burn it.

What is it?

The human soul, he said.

I thought he mocked himself. What did I expect? Certainly not art.

I swear, I told him, that I shall not damage this in any way.

I was being truthful. I would have protected it even if it was the ravings of a paranoid schizophrenic, which is exactly what I thought it was.

Give me, he said. You can read it when I'm gone. He was, finally, very gentle, touching my face so affectionately he might have been a doting uncle. Good man, he said. I know you will look after it.

I had thought his hatred of me all gone, but recently I have come to wonder if, even when he seemed so gentle, he was secretly relishing the notion of making me a bicycle mechanic. So like him. To trick me into living my own lie-*ah*? Lock myself in a pit of oil and gasoline. Did he wish his fate to be mine? If so, he hid his feelings until my daughter returned with the *tow too fah*.

He did not die until the following day but his demise, unlike his life, was peaceful, and he held the book against his chest until the very end.

49

You have seen it coming. I was treating the wrong disease, and he died not of Graves' disease but of a rare leukemia, myelo-proliferative disorder. The leucocytes had accumulated near the eyes, which is what turned them into jellyfish. He died of cancer.

The coroner was an Indian chap. Furious with me. I had impersonated a doctor. Smuggled drugs. I should be hanged, he said, except he could not see how that would benefit the family.

Leukemia was recorded on his death certificate but this had no meaning to the woman and the girl, who were soon telling the neighbours that the *hantu* had sucked the blood from Mr Bob.

It is hard to believe the monster had been so loved, Mem, but they wept for him on Jalan Campbell. They had seen the way he cooed and fawned around the little girl. They would never understand how he had fed off her, stolen her very life to fertilise his ego. It was not only Tina he devoured. Every child in that street was fuel for his forge. He was a user and a thief, yet tears were shed for him. My role was to be his cause of death.

But I had won as well, so I thought. I had my daughter. She did not love me then but I did not doubt that she would learn. And while she spurned me, my life was not a desert.

I was sustained by his strange and fearsome book. *My Life as a Fake.* What an accusation! It was to me it spoke, and had been willed to me directly, but I knew the women would not like me touching it. So I read it in secret, taking little trips up the stairs when I was at home alone. I was at it like a hidden arak bottle, going back for more of the harsh, bitter taste. *Satu lagi.* Just one more sip.

Certainly, Mem, I was as cunning as a drunk and it was several months before they caught me at my studies. *Wah!* You never saw such rage. They scratched my hands with their fingernails but that was nothing. I must put the volume down at once. The little scarface threatened what would happen if I erred again: sharp knife in the night.

My daughter smirked.

After this time, my heart hardened against her.

She had been used and abused and it had made her cruel and ignorant. I should have felt great pity but suddenly I loathed her. As you loathe someone who has betrayed you, cheated, lied, used you like a toy, made profit from everything that is good in you. This was not her fault, but that did not stop me hating her.

In spite of this, as you have seen, I continued to serve the creature's interests, for even if I could have abandoned the family I would never leave that work of art alone and unprotected.

I was patient, Mem, and I waited, because I knew one day you would come, or someone like you. Such a bet to place-*lah!* What chance you would find me reading Rilke? My life was almost a waste, but now, Mem, I will fetch you the book.

He stood. He was quite shaky, I thought. I'll come with you, I said.

No, no, you must not. At seven o'clock they will go together to the railway station. There are bicycle parts coming from Singapore. I must be there to mind the shop.

Very well, I said. So you will be back here by seven?

By seven-fifteen – he smiled – you will have the book.

I was distracted, I think, at that moment. Signing the bill. I did not pay particular attention to his departure.

50

Chubb left me with the dreadful problem of how to endure the three hours between now and his return. I packed and repacked my case – toothbrush, unwashed clothes, the free postcard of the ghastly Merlin. I ate the horrible hotel biscuit whose charms I had so far resisted and drank a glass of musty water. Then what? I was stuck ages away from the moment when I would finally hold that rough and slippery volume in my hands. From there it was another eternity until Charlotte Street, where I might feast contentedly on my treasure, its foreign stippled skin bathed in watery London light. In that far-off happy time I would copy every line by hand, not merely for safety – though that too was much on my agitated mind – but to learn it inside out. This is how I'd first read Milton, aged fifteen, and perceived what my dull lesbian head-mistress would never see: that it was Satan for whom the poet felt sympathy. Back in London I would use my pencil as an instrument of worship, using it to plumb the logic of McCorkle's ripped and rumpled map.

But how the time did drag in that dreary hotel room. And when night fell a full seventy-five minutes remained and I was irrationally frightened that the wet octopus of Kuala Lumpur would manage to suck my book into its fishy maw.

Downstairs, I sought the bar. No members present, as they say. I was reduced to ordering a curried-egg sandwich and a Tiger beer, and as the first wash of bubbles touched my throat Slater sat down opposite me. His brow was stern, shadowed, like deeply eroded rock.

Don't, he ordered.

I thought he was forbidding me the beer, which would have been out of character, to say the least.

Keep away from those women, he said, whatever you do.

You know, John, that's exactly what I was going to say to you. The young one particularly.

Micks, please. Get off it.

Oh, you weren't seducing her?

He ignored that. What are you hatching? he said. I have been sitting over there watching you. You are in a complete bloody state, so please do tell me what you're up to because I don't think you understand exactly where you are.

Don't be ridiculous.

Have you sent mad old Chubby off to steal that book again? Yes? I'm right?

I would have denied it but had no defence against his angry eyes.

You must call him off, he said. Those women are the dogs of hell.

Yes, but as it happens the dogs are at the railway station.

They're on to you, Micks, believe me. You'll never see that manuscript.

You know that?

I said *they*'re on to you.

How could he know? It was impossible. Yet he succeeded in making me believe that my treasure was about to be snatched away and I simply could not bear it. I stood and rushed out into the hot night. The bill, I imagined, would detain him for a moment, but as my cab pulled out of the congested drive I saw him entering the one behind, and now I supposed we would be like creatures in a bad movie. In order to confuse my pursuer I directed the driver to the

Coliseum, which I recalled was a short walk from the shop-house, and there I jumped out and dashed into the throng. Assuming Slater was behind me in the traffic, I crossed the street and soon was in a very questionable lane. In the adjacent alleyways, illuminated by their own flashlights, were women in short dresses whom I knew to be men. Someone called out to me and I splashed off through the puddles. I emerged onto Batu Road disorientated, and although I pushed rather violently through the crowd I was not confident of my direction.

How relieved I was to see the familiar police station and then, diagonally across Jalan Campbell, the bicycle shop, its roller door wide open, the clear white light spilling out into the smoky night. There was no-one inside! That surely meant the women were at the station, just as Chubb had said. I threaded my way through the tangled bicycles, calling out hello as I ascended the stairs. I heard a thump. Chubb, I thought.

Upstairs there was sufficient light to reveal Mrs Lim lying on the floor with Tina kneeling at her side. The girl turned towards me and in the glow from the window I could see that her luscious top lip was split open like a burst sausage, blood washing her teeth black as betel.

I don't know what I said but I certainly believed, even before understanding what had happened, that I was to blame.

Mrs Lim tried to sit up, then groaned and fell back to the floor. She too had been cut and her blouse was dark with blood. The floor around them was shining, black and wet.

What had Chubb done? What horror was I responsible for? I got no answer. They stared up at me as if at the enemy, eyes narrowed.

I asked again and cannot remember how I put it, but the girl's answer was in the rough Australian accent she had inherited from McCorkle: The mongrel-*lah*. He ran away.

It was Mr Chubb who did this to you?

Mrs Lim gasped and pointed towards the window.

But the window was barred. No-one could have escaped through it.

She continued pointing and then I saw, beneath the sill, what I took to be a pile of abandoned boots and clothes.

They kill him, Mrs Lim said. We could not stop them. They try to kill us too.

I cannot describe the confusion of my mind as it attempted to explain what my eyes were seeing. The last thing my brain would tell me was the truth. From the lane outside came an old man's voice – *paper lama, paper lama* – and I walked to the window. On the floor below was the pile of clothes. The light was slightly blue, making Chubb's shoes appear almost purple. There was something else: I imagined it was a dog. I don't know what I thought exactly, but I know I reached down and felt meat, as raw as in a Chow Kit butcher's shop. Then I saw the soft burr of that beautifully shaped monk's head, and I knew at last what it must be. *Sparagmos.* This was the horror at the poem's end. The man I had spent the afternoon with was now dismembered, his warm blood on my hands and spreading like honey across the floor.

Suddenly I was kneeling and then Slater was there, his big hands underneath my arms, pulling me to my feet.

Come, he said, we must go.

I decided he was afraid that the attacker would return. As he pulled me towards the stairs I insisted that the women come with us. When they would not budge I thought they wished to bravely guard the book.

Come, I said, bring the book with you.

Book gone, said Mrs Lim. Stole the book.

On her hard, square face was a sheen of satisfaction I could not understand.

Come, said Slater. Micks, darling, you must not stay.

The Chinese woman's face was so strange. By now it was clear, even to me, that she did not wish me well.

Micks, do as I say. Come now.

Confused as a drunk who dimly understands she has given offence, I permitted him to escort me down the stairs and out into Jalan Campbell and across to the police station, so conveniently close.

We were treated with the utmost seriousness and taken immediately to a kind of conference room. Then I was shown to a separate, smaller office. I was given a towel and bowl and only then did I fully appreciate that my hands and arms were bright with blood. As I washed I brooded that the women were alone and unprotected. I recall very little, only that I was extremely cold and they gave me a blanket and took my statement. No-one removed the bowl. Whenever the door opened or closed, the surface of the red liquid shook. It was Chubb, his substance, the blood that had coursed through his beating heart.

When they told me I could go, John Slater was waiting by the door. He gave the policemen back their blanket and wrapped his jacket round my shoulders. Everything I had hoped for was lost, gone, dead.

Back at the Merlin, a wedding party was spilling into the foyer. I badly wanted a drink but Slater bundled me into the lift. There were three men in the car with us – Japanese, I think.

Slater got me inside his room which, unlike mine, turned out to be very well provisioned. He poured me a large single-malt but not even its distinctive peaty flavour could mask the taste of blood.

Slater sat on the bed opposite me. Micks, darling, he said quietly, do you understand what has happened?

Poor Christopher is dead. The book is stolen.

You understand the women are lying?

No, I saw him. He's dead.

Yes, but didn't you see the mad triumph on their faces?

They were in shock, I said. They'd been attacked.

They're lying, darling. About bloody everything. Didn't you see the book? It was sitting on the shelf where it always is.

He fetched a big tub of cold cream and a box of tissues and, without asking permission, began to clean my face. I had no idea of my condition, blood all across my cheeks and ears. God knows what I had done.

You have cold cream, John?

Shush.

He cleaned my neck and arms, and then took a cotton bud to my blood-lined nails. It had taken me years to realise that, for all his faults, John Slater was truly very kind.

I was sure you were going to notice the book, he said. You're a lucky girl not to have.

How am I possibly lucky?

Darling, don't you understand yet? They killed him.

Then who attacked them?

They did it to themselves.

I did howl then, most horribly, and the dear man held me and did everything he could to give me comfort.

Though I thought I now understood exactly what had happened, it would take me an awfully long time to accept the full extent of the horror that had occurred in the shrine on Jalan Campbell, and even back in London I could not grasp it firmly, not least because I had no sensible explanation of McCorkle himself.

The result, of course, was that I was left with a wound that would not heal no matter how I tended it, and tend it I did, obsessively, until even Annabelle was forced to tell me I had become a bore. I expelled her for her honesty. I did not care. I was now above such scrapes and hurts for I had turned into one of those 'sad friends of Truth' Milton describes in his *Areopagitica*: 'such as durst appear, imitating the careful search that

Isis made for the mangl'd body of Osiris'. The body of truth, he meant, dismembered and scattered – in Greek, *sparagmos*.

I now commenced to travel compulsively 'up and down gathering up limb by limb' of that horrid puzzle. It was this quest that sent me journeying out to Australia at a time when I could scarcely afford the bus fare to Old Church Street, and at the end of all this ridiculous expense and anguish the only 'fact' I could be certain of was that McCorkle had a physical existence and it was separate from Chubb's.

This I would not accept and so I laboured madly on, stubborn as a goat, writing pestering letters, borrowing money, imperilling *The Modern Review*, getting sucked deeper and deeper into the morass until, one dark winter's afternoon on Oxford Street, I suffered what is politely called a nervous breakdown.

It was certainly not John Slater's idea that I should return to K.L., but when this was deemed important for my convalescence he behaved like the dear friend he had become, and this time he did not slip away to Kuala Kangsar. No-one, certainly not the genius doctors at the Tavistock Clinic, had ever considered the possibility that the two murderers might be exactly where I had seen them last and that the sight of them would not be therapeutic in the least. By 1985 Jalan Campbell's name had been changed to Jalan Dang Wangi, but the bicycle business was just as it had looked thirteen years before and the old black vise still sat where Chubb had left it, on the floor inside the door. Seeing that ugly device did rather wrench my heart and I would have paid any price to have the dear old puritan alive, with his wry sweet smile and his sniffy snobbery, his desperation to tell the story of his sad, unlikely life.

One can assume that McCorkle's manuscript remained in the shrine upstairs, although by then it seemed as foul to me as the disgusting giant orchid with which Mrs Lim had first attracted the poet's attention.

Tina was by now in her thirties, and if she did not appear to recognise the tourists at the door, the scars made her perfectly identifiable to us. We remained there only a moment, until the Chinese woman looked up from her abacus. John doffed his hat and she, for her part, raised her upper lip to display the lethal edges of her small white crooked teeth.

AUTHOR'S NOTE

Australian readers will have noted certain connections between Bob McCorkle and Ern Malley. Indeed, McCorkle's early verse is lifted word for word from Malley's 'The Darkening Ecliptic', first published in the literary magazine *Angry Penguins* in 1944.

Of course, Malley's poetry and biography constituted a hoax conceived by two talented anti-modernists, Harold Stewart and James McAuley. These conservatives wrote not only the verse I have borrowed for Bob McCorkle but also the wonderful letters they attributed to Malley's equally fictitious sister, which fabrications also appear in *My Life as a Fake*, though in much-abbreviated form.

The editor of *Angry Penguins,* Max Harris, having already been humiliated, was then called into court on the same charges faced by my fictional David Weiss, and I have drawn from transcripts of his bizarre trial.

'I still believe in Ern Malley,' Harris wrote years later.

I don't mean that as a piece of smart talk. I mean it quite simply. I know that Ern Malley was not a real person, but a personality invented in order to hoax me. I was offered not only the poems of this mythical Ern Malley, but also his life, his ideas, his love, his disease, and his death ... Most of you probably didn't think about the story of Ern Malley's life. It got lost in the explosive revelation of the hoax. In the holocaust of argument and policemen, meaning versus nonsense, it was not likely you closed your eyes and tried to conjure up such a person as the mythical Ern Malley . . . a garage mechanic suffering from the onset of Graves' Disease, with a solitary postcard of Durer's 'Innsbruck' on his bedroom wall. Of someone knowing he is going to die young, in a world of war and death, and seeing the streets and the children with the eyes of the already dead.

A pretty fancy. It can have no meaning for you. But I believed in Ern Malley. In all simplicity and faith I believed such a person existed, and I believed it for many months before the newspapers threw their banner headline at me. For me Ern Malley embodies the true sorrow and pathos of our time. One had felt that somewhere in the streets of every city was an Ern Malley . . . a living person, alone, outside literary cliques, outside print, dying, outside humanity but of it . . .

As I imagined him Ern Malley had something of the soft staring brilliance of Franz Kafka; something of Rilke's anguished solitude; something of Wilfred Owen's angry fatalism. And I believe he really walked down Princess Street somewhere in Melbourne . . .

I can still close my eyes and conjure up such a person in our streets. A young person. A person without the protection of the world that comes from living in it. A man outside.

ACKNOWLEDGEMENTS

Four of those I wish to thank are poets whose names are not unfamiliar, while another, Sir Frank Swettenham, was a colonial administrator now of dubious repute. During the three years it took to write this novel I have been touched by the generosity of family and friends, and those so close it is often hard to tell the difference – Maria Aiken, Carol Davidson, Peter Best, Gary Fisketjon, Michael Heyward, Paul Kane, Alec Marsh, Patrick McGrath, Sharon Olds, Robert Polito, Jon Riley, Deborah Rogers, Mona Simpson, Betsy Sussler, Binky Urban, and of course Alison Summers. Two gifted Malaysian writers, Rehman Rashid and Kee Thuan Chye, were selfless in the assistance they offered one who had come to them as a stranger. If this book contains errors of locution or history, the fault is mine, the stranger's. Another Malaysian writer, Dr. M. Shanmughalingam, not only offered advice and friendship but also allowed me to read his unfinished autobiography, which proved invaluable to my understanding of the Tamils who are such an important part of Malay society. In Kuala Lumpur, Victor Chin provided me with an intense tutorial in shophouse culture. Khoo Salma Nasution, the author of *Streets of George Town, Penang*, was a powerhouse; on my third visit to that almost perfect island, she found me an entire lifetime's worth of places and memories which have made their way, sometimes coded, mostly transmuted, into this narrative. Lastly I must thank John Dauth, the former Australian High Commissioner in Malaysia, whom I am now pleased to call a friend; and also Simon Merrifield, presently Counsellor at that same High Commission, who organised that memorable dinner when, straight off the flight from New York City, I met with so many of Malaysia's great minds and spirits. In a novel which contains its fair share of Ezra Pound, it is perhaps appropriate to conclude with the last lines of his translation of Rihaku's 'Exile's Letter'.

> What is the use of talking, and there is no end of talking,
> There is no end of things in the heart.
> I call in the boy,
> Have him sit on his knees here
>   To seal this,
> And send it a thousand miles, thinking.

155